DEATH
AT THE
GATES

BOOKS BY KATIE GAYLE

KATIE GAYLE

DEATH
AT THE
GATES

bookouture

Published by Bookouture in 2021

An imprint of Storyfire Ltd.
Carmelite House
50 Victoria Embankment
London EC4Y 0DZ

www.bookouture.com

ISBN: 978-1-80019-665-0
eBook ISBN: 978-1-80019-664-3

CHAPTER 1

Pip woke to the smell of burnt polyester. Or perhaps it was nylon. The night before was all such a blur. One moment her boss, Henrietta, director of the Museum for Movie Memorabilia and Costumes, was welcoming the press and favoured patrons to the grand opening of the 'Swinging 70s: Stairway to Heaven' exhibition at the newly revamped museum. The next… Poufff!

Pip had thought it a grand idea to arrange a fire juggler for the opening, and it certainly had looked dramatic when the young woman came tumbling in with a flaming torch. It was even more dramatic when the torch touched the tassels on the waistcoat displayed next to the little stage where the Led Zeppelin tribute band was performing.

Pip rolled over, buried her face in the pillow, and tried to block out the awful scenes from last night. She could still hear the whooshing sound when the would-be Robert Plant's hair went up. And the screams from the audience as the flame travelled rapidly through the synthetic fabrics. And finally, Henrietta's distraught face as she surveyed the carnage, and her cold voice: 'Epiphany, I never want to see you here ever again. You're fired.'

A groan of shame and despair escaped her. Pip couldn't believe she'd messed up again and lost another job. The worst of it was that things had been going so well. She liked the place, the clothes. The weirdo people. They liked her. She had solved a mystery and tracked down the stolen prize exhibit, the red dress Julia Roberts wore in *Pretty Woman*. She'd been the hero of the hour.

Her cat, Most, jumped up on the bed. Sweet girl, she was coming to comfort her. 'Hi, love,' Pip said, lifting her teary face from the pillow and reaching out to touch the cat's tabby head. Most sniffed her hand quizzically and stalked to the bottom edge of the bed, settling down on the far corner, facing away from Pip. She might even have actually wrinkled her nose in disgust. Even her beloved three-legged rescue cat hated her. How was she ever going to get up and face the world?

There was a soft *rat-a-tat* on the door.

'Pip? You up?'

Oh God. Her flatmate, Tim, had witnessed the disastrous opening. And so had her sister, Flis. And her friend Jimmy. And even Mummy. There was no end to the humiliation. She put the pillow over her head and waited for Tim to go away.

'Coffee's ready. And I made your favourite banana pancakes,' said Tim.

Perhaps if she played dead *everything* would go away.

'Pip, I'm coming in, OK?' he said, and she heard the door open.

'Come on, Pip, you'll feel better if you get up. Coffee and pancakes. We can talk about things.'

'Don't want to talk. Especially not about things. Things are the worst thing.'

Her words were muffled by the pillow, but Tim still heard her. 'That's OK, we don't have to talk. We'll eat the pancakes and look at the cats.'

Pip sighed. It seemed unlikely that she was going to just quietly and painlessly die, as she hoped. Which meant that she would have to get up at some point. A fresh surge of horror went through her at the thought, but then again, she *did* like pancakes. And they really were much better hot. She raised her head and sighed.

'OK. Pancakes. No talking.'

He smiled his lovely smile and withdrew. Most followed him out. Pip gave a last groan into the pillow and swung her legs to the floor. She would have to face the world sometime. Might as well be for pancakes.

Tim gave no indication of finding the enforced silence awkward. He hummed as he put the pile of banana pancakes on the kitchen table, together with the butter, jam and syrup. He seemed perfectly content as he placed their coffee cups down in front of their places. He muttered a few niceties to Most and to Smokey Robinson, the grey kitten they had kept from Most's litter. Then he sipped his coffee and chewed his pancakes contentedly without a word. It drove Pip nuts.

'Well, aren't you going to say something?' she snapped grumpily.

'More coffee?' he said pleasantly.

'No, thanks.'

They retreated into silence. Tim looked dreamily out of the window. Pip followed his gaze. Nothing to see, just clouds and treetops.

'Go on, spit it out,' she said.

'Hmmmm?'

'Whatever it is you want to say, say it.'

'Oh, I thought you wanted no talking.'

'Well, you seem to want to say something.'

Which wasn't true. He was calm and peaceful; she was the one jiggling her knee and stressing.

'OK, well, just to say, I'm sorry about last night. I know it's very upsetting for you, and for what it's worth I think you were very unlucky, being fired. It was just a horrible accident. As you always say, it could have happened to anyone. It wasn't your fault.'

'Whose fault was it then, Tim? The fabric manufacturers of the 1970s?'

'That's exactly who! Those dangerous lunatics with their highly flammable materials. It's a wonder anyone lived through the 1970s without being burnt to a crisp.'

'Especially with all the smoking they did back then,' said Pip, warming to the banter in spite of herself. 'Not to mention those giant flaming joints.'

'And dancing round those bonfires and campfires. Like at Woodstock.'

'You are right. I'm not at fault. It was the decade. In the immortal words of the Jacksons, blame it on the boogie,' she said, doing a very poor imitation of that popping thing MJ used to do with his head.

She took her last sip of coffee, put down the mug and said, 'Thanks for the pancakes. I'm going back to bed.'

She was still there three hours later, trawling through Twitter, trying to avoid news articles about the fire at the museum – a spectacular picture of the faux Robert Plant's blazing locks was doing the rounds – when Tim was back, *rat-a-tat* on her bedroom door.

'I'm popping out. Want anything from the shops?' he asked casually.

'A small bottle of arsenic and a large bottle of vodka.'

It was a joke, but she didn't pull it off.

'Hey, Pip—'

'Nothing I need,' she cut him short.

'OK, see you later.'

A while later she heard his key in the lock as he returned, and felt the little tinge of pleasure she'd come to feel when he arrived home.

Then she remembered that her life was shite and she was stupid and useless and jobless, and the momentary pleasure disappeared.

There was some muffled sound from the kitchen – the familiar clatter of the cats' bowls, the opening and closing of the fridge – and then again his *rat-a-tat* on the door.

'OK. Enough with the self-pity. Time to get up. Go have a shower while I get lunch started.'

'It's not self-pity,' she said, self-pityingly.

'Go on. Shower.'

Admittedly, she felt somewhat better after a good dousing of hot water, and it was a relief to inhale the fragrance of ylang-ylang on her hair instead of the stench of burnt plastic and smoke. What was a ylang-ylang, come to think of it? Or was it an ylang-ylang? It was in everything these days. There must be great fields of the stuff somewhere. Or swarms. Or flocks. Or whatever. She hoped it wasn't a cute mammal – a gerbil from Indonesia or something – that would be terrible. She stepped out of the shower, dried and dressed, and went through to the kitchen.

'They were out of arsenic so I got us a Chardonnay,' he said, gesturing to the bottle. 'Open it up, pour us a glass.'

'You are the best flatmate,' she said, taking the corkscrew from a drawer. 'Really.'

'You'd do the same for me.'

'I promise that if you ever set fire to your place of work, destroy priceless vintage items and lose your job dramatically in front of your family and friends, museum patrons and the media, I will definitely make you pancakes and buy you wine.' Pip poured and handed him a glass.

'Good to know.'

They sat together a while in silence, sipping their wine.

'You know, Tim, I've had a lot of jobs in my time. A *lot* of jobs. Many of them have ended not so well. A few of them have ended disastrously. To be honest, I never really cared. But this job was great. I loved it. I was good at it. And it ended in the worst way of all, and I feel just awful.'

Appallingly, tears slipped down her cheeks. She put her glass on the table. 'I'm going back to bed.' But just as she got to her feet, the doorbell rang.

CHAPTER 2

'Expecting anyone?' Tim asked.

'No, you?'

He shook his head and went to the door. Pip tried to sneak into her bedroom and avoid whoever was at the door, but she was too slow.

As Tim opened the door, the visitor threw herself at him, burying her face in his chest. Pip could hear sniffing and crying and some indistinct gabbling. Tim held the shaking, heaving young woman and pulled her towards him, closing the door behind them.

'What happened? Are you all right? Talk to me,' he said in alarm.

Pip observed the scene with interest, her heart sinking slightly. Was this some heart-broken girlfriend of Tim's that she hadn't even known about? If so, she looked awfully young. Pip frowned, and Tim must have seen her.

'Pip, it's my sister, Claire. Remember?' he said.

Pip remembered being introduced to the girl – a female, teenage version of Tim, with his dark hair and gold-flecked eyes – at their cousin's engagement party. Claire had run off almost immediately to join the youngsters on the dance floor.

Claire raised her tear-streaked face and turned her puffy eyes on Pip, then collapsed into a fresh round of crying. Was she hurt? Pip couldn't see any sign of injury, thank God.

'I'm going to be expelled…' she wailed.

'Now, I'm sure that's not true. Let's just calm down,' Tim said soothingly, shooting a 'help me' glance at Pip. 'Just tell us what happened, and we'll do what we can to help you sort it out.'

'I'm in big trouble, I don't... I can't... The school says that I, that I... I'm going to be...'

School dramas. The very last thing Pip needed to hear about.

'I'm innocent, I swear,' cried Claire.

Pip sighed inwardly. She knew this roundabout. She herself had repeatedly got into trouble at school. Bad trouble, the sort of thing you can be expelled for. And she was always, always innocent. At least that's what she told her teachers, her mother, the local police, and once, when things went properly wrong, the SAS unit of the British Army. But the less said about that, the better. It could have happened to anyone, really. Whatever was going on with Tim's sister, Pip wanted nothing to do with it.

'I'll leave you to it,' she said, heading towards her room. 'Going back to bed.'

'Pip...' Tim shot her a pleading glance.

'Good luck,' she called her over shoulder, scooping up Most and leaving the siblings behind.

She had no sooner settled under the duvet and opened up her phone for a brain-rotting session of flicking through social media than Tim was back.

'Pip,' he said, knocking and opening the door at the same time. 'Please come, I need your help.'

'I don't know what I can do about that.'

'It's a misunderstanding. I can tell you she's a totally straight-up, honest girl. She would never lie to me.'

'Look, Tim, I don't know Claire at all, but in my experience...' She struggled for the right words to express her absolute belief in Claire's honesty, along with her complete scepticism about her innocence. 'It's just that at school, when things go wrong, it's not always easy to fess up. Sometimes, just to keep out of trouble, a person might be tempted to go for the outraged innocent defence, when in fact she maybe let things get just a teeny tad out of control.'

'Not in this case. If she tells me she's innocent, I believe her.'

It really was very sweet, how convinced he was of his sister's innocence. Nonetheless, based on no evidence whatsoever – but years of personal experience – Pip would put money on his being wrong.

'Please, Pip. Just come and listen. You've got good instincts.'

'Yeah, great instincts. Like inviting a fire juggler to an acrylic convention,' Pip said glumly. 'I don't know, Tim, I'm not sure I want to get involved. Knowing me and my poor judgement, I'll only make things worse for you and your sister. You'd be furious if I accidentally set her on fire.'

She picked up her phone again, giving him a very firm message – she wanted nothing to do with Claire's problem.

'Pip, I'm asking for your help.'

'I don't—'

'I'm always here for you.' His eyes flashed as he said this. 'When you needed me on your investigations, or to pick you up after some disaster, did I ever say no? Did I ever let you down?'

It was true. Tim had helped her out time and again. Pip felt awful.

'You're right. You're absolutely right,' she said, throwing her phone down on the bed. 'Let's hear what Claire has got to say. Perhaps she's as innocent as you say. Anyway, it's probably not as bad as she fears. You know what schools are like, everything's a drama. Let's hope it's just some misunderstanding that we can help her with. I'll keep an open mind.'

'Thanks, Pip, I appreciate that. And you know, maybe you've got a point. It could be something minor that's been blown out of proportion, and we'll get to the bottom of it nice and quick and put the whole thing to rest. And have some more pancakes.'

As it turned out, that was not the case.

CHAPTER 3

Claire sat hunched over the cup of tea Tim had made for her, the steam drifting up to her face while the tears ran down. A ginger biscuit lay in her left hand, undipped.

'Come on, sis,' said Tim gently. 'Just tell us what happened so we can help.'

Pip couldn't help but notice that 'we'. She only hoped that whatever the problem was, 'we' could solve it quickly and simply so that Tim would stop worrying about Claire and she, Pip, could get started on finding another job. Or go back to bed. Either, really.

'Start from the beginning,' she said to the girl.

Claire wiped her tears and her nose on the sleeve of her school jumper, gave a huge dramatic sniff, and said, 'Well, it all started with the science test. It was the mid-year exam, so it was really important to do well. And you know science isn't the easiest…'

'Not her best subject,' Tim explained to Pip. Then added proudly, 'Claire is more of an art and history buff, gets top marks in the class for those subjects.'

'That's the thing,' said Claire. 'I was determined to crack this science test. I needed to bring my average up. I gave it my all. I worked super hard and I got eighty per cent. My best mark ever.'

'Wow! Well done, sis!' Tim beamed. 'I told you you could do it.'

'Except that's where it all started to go wrong,' she said. 'After the results came out, Ms Peters, the headmistress, called me to her office. I was pleased that she had noticed the turnaround in my mark and wanted to congratulate me. She asked me to tell her how

I did so well this time and I told her. I said I'd read the notes and then practised the equations from past papers like the teacher told us, and it just sort of clicked.'

Smokey Robinson, that little grey scrap of a cat, jumped up and settled into Claire's lap, kneading into her blue-and-green tartan skirt with his tiny paws and purring his loud kitten rumble. It was weird how cats instinctively knew who required their ministrations. She gave him a stroke and seemed to grow a little calmer. Most looked on proudly.

'Anyway, then she asked me who I was friends with, which was, like, weird, because what's that got to do with anything, but I told her a few names. And she asked how well I knew Ruby and Amelia.'

'Who are they?'

'Just two girls in my class. They're fine. We're friends, but we're not like *friend* friends. They're not in my group, or anything.'

Teenagers and their endless friend dramas. Pip remembered them from her own teen years – the little gangs, the falling out, the making up, the gossip, the big to-dos about nothing at all. It seemed the so-called big problem was going to be one of those.

Claire continued, 'And then Ms Peters started asking me all sorts of questions about the paper. She said the school knew that the exam paper had been leaked, and they were going to get to the bottom of it and when they did there would be Big Trouble. She said that this was a criminal matter!'

There was a fresh round of tears from Claire, and a new round of patting and tutting from Tim.

'Go on, sis,' he said. 'Finish your story, then we'll talk about what to do.'

Claire sniffed, and went on. 'Ms Peters wanted to know who Ruby and Amelia and I got the paper from. She said if I gave her the names of who was responsible for leaking the papers, it would be treated as an internal disciplinary matter by the school and…

and… and…' Claire's tears were dropping heavily onto the little cat at this point, and although his spine twitched with each tear, sending a ripple down his back, he stayed in place. 'And she wouldn't have to hand the matter over to the police.'

She let out a great wail. 'I don't want to go to jail!'

'No one's going to hand you over to the police, and you are not going to jail,' said Pip brusquely. 'We're talking about a spot of cheating here, not stealing the Crown Jewels. So please, put that out of your mind.'

'Really?' Claire asked, brightening visibly at the news that she wasn't about to be detained at Her Majesty's pleasure. 'You're certain?'

'Of course,' Pip said, with rather more confidence than she felt. She wasn't a lawyer, after all. Or a cop. Or, in fact, an investigator. And that one night in jail after the tractor incident didn't make her an expert on the criminal justice system. 'We can sort this out, I'm sure.'

'I told you Pip would help. She's an experienced sleuth,' Tim said, rather overstating things. He patted his sister on the shoulder and gave Pip a grateful-puppy look. 'Don't you worry.'

'Let me ask you a few questions,' Pip said, and pulled out her notebook.

She had a new one, a gift from her friend Jimmy, and it was even more ridiculous than the notebooks she'd used on her previous two cases. This one had a huge blue eye in the centre and it was a sort of 3D-hologram thing, so as you moved it, it blinked open and closed, and the psychedelic swirls and squiggles that surrounded it moved too, wriggling and squirming. On the cover and on each page were the words 'See the Light'. It was truly ghastly and actually quite disconcerting.

Goodness knows how long Jimmy had searched to find such an awful item.

'Tim,' she said. 'Why don't you go and get some more tea while Claire and I get started.'

'But we've just had tea, I'm sure nobody…' She shot him a look with just a tweak of a raised eyebrow, which stopped him mid-sentence. He cottoned on. 'Oh yes, of course. I'll go and make tea.'

Once he was safely out of the room, Pip turned to Claire.

'Claire, I need to know the truth. You can tell me and I won't judge. Did you buy the exam paper?'

'No. Hand on heart. Swear to die.'

'Did you see the exam paper before the exam?'

'No.'

'Did anyone tell you anything about what might be in it?'

'No. I prepared well and worked hard. I promise.'

Pip looked into her eyes – so like Tim's – and tried to gauge her. Her instinct was to believe the girl. She looked, well… she looked innocent. She seemed to be telling the truth. But Pip had been wrong about this many, many times, and had given lots of convincing fibbers and scoundrels the benefit of the doubt – starting with just about every man she had ever dated. Nonetheless, right now Claire didn't seem like a devious cheater.

Tim came in and put a tray of fresh tea on the table.

'Are Mum and Dad freaking out?'

'I haven't told them.'

'What? Didn't the school…?'

Claire explained that their parents had gone to the Cotswolds to nurse a great aunt, and nobody knew quite when they would be back.

'I don't want them to know. They will go nuts, you know what they're like.'

Tim nodded and gave a slight eye-roll. Pip filed that away for future consideration, realising she knew next to nothing about Tim's family other than that his cousin threw a fine engagement party, and now, that they were the type of people who would look after a sick great aunt.

'That's why I came to you, Tim. The school was going to phone Mum, so I told them my parents were away and you are my guardian, but you were in a meeting all day and I would get you to phone this afternoon. Just tell them you've spoken to me, and you believe me. Then they won't have to involve Mum and Dad. It'll all blow over.'

Funny, that was what Tim had hoped for – that it would all blow over.

Claire held her phone out to him, the number up on the screen ready for him to hit dial. 'Here. Just phone Ms Peters. Schools hate drama. They'll back off, I know. Please, Tim, please.'

Tim reached out and took it.

CHAPTER 4

More than a decade since she'd finished school, here Pip was, waiting nervously outside a headmistress's office. She felt the familiar jitters. She had spent quite some time waiting outside various offices for various headmistresses to call her in, to explain various misunderstandings and misdemeanours.

Things hadn't changed much, she noted. The implacable secretary with the sensible skirt and blouse and the pearls, at her desk, tapping away at a keyboard. The cabinet of silverware – cups and trophies and accolades for this and that. The portraits of the previous incumbents; the headmistresses of yore, their severe faces and rigid helmets of hair fixed forever in oil paints. The school smell of polish and boiled potatoes and hormones and floral spray-on deodorant.

She examined the wooden plaque directly across from her, listing the girls who had been made Head Girl in the years dating from 1965 to 2005, a name alongside each year. What was Mary Jane Marlboro doing now? she wondered. Or Harriet Glenferness. Or Petra Smith. Or any one of those forty women who had preceded Claire at this school, and earned the honour of being a student leader.

Did their brains stand them in good stead? Did they find success and happiness? She hoped so.

Did any of them filch an exam paper and cheat on the exam? She suspected not.

Tim had probably not spent as much time as Pip outside the headmistress's office awaiting admonishment. Nonetheless, he looked nervous too, his knee bouncing up and down. He had phoned, as Claire requested, and tried unsuccessfully to put the matter to rest. But Ms Peters hadn't 'backed off' as Claire had predicted. The whole thing hadn't 'blown over' as Tim had hoped. Instead, he had been summoned to the school for a meeting with the head to discuss the exam paper matter.

The door to the headmistress's office opened, and the headmistress stepped out. Pip tried to remind herself that she was definitely not in trouble about anything, and didn't need to feel quite so nervous.

'Mr Linden, please come in. I'm the principal of Hurlingham House, Alexandra Peters,' she said, offering her hand.

Her portrait would make a nice change in the gallery of battle-axes, thought Pip. The woman was young – maybe forty or so – and friendly looking. Instead of the helmet style preferred by her predecessors, she had a head of narrow braids that brushed her shoulders. She smiled warmly at them. Pip relaxed a little at the sight of her.

'Tim Linden, Claire's brother,' he said, shaking her hand.

Ms Peters looked quizzically at Pip.

'This is Epiphany Bloom, um, a family friend,' Tim said.

Pip said hello, without elaborating on the reason for her presence, and they settled at a round table in the office. The place was light and cheery, the wood panels painted white and decorated with photographs of healthy, happy young women playing hockey, or declaiming from the stage, or caught in mid-air, tucked in a pike above a swimming pool.

'I'm sorry we have to meet under these circumstances. I believe your parents are out of town and you are Claire's guardian in their absence?'

'They've asked me to handle the matter.' Tim nodded, pale-faced. His Adam's apple bobbed up and down as he swallowed hard. He was a terrible liar. Pip liked that in a man.

'Thank you for making yourself available. I wanted to speak to you alone to start with, so I've asked Claire to join us in five minutes. Claire is a lovely girl and a good student,' Ms Peters continued. 'But you must understand that cheating is a very serious offence. We have a zero tolerance policy – if it turns out she cheated, it will be on her school record. She would be prohibited from any student leadership positions. It might even affect her chances of getting into certain universities.'

Tim paled at the thought. 'Yes, of course, it *is* very serious. And we take it very seriously too. But the thing is, Claire is adamant that she's innocent. She assures me she didn't cheat. I believe her.'

Ms Peters nodded. 'Yes, she said the same to me. I would like to believe her, I really would, but look at this.'

She took a file off the top of a pile on the side of her desk and opened it, flipping through to find a page of numbers arranged on a grid.

'Claire's science marks.' She put it on the desk between them and pointed to it with a pen as she spoke. 'Solid low- to mid-sixties all year, you see? And then here, this most recent test, eighty per cent. A big jump. You can see how that might look suspicious.'

'But she explained the improvement,' said Tim. 'She really worked hard at her science. Went over the notes. Did the past papers.'

'Yes, she told me the same thing. Granted, it's possible – if extremely unusual – for a student to make such a big and sudden improvement. But then have a look at this.'

She pulled out a second sheet of numbers, and a third. Again, she pointed at them with the tip of her pen as she spoke.

'Two other students in the same class. Ruby Stern and Amelia Duncan. Less than solid mid-fifties, both of them, all year. In some tests they only just scraped by the fifty per cent mark. And here they are with seventy-three per cent and seventy-five per cent respectively on the most recent exam. They completely denied it, of course. But it was the same exam in which Claire made such a sudden improvement. You can see how such a coincidence might look, er, surprising.'

It looked dodgy as anything, frankly. Pip wouldn't admit it to Tim, but she was less convinced of Claire's innocence in the face of this evidence.

'The thing is, Mr Linden, this looks very much like an exam paper leak. Or theft.'

She paused a moment, as if unsure whether to speak, and went on. 'Strictly between you and me, it's not the first time. There have been two other such incidents that we're aware of this term. It's starting to look like a pattern. Now, I don't want to have to get the authorities involved at this stage…'

'No, of course not,' Pip agreed vehemently, and added slyly, 'Something like that would reflect poorly on the school. Very bad publicity.'

Ms Peters looked surprised to hear she could speak. She'd sat there like a turnip since they had arrived.

'Epiphany has some experience with the media,' said Tim, entirely inaccurately, by way of explanation. Pip's sister, Flis, ran a massively successful blog and Pip had once pretended to be a journalist on it in order to get to a potential kidnapper. She didn't think that really counted as media experience.

Ms Peters went on. 'As I said, I'm reluctant to bring in the police and risk this getting out. You are correct, this is not the kind of publicity a school with our excellent academic reputation wants. But I do need to get to the bottom of it.'

Tim leaned forward, and began to speak in his earnest way. 'I understand. That's why I brought Pip, you see. She's experienced in conducting discreet investigations.'

'You're a private investigator, Ms Bloom?' Ms Peters asked, turning to Pip.

'I don't really like to use the term, or to label what I do. But I have managed on occasion to find things. Missing things. A boy, once. And a dress.'

She sounded like a twit, and Ms Peters clearly thought so too. 'I'm sure that was very good news for the owners, but the school environment is quite tricky. The governing body, the parents; I'm not sure it would be appropriate. This isn't a missing dress.'

'Ms Peters, please.' Tim turned to the principal and said, in a tone somewhere between begging and charming, 'Before you go to the police, just let Pip – Ms Bloom – investigate. Give her a week or two and if there's no progress, then call the police, by all means.'

Ms Peters thought about Tim's proposal for a moment. 'I can't say I like the idea of a private investigator poking around the school. But I can't say I like the idea of escalating this to the board either. Let alone to the Education Department.' She gave an almost imperceptible shudder. Pip could see her mulling it over, imagining the many ways in which an exam scandal at the school could devastate her career. She sighed. 'All right. I'm prepared to consider your suggestion. Tell me how you see this working.'

Tim stammered. 'I, um, well, I'm not quite sure about how, exactly. Pip? How would you go about getting to the bottom of this?'

'I guess I would interview some of the girls. Ruby and Amelia, to start with, and then others.'

'I'm afraid I can't allow you to formally interview students,' said Ms Peters firmly, shaking her braids. 'Any investigation has to be unofficial and undercover. Below the radar. The parents in this school pay a great deal of money to send their daughters here. They are, for the most part, powerful and influential people who do not take kindly to the intimation that their offspring are cheats. Some of them are… Well, let's say they wouldn't respond well to the girls being accused.'

Tim shot Pip a look, as if he knew the type.

'We can't confront the girls or alert their parents until we have more information. And actual proof.'

'That's where Pip comes in. Information. Proof,' Tim said, with confidence and a beaming smile that could melt the heart even of a headmistress. Pip felt somewhat less confident and beaming herself. Where would she start? It was hard to think, with a sound of ambulance or police sirens in the background distracting her.

'Maybe if I could find a way to mingle with the students,' she suggested. 'Even the teachers. There might be someone from the staff involved.'

'The teachers? Oh, I'm sure not. Our teachers are some of the best in the country!'

Pip decided to ignore her protestations, and brag a bit. 'When I found that very valuable missing dress, I did it by going undercover at the museum the dress was stolen from.' There. That would put an end to comments like 'this isn't a missing dress'.

'And you can do this without anyone realising who you are?' asked Ms Peters, sounding doubtful. Pip didn't blame her, really.

'I'm sure I can,' lied Pip, who wasn't sure of anything of the sort. 'It's the difference between an interview with an investigator and a casual chat that's key. Suspects will give away all sorts of things if they don't know who they're talking to.' She tried to inject some authority into this statement, and it seemed to work.

Ms Peters nodded. 'Yes. Instead of going in and interviewing, something more low-key. Chats, as you put it.'

'Exactly,' said Pip. 'Low-key. Ear to the ground. Maybe coming into the school as, um…' Pip racked her brains, but the ambulance siren was now so loud that she could hardly think. 'Perhaps as, um…'

Before she could come up with a brilliant idea, or finish her sentence, there was a knock on the door. The secretary popped her head round and said, 'Sorry to disturb you in a meeting, but it's an urgent matter.'

'Yes, Mrs Jenkins, what is it?' Ms Peters said.

'I thought you should know, Mrs Hatfield has gone into early labour in the middle of the Year Nine netball lesson, ma'am; the ambulance is here.'

'Oh goodness, thank you, Mrs Jenkins,' said Ms Peters, her kind face suddenly concerned.

'Perhaps,' said Pip, with a smile. 'Perhaps I could come in as a substitute sports teacher.'

Ms Peters nodded, and then excused herself to go and wish Mrs Hatfield well. 'I'll be back in ten minutes,' she said. 'Mrs Jenkins, please do bring our guests a hot drink while they wait.'

Pip was grateful for the pause, which allowed her to think about how this could work, so she was ready for Ms Peters's return. Unfortunately, she had very few ideas.

'So,' said Ms Peters, returning to her office ten minutes later, and settling herself back in her chair. 'The PE teacher idea is inspired. But what is your strategy, Ms Bloom? How do you intend to expose the exam leak ringleader?'

Pip stammered a bit and said, 'Well, my first step will be to get close to the two girls who were likely to be cheating. Ask them to help me with… sports things. Get a feel for them.'

'Yes, I can arrange for you to teach their classes, so that will work.'

'I'll ask them some leading questions, without letting on that I'm particularly interested in them. Or in exams. Maybe ask for some advice. Something exam-related. Or…'

There was an awkward silence as they both reflected on the hopelessness of this so-called plan.

'I could tell them I'm setting an exam myself!' Pip said, triumphantly.

'Yes, I see where you're going with this,' said Ms Peters approvingly. She did? Pip didn't. Unless...

'A sting operation,' said Pip, as if that had been her plan all along.

'That sounds like a good idea to me,' said Ms Peters. 'Tell me more about how it will work.'

Pip's brain whirred, trying to develop a plan on the fly – which was, to be fair, where most of her plans were developed.

'Well, as I said, my idea was to set an exam, a written exam, and let everyone know that's happening. Then leave the exam somewhere... I'll work out the details once I have the lay of the land. Let me get a feel for the place and the girls, and I'll fine-tune the plan.'

'Good, good,' said Ms Peters, nodding happily, as if the whole affair was well on its way to being settled.

'One important thing,' Pip said, giving Ms Peters a serious look. 'No one else must know. Not the girls, nor the science teacher. Just you and me. We can't risk the perpetrator being tipped off.'

'Of course. Just us. Believe me, I do not want this getting out. You have no idea how fast rumours travel in a school environment. The Car Park Mafia would be all over it in a heartbeat.'

Ms Peters sighed wearily, as if recalling other such incidents, then turned back to Pip with a smile.

'Thank you for your expertise, I think your plan is a good one. Keep me posted,' said Ms Peters. 'We'll pay you for your time, of course. And additionally when the matter is taken care of. I will give you something upfront just to tide you over – how does one thousand pounds sound?' Pip felt a wave of relief. Getting fired from the museum had left her in an awkward financial position.

'Thank you, Ms Peters,' she said.

'Oh, do call me Alexandra,' she added warmly. She really was a very strange headmistress, in Pip's experience, which was large and spanned continents. Pip wanted to please her, which was a completely new feeling when it came to headmistresses. She needed to crack the exam leak wide open, and Ms Peters would like Pip forever.

CHAPTER 5

The idea that had come to her in a flash of brilliance now seemed rather rash. Going undercover as a sports mistress presented a number of problems, Pip realised, as she pottered around the kitchen, feeding the cats and waiting for the kettle to boil. Most intractable amongst the problems was that Pip had only the vaguest idea of what a sports teacher actually did, or in fact what sport was, having bunked most of the physical education sessions in her various high schools.

Pip had been a complete klutz from birth, according to Mummy, dropping her rattle and missing her porridge bowl and slipping in the bath and tripping down the stairs and constantly breaking things.

'It was like having a deranged Labrador puppy,' said Mummy, who actually had a deranged Labrador, which had once been a puppy, and she seemed to find him rather easier to deal with than Pip.

After years of being picked last for every team, every time, and tripping and fumbling her way through games, Pip had had the foresight to invent a fake heart murmur when she entered secondary school.

'Yes, I'd love to try out for hockey, miss. I know Mummy is worried about my heart, and the doctor too after the incident, but it'll probably be fine. He was almost certain…'

After that she'd been happily relegated to the social badminton team, where one of her fellow team members had an actual prosthetic leg. Pip loved social badminton and was considered rather good at it, given the exceptionally low standard of the players and the game. That was the modest highlight of her school sporting career.

Having explained to Claire that she would be standing in as the sports coach, and that Claire must pretend not to know her, she asked her what Mrs Hatfield usually did.

'Teaches sports,' said Claire. 'It's ever so boring.'

'But how does she do it?' asked Pip. 'How does she teach sports?'

'I dunno,' said Claire, unhelpfully. 'She tells us what to do, and we do it. And sometimes she shouts and says, "God help me, what a bunch of fools you are," and walks out.'

Pip had banked the last piece of information for emergencies, but felt she needed more research.

She settled down with a fresh cup of coffee. She started, as always, with Google. 'What does a sports teacher do?' she typed.

Google, as always, was completely useless: 'Aspiring sports teachers typically hold a Bachelor of Education (B. Ed.)…'

You needed a degree to tell children to run round a field? How ridiculous! Anyway, it was much too late for that. Pip had four-fifths of a degree in English Literature, and that would just have to do. She couldn't possibly get a Bachelor of Education by tomorrow.

'…instruct students in key concepts and skills related to physical fitness and specific sports…'

Skills? Key concepts? Heck, no. There was no way she could tell someone how to hold a tennis racket or run faster, or determine whether a particular hockey player had committed a fowl. Or, come to think of it, was it a foul? That would certainly make more sense, now that she thought about it.

'…organise practices, lead drills… Use practicals, exams, tests and assignments…'

Oh, for goodness' sake. What, a netball exam? She put the phone down on the table and sighed.

But she did know a sport! She smacked her hand on her head in a cartoon gesture of realisation. Boxing, of course!

Pip had, in recent months, been training at The Glove Box with Jimmy. She was surprised to have discovered a talent and enjoyment in smacking the hell out of a punch bag or set of pads. She was fitter than she'd ever been and was even developing some skills.

Hah! She had a sport. She had skills. She was a sporty girl with sports skills! She was going to be fine.

With that in mind she changed into her kit and headed out for The Glove Box. She'd train for a bit – getting hot and sweaty always seemed to bring on good ideas, like that time she'd thought about adding crispy bacon to Tim's trademark banana pancakes, and when she got home they did just that and it was amazing. While they trained, she'd tell Jimmy about the exam scam and pick his brains about how to develop the sports teacher persona.

Once he'd finished laughing at the idea of her passing herself off as a sports teacher, Jimmy was quite helpful.

Making a big show of wiping the tears of mirth from his eyes, he said, 'Forget skills. You'll never pull that off.'

She had to agree with him on that one.

'You're only going to be there for a week or two, so your best bet is to let them get on with the game, whatever that is. So, if it's hockey – the one with the curved stick and the—'

'I know what hockey is,' she said grumpily. It was annoying to have to put up with his cracking jokes at her expense, but she did need his help. 'It's the one with the chickens. I mean the fouls.'

Jimmy looked baffled, but continued his instructions. 'Whatever the game – hockey, netball, whatever – first off, you divide them into teams.'

'How many in each?'

Pip went to her bag and extracted her hologram eye notebook, ready to take notes. He smiled, pleased to see her using his gift.

'There are different numbers for different games.'

'That doesn't seem sensible.'

'Scrap that. Tell them to divide themselves. And Pip, take this down, it's important...'

She stood to attention, pen poised. He danced around the bag.

'Whatever you do, don't ref the game. You have no idea how to do that. Because you don't know the rules.'

'Noted,' she said, noting it in her notable notebook.

'Let one of the kids ref.'

'Good idea.' More scribbling. 'But what do I do when they're playing? If I'm not reffing... refelling... referring?'

Jimmy bounced on his toes, punctuating his sentences with an uppercut, then a cross.

'Refereeing.' *Thwack.* 'Just stand on the sidelines with your arms crossed, staring stony-faced at them as if you're looking for areas of technique that you can improve on.'

Thwack.

'Don't say a word. Don't engage. Look as unapproachable as possible. Get some sunglasses.'

Thwack. Thwack. Thwack.

Pip wrote down 'stony' and 'sunglasses'.

Jimmy was well into his stride by now, bouncing and thwacking and talking. 'Oh, and fitness training. It's useful for filling in the time and tiring them out. Feed them a story about how fitness is the basis of all success and yada yada yada. Whenever you're at a loose end, make them run round the field or do some of the drills you

and I have been doing – jumping, hopping, squatting, punching,'
he said, smacking the bag as he mentioned each drill.

'That's a good idea, Jimmy,' she said, feeling a bit better about
things. 'So, between the fitness and the game, it's not as if I'm going
to need a lot of actual knowledge. Like, "this is how you throw a
netball" sort of thing.'

'Yes, stay away from telling anyone how to do anything.'

'OK great, I've got what I need.'

She left with a page of notes, thanking him profusely.

'Hey, you should get me to come along some time. I'll set up a
punch bag, we can show them some moves.'

'Great offer, thanks Jimmy.' She wondered how a room full of
schoolgirls would react to Jimmy, who looked like he had wandered
off the set of *Prison Break*.

'Supper at the diner when I'm done with this little job?' she
said. 'Burgers on me.'

He waved her off, chuckling to himself. 'Let me know how it
goes. I'm looking forward to a full report. And to dinner. A lot.'

CHAPTER 6

Pip hit the malls at the weekend and purchased two bright shiny tracksuits – if that's what they were still called – and a new pair of trainers. The purchasing of the trainers had been particularly stressful. Who knew that there was so much variety?

First she went to a shop full of sneakers only to discover they cost more than handmade Italian boots and they weren't actually for playing sports in. To avoid a repeat of that embarrassing misunderstanding, she went to Sports Stuff, which was very obviously a sports store that sold sports equipment and sports shoes.

A young man slouched over to her, a touch of reluctance in his offer of assistance.

'Hi. I'm looking for some sports shoes.'

His expression was familiar to Pip – that of someone holding back a smirk, but not trying very hard. She would have liked to give his smirky weasel face a smack.

'What will you be using them for?'

'Sports.'

'Like what?'

'I guess hockey, and—'

'Well, if you're wanting hockey boots, that's another matter entirely,' he said officiously. 'Follow me.'

'No, I don't need hockey boots, just something all-round.'

'All-round?' He raised an eyebrow, and with it, a sort of miniature dumbbell that pierced it.

'Yes. A pair of shoes for all different sports.'

'Will you be running?'

'Yes.'

'So you need running shoes.' He gave a supercilious look at her feet. 'And you are pronated?'

'No, I was conceived naturally, as far as I know. But what's that got to do with anything?'

'Your feet. They are pronated. They roll inwards.'

'I didn't know that,' she said, looking at her treacherous feet. She'd thought they were fine and now discovered they were not.

'It puts a lot of strain on your joints. Hips, knees and so on. I can give you some special shoes, or a neutral shoe with inserts to help correct the deformity.'

This excruciating conversation went on for some minutes. When she could bear it no more, Pip left.

Exhausted by her trials, Pip decided to try one more shop, and a new approach. She marched into the next sports store and said to the young woman standing by the shoes, 'Hello. I require stable, not very stylish footwear for playing games in. Size eight. I don't want to spend a fortune and I don't want to answer any questions.'

The girl nodded without speaking and went to the storeroom, coming back with a single shoebox, which she handed to Pip without a word.

Silently, Pip tried the shoes on. She walked to the mirror and back. The sports shoes were stable and comfortable and the right size. She looked at the price tag – quite considerably less than Italian boots.

'I'll take them,' she said. 'Thank you. You're the best sales assistant in London.'

*

Pip arrived at school on Monday feeling pretty chuffed with her sports mistress outfit. The drive to Kent had been tedious, with various road detours where things were being built; housing developments and shopping centres, mostly. But, in a most un-Pip-like turn of events, she had still arrived on time, and even managed to find a parking space in the staff parking, inserting her ancient yellow Mini between a battered Toyota and a shiny Range Rover. She felt ready for the day. As long as no one threw a ball at her – she could never lose the impulse to duck – she should be able to pass herself off as athletic. She wondered if she would be given a whistle, or if she should have bought one of her own.

She was to meet with Ms Peters after assembly, so once again she found herself under the watchful eye of the secretary and the ghosts of principals past.

'I've got a few minutes before classes start,' said Ms Peters, looking at her watch. 'Let me show you around.'

The staffroom was a bright and pleasant space furnished with sofas, rugs and small meeting tables. The teachers were milling about, chatting; mostly women, but one or two men were sprinkled about. Pip spotted a very proper older fellow, and a young, pale, Gothic-looking chap. She liked that about schools – you got all sorts.

Ms Peters briefly called for attention and introduced Pip as the substitute sports teacher. 'Please make her welcome,' she said. The assembled teachers smiled and nodded with friendly disinterest before going back to what they were doing. Clearly it was not worth investing too much time in substitutes. But Pip would need background information and office gossip – so she would have to make some connections.

She joined a short, orderly queue at the gleaming cappuccino machine. 'Nice to start the day with a good cup of coffee,' she said chattily to the woman in front of her.

'Oh yes, a top-notch bit of equipment this is. A gift from a grateful parent. I'm Marie Stone, by the way. Geography.' Marie looked as if she had scaled a few mountains and forded some rivers in her time – fit and no-nonsense, in a zip-up fleece and sturdy shoes.

'Good to meet you,' Pip said, restraining herself from making a Stone/geology joke – the Geography teacher must have heard that one a million times. 'That's quite a gift. They must have been nice parents.'

'I don't know about that, but I do know they were very grateful. Their daughter left here with a full house of A-stars and a place at Oxford, if I remember rightly. Very grateful. And so they should be. I don't know who worked harder, me or the girl, to get those marks,' she said, and added, 'I think I was as proud as she was when that First came through.' Marie's coffee was now steaming fragrantly in her cup. 'Cappuccino?' she asked Pip, and pointed to the right button.

'I've heard so much about the school – I'm pleased to have a chance to teach here for a bit,' said Pip, in a display of new-girl enthusiasm. 'You know, I'm hoping that if I do well here, they might find a permanent place for me some day. Any tips?'

'Steer clear of the parents,' Marie said with a wicked laugh. 'Don't be fooled by the cappuccino machine.'

'Are you scaring the newbie, Marie?' The tall, grey-haired man who Pip had spotted earlier was behind her now, empty cup in hand, awaiting his turn at the grinding, steaming behemoth. 'Jeremy Horn. Classics. You'll be all right with the sport,' he said with a dismissive wave of his hand. 'It's just a bit of fun and fitness, we're not a very sporty school. Anyone with any sports ambition is with a private coach or boot camp or what have you. The pressure's in the academics. That's where we earn our keep.'

Her coffee ready, Pip moved aside and let him take his turn, positioning his cup under the silver nozzle.

'Yes, I hear the school promises excellent results,' said Pip. 'It must be very demanding for you teachers.'

'It is, but everyone here knows the drill. They employ the best, pay better than any other school, and look after us very well. Good pensions, generous financial incentives for the girls' good marks, fine facilities…' He made a sweeping hand gesture, taking in the tasteful furnishings, the plates of biscuits, the sparkling coffee monster. 'All they ask in return is your soul. A Faustian bargain indeed.'

Jeremy Horn barked an abrupt laugh at his own joke, but it didn't reach his eyes. Marie tittered too, and nudged him with her elbow, while Pip tried to remember who Faust was. A deal with the devil, if she remembered correctly. She wondered if one of the group of teachers who were sipping their hot drinks and packing up their baskets and briefcases was the devil behind the cheating scheme.

Marie said to Pip, 'You could do a lot worse than end up at Hurlingham House with this lot. Some of the finest and most committed teachers in England.'

'It sounds wonderful. What about the girls? What are they like?'

'Lovely, most of them. You know teenagers – you do get some troubled ones; the bullies, the eating disorders, what have you.'

'Is there a lot of pressure on them, then?'

'Oh yes,' said Marie, with what might have been a very small eye-roll. 'Their parents have high hopes and high expectations in terms of marks. There's no question that they expect their daughters to perform. And believe me, they pay enough money for the privilege. The final hurdle, of course, is university entrance. That's the real prize. And the girls know it.'

'And they'll do anything to get it,' remarked a voice behind Pip. Pip turned. 'Janice,' said an older woman, reaching out her hand to shake Pip's. 'English.'

'Anything?' said Pip.

'They're like a pack of hungry lions, these girls,' said Janice. 'Turn your back for a second and they'll eat you. You and each other. This might be the best teaching gig in southern England, but it takes skill and experience.' Pip wondered if this was a dig at Pip's own glaring lack of either.

'On one side you have the girls,' agreed Marie, 'and on the other the teachers. All chasing the golden grail of excellent grades and top university entrance. All determined to achieve the same thing.'

'It sounds very… stimulating,' lied Pip. Actually, it sounded like a school full of people who would have every reason to cheat. Where was she even going to start?

A bell rang, and the teachers disappeared like leaves in the wind. Pip headed in the direction of the sports field with butterflies in her stomach.

CHAPTER 7

A hand went up. 'Ms Bloom?'

'Yes.'

A short girl with two long mousy braids asked, 'Is the test for marks, miss?'

'Oh yes, definitely for marks. Lots of marks. It's very important. And could you all give me your names when you speak so I can learn who's who.'

'Ruby, miss.'

Another hand went up. 'Amelia, miss. But, miss, we don't have exams in PE.'

'You do now. This is the first year it's been instituted. I am surprised Mrs Hatfield didn't mention it to you. She probably forgot, what with the baby and so on. A memo came last week from the Department of Education… of Sport… of Sport Education…'

A forest of arms appeared in front of Pip, and her stumbling explanations were drowned out by the chorus of girlish voices which rose from the crowd.

'But we never…'

'When's the…'

'And what about…?'

'But, miss…'

'My name is Grace Faith, miss,' a forceful drawl broke through the noise, and the rest of the group seemed to quieten. 'What is the test on?'

'It's on sport,' Pip said firmly. 'And fitness.'

'How can we swot if we don't know what it's on, miss?' said the girl, tossing her head to flick her ponytail over her shoulder and regarding Pip with a cool look that bordered on insolent.

'What would you put into an exam of this sort, girls?' Pip asked, turning to the group. She was rather pleased with herself. This was the sort of annoying switcheroo teachers were always pulling.

'The rules for different games,' Claire said helpfully, getting the ball rolling. Pip gave her a tiny, grateful smile.

'Scoring, I guess?' said Ruby.

A few more piped up.

'Teams – like, who does what.'

'How to build strength.'

This was quite helpful; Pip wished she had her notebook. 'Exactly,' she said. 'You see? Nothing to worry about.'

Another round of questions erupted. Pip longed for the days of 'seen and not heard'. She raised her hand and her voice, and adopted what she hoped was a teacherly tone. 'There will be an exam, as required by the Department, in our lesson on Wednesday. There is no specific topic or content. You will be tested on general aspects of sport. The test is very important. Please take it seriously; it will count towards your final year mark, which as you know is very important for, um, university entrance, and, er, life.'

There was a rumble through the crowd, but it soon died down under her attempt at a teacher's glare.

'You all right, miss?' someone asked from the front of the pack. 'Your eye…'

Pip ignored her. 'Now, I don't want to hear any more about the test. Let's get on with the lesson. Today we'll be concentrating on fitness training.'

There was a low groan.

'I want to see where your strengths and weaknesses are, where we need to focus for the term. Get ourselves fit and fast for the season.

Lean and mean.' Pip had noticed, from watching Tim watch the pre- and post-game interviews on the sports channels, that most sports commentary was just a whole lot of meaningless phrases, arranged in various orders, and repeated ad nauseam.

'There's no glory without going the extra mile,' she said in what she hoped was an inspiring manner. 'No gain, no pain,' she added, with a small air punch.

'It's no pain—' interrupted another.

'Enough chitter chatter,' Pip cut in, rather pleased with her teacherly tone. 'Go on. Run.'

The girls looked back at her glumly.

'Where to, Ms Bloom?'

'Around the field,' she said, rather snappily. Children were exhausting.

'How far?'

Pip tried to recall how long the field was, and how far a full circuit would be. 'Run round the field five times to the right to start with.' For want of a better idea. 'Then turn round and run five times the other way. Widdershins.' More dubious looks.

'Widder—'

'Widdershins. It means anticlockwise,' said Pip. It didn't say much about the English department that none of the girls knew the word. Although, Pip herself only knew it because she had worked at a pub of that name in Galway. She made a mental note to include the word in the exam.

'Go on!' she said, punching the air. 'Give it your all!'

They moved off somewhat reluctantly, and then a few of the fitter, more eager girls picked up the pace, plaits and ponytails swinging behind them as they headed off round the track. The rest jogged after them, with less speed and grace. Claire was in the middle of the pack, and raised her eyebrows questioningly at Pip, but Pip wasn't sure what that meant. Well done? Terrible job? WTF? A few slackers plodded reluctantly at the rear, Ruby among them.

Having successfully got the girls off her back, Pip felt more relaxed. Now she could think of her next steps in the investigation. She sat on a low retaining wall with her back to the sun, donned her sunglasses and looked stern as per Jimmy's advice, and considered her mental to-do list.

Of course, she needed to get that exam paper written. Pip saw a lot of Google in her future. Perhaps her sister, Flis, would help her; she had been quite a good tennis player in their youth. She would like to somehow get Amelia and Ruby alone, so she could speak to them individually, get a sense of who they were. But she had no idea how to do that without tipping them off.

She was distracted from her to-do list by some sort of commotion on the field. The run around the circuit had come largely to a halt, with girls running from both directions to mill and mingle in the centre. There were raised voices. The atmosphere appeared quite charged.

Pip stood up and made her way back to the field. 'What's going on?' she called, but the girls were too busy talking and gesticulating to hear her.

Someone was on the ground. Pip's blood ran cold. *Oh God.* Her first day at work, her first hour in fact, and there was already an incident. Possibly a bad one. Why did working life have to be so very hard?

Picking up her pace, Pip jogged onto the field, her new shoes rubbing slightly at the heel.

The girl on the ground was working her way into a sitting position now, which Pip took as a good sign. She wasn't dead, at least.

'Are you all right?' Pip asked, as she neared the huddle around the fallen girl. Through the crowd she saw that it was Ruby.

'Louisa ran into me…'

'I didn't, you ran into me…'

'But Ruby was—'

'Girls, come on…'

'You weren't looking…'

Were they always like this, a squawking flock of seagulls?

'GIRLS!' Pip shouted in her most authoritative voice. 'Quiet down and let me through.'

The squawking reduced to a low grumble and Pip was able to reach Ruby. 'Are you hurt? Can you stand?' she asked, holding out a hand.

'Yes, I just tripped,' said Ruby sulkily, brushing grass from a graze on her knee. 'The girls at the front had finished their five, and they turned around and ran straight into the rest of us, so…'

'Sorry, but it wasn't our fault,' said Grace Faith, who Pip recognised as one of the front runners. 'We were told to turn round. Usually we would all just go round the same way. But Ms Bloom said we had to go in the other direction, which when you think about it…'

The seagulls piped up in enthusiastic support.

'Grace Faith is right…'

'Like Grace said, we always—'

'That's enough, thank you, Grace Faith.' Pip realised, now she thought about it, that perhaps having them change direction wasn't the cleverest idea. 'OK, girls, you do another five laps. Clockwise, this time, all of you. Ruby, you come with me.'

Pip couldn't believe her luck that it was Ruby who had got hurt, if anyone had to get hurt at all. She took her through the changing rooms in the sports pavilion, to her little office, thinking about how she might approach this. Amelia trailed behind and lurked by the door, seemingly undecided as to whether to follow them in or not.

'Come in. This is my office. Here's my desk, where I prepare my tests and exams,' Pip said, gesturing to an unremarkable office desk. 'And the drawers there, where I keep my notes and papers. And here are my chairs. Sit.'

Looking somewhat bemused by the tour of the furniture, Ruby sank gratefully into one of the chairs while Pip fetched the first aid kit from a shelf. Ruby did not strike Pip as a natural athlete.

'It's OK, ma'am. I'll just rest it, it'll be fine.'

'Now, let me look at that knee,' she said. She had done a first aid course when she'd worked at the ski resort in Verbier. Ruby stretched out her leg. It was just a little graze with a bit of dirt and grass around it. The injuries you saw when American tourists with two left feet and a Glühwein inside them hit the Alps did not bear thinking about. Once you've removed the tip of a ski pole from someone's thigh, a minor grass burn is child's play.

'Is it bad?' Amelia asked from the doorway.

'Just a graze. I'll clean it up a bit,' she said, taking out a ball of cotton wool and a bottle of Dettol. As she dabbed at the wound, she tried to engage Ruby in a chat.

'Do you like sports then, Ruby? What's your favourite?'

'Um, tennis? I'm not very good, but…'

'We can't all be sporty. I'm sure you have other subjects that you are good at…'

Ruby pondered this glumly. 'I quite like biology. I s'pose I like nature. Photography.'

'So you're more of a science girl?'

'Not really.'

'An all-rounder, I suppose. I was like that at school. Sometimes it takes a while to find your niche.'

Pip herself was still looking for her niche, after a circuitous route through all manner of jobs, from an almost-success in investigating to a would-be career in museum curation, and now a fake identity as a high school sports teacher. She sighed and continued briskly, 'It's more important to have a good school experience, try new things, make nice friends.'

Amelia gave a small *pff* of nasal exhalation. 'Good luck with that. Some of these girls…'

She stopped herself and seemed reluctant to finish the sentence.

Pip employed her often quite successful technique of sitting quietly and waiting expectantly.

It worked. Amelia said, 'There are a lot of spoilt brats here.'

'Ah,' said Pip, nodding.

Ruby elaborated. 'Girls who think they own the place just cos Daddy's got a big job in the City, or is a property developer, or chairman of the board. The sort that get whatever they want.'

'I know the type,' Pip said encouragingly – and truthfully – selecting a large square plaster from the first aid box. 'The girls to whom everything seems to come so easy.'

'Exactly. Top marks. Good-looking boys. Hockey captain. The perfect ponytail. Not that I care about it.'

That last bit seemed most decidedly untrue.

'It's hard. You just have to be yourself, find good friends, do your work and do what you know is right,' said Pip, peeling the back off the plaster and positioning it over the graze.

'I guess so. I try…' Ruby said, squirming uncomfortably in her chair. 'Me and Amelia…' She looked over at the other girl in the doorway. 'We've got each other.'

Pip stood up and rested her hand on the girl's shoulder. 'All done. It should be fine now. Thanks for the chat, Ruby. And don't forget the exam next week. In fact, I must get on with setting that. It looks like I'll be spending the afternoon here at my desk,' she said, patting it as if it were a large dog.

*

Ruby had just left when Claire poked her head around the door.

'Thought I'd just see how things are going?' she said, slipping into the office. 'Any leads?'

'Oh Lord,' said Pip, putting her head in her hands. 'It could be anyone at this stage, Claire. Anyone. Every girl and teacher in this school has a motive to cheat.'

'The teachers would never cheat,' said Claire, decisively.

'It's sweet that you think that,' said Pip. 'But the reality is that this seems to be a really great school to work for – but you have to get the marks. Seems to me that they've all got every reason to help girls cheat.' She looked at Claire. 'Have any of them ever hinted at anything?' she asked. 'You know, dropped an odd hint about extra help, that sort of thing.'

'Pip, they all offer us extra help, it's their job. But they wouldn't cheat because of Mr Packerton-Jones.'

'Mr Packerton-Jones?' Pip searched her memory and came up blank. 'Who's he?'

'Mr Packerton-Jones was before my time, but people still talk about him,' said Claire. 'He was the best teacher the school had ever seen. And then Ms Peters became headmistress, and she realised that Mr Packerton-Jones had been getting the exam papers from a friend on the exam board, and basically teaching his classes the exam questions, so they'd all get top marks. She fired him, and he lost everything. His pension, his reputation, everything. He couldn't get a job after that.' Claire's voice dropped. 'People say that he lives in a tent next to the Thames, and that when it's exam time you can see him pacing along the paths. Daddy says that now people know not to mess around on Ms Peters's watch. So the staff wouldn't cheat. I'm telling you.'

Pip thought about what Claire had told her. It wasn't to say that it was impossible that a staff member was involved. But at the same time, it seemed unlikely a teacher would risk everything just for some high-school girl to get into their first choice of university. The cheating most likely came from the girls, but Pip wouldn't rule the staff out yet.

CHAPTER 8

The front door had been painted again, this time in a fiery red. Pip liked it better than the pale lemon colour that had preceded it, but not as much as the duck egg blue of last summer. Not that there was any point in getting too attached to her sister's paint choices. Flis changed the colour of the front door at least twice a year, sometimes more if the mood took her.

Camelia opened the door and flung herself at Pip's legs. 'You're here!' she cried dramatically. She was a very dramatic child, and always greeted Pip as if she'd just returned from a year at the Russian Front. To be fair, that had only happened once, and it was a month, not a year. That relationship had *not* gone the way Pip might have hoped. 'I've missed you, Aunty Pip! Would you like to see my science project?'

The child was eight. How did she have a science project? And where did she find the time, what with the Mandarin lessons that her father, Peter, insisted on and the mandala dancing that Flis chose? They each got to pick a new extracurricular for Camelia and Harry to try every term. Last term it had been astronomy (Peter's choice) and astrology (Flis's). 'I'd love to, but let me get in and say hello to your mum first, OK?'

A damp fungal odour greeted Pip when she stepped into the house. It smelled of wet carpets. Maybe there had been a leak or a flood or something. She followed Camelia to the kitchen where Flis was at the stove, partially obscured in a cloud of steam. The flooded carpet smell was overpowering by this point.

'One more crone and we could be the witches from *Macbeth*,' Pip said, leaning in for a quick hug and pore-opening facial steam. 'Did you remember the eye of newt?'

'They were all out of newt, I had to use salamander,' said Flis, giving the cauldron a stir. 'Actually, I'm trying out a new recipe for the blog. It's immune-boosting fresh turmeric, kale and bok choy in a mushroom broth. Doesn't it smell divine?'

Pip didn't mention the wet carpet.

'Such a pity you're allergic to mushrooms. If I'd known you were coming I'd have made something else. You can have some of the bok choy.'

'Thanks, Flis, but not to worry. I'll just have some toast or something. I like the new door colour.'

'It's for the Year of the Pig,' Flis said, enigmatically. 'Let's have wine.'

Flis was always trying to give up wine and carbs and basically anything that made life halfway bearable, in the service of making life halfway longer. She'd devised a complicated set of rules for what was allowed when – weekends, full moon, birthdays, the week of the summer solstice, and so on. Pip's visits were a loophole. If Pip visited, Flis allowed herself wine, no matter what day it was, or even what time – in this instance, five thirty on a Monday. She was always very pleased to see Pip.

Determinedly ignoring the Pig remark, and focusing on the wine suggestion, Pip opened the fridge and extracted a half-full bottle of Chardonnay.

'Not that! It's my science project!' Camelia shrieked. 'It's wee.'

Flis explained, 'We are testing the homeopathic properties of acids and—'

'Don't tell me,' said Pip, feeling sick. 'I don't want to hear about it. Putting wee in a wine bottle? How can you do something so reckless? Is there any actual wine in this fridge?'

She pulled out an unopened bottle, opened it and poured them each a glass. After a deep and suspicious sniff – yes, definitely Chardonnay – she took a cautious sip.

'Soup will be about ten minutes. How's the school thing going?' Pip had filled her in briefly on the phone. 'Have you solved the mysterious case of the exam paper theft?'

'Working on it.'

'When we were at school, cheating meant writing a few notes on the inside of your hand. And now they're stealing whole exam papers.'

'The kids of today…' Pip said, taking a long sip of the wine. 'Actually, I need your help with something. Sports related. You were always quite good at that sort of thing at school.'

'Not really. Only compared to you. In the land of the blind, fun-eyed Sam is king.'

After absorbing this wisdom, Pip let it go, and explained the situation with the bogus exam paper.

'Surely they don't do exams in PE?' Flis was as incredulous as the girls had been. 'I've never heard of such a thing.'

'Don't worry about that,' Pip said, waving away her concern. 'I told them it's a new thing. Education Department, you know. Policy. Standards. I thought we could do something on rules. And a section on fitness.'

She pulled out the ridiculous notebook.

'What about famous athletes?' said Flis.

'Great idea. And what is the offside rule?'

'It's when you can't go past the other players, for some reason. Remember? They explained it in that film, *The Full Monty*.' Flis waved her hands around in illustration, as if a picture of the offside rule might appear in the air in front of her.

'I mean, we can ask that for a question. "What is the offside rule?"'

'Oh yes, good one.'

Pip then had the bright idea of Googling 'interesting sports facts', which was absolute gold.

'Gosh, Flis, did you know that early baseballs were made from a variety of strange materials, including the foreskin of a horse, and sturgeon eyes.'

'Both together, or either or?'

'It doesn't say.'

'Anyway, I don't think it's right to take a surgeon's eye,' mused Flis. 'They need them to operate.'

Pip let that one go. 'No matter, I think I've got enough. Thanks for your help.'

Flis announced that the soup must be ready, and went out to round up the children. They arrived in a clatter with Peter trailing behind.

'Hey, how's the, ahem, sports mistress?' he asked, making ironic air quotes with his fingers. He had a wry twinkle in his eye.

'Fit as a fiddle. Getting to know the girls and see what's what.' Pip liked her brother-in-law and thought him immensely tolerant of Flis's peculiarities, not to mention her cooking experiments. He was the very soul of good-natured ordinariness.

The children were less accepting. 'What's that smell?' asked Harry.

'Delicious soup,' said Flis brightly. 'Lovely bok choy.'

'Can I have some of Dad's supper?'

'Me too,' said Camelia. 'What's Dad having?'

'Peter is doing the keto diet,' Flis told Pip. 'The sad thing is that it's all about high protein, so there's a lot of meat and he can't eat the meals I test out for the blog, poor poppet.'

Peter looked downhearted, or tried to. Pip caught his eye and a look passed between them. He knew that she knew that he had happened upon a strategy for cleverly avoiding interminable kale and turmeric-based meals without hurting his wife's feelings.

'That's a pity,' she said. 'It smells delicious. Yum.'

'Come on, kids, I'll fry us some chicken breasts,' he said.

'Yay!!!!'

While Peter and the kids cleared up after supper – Pip had managed to cadge a chicken breast to go with her side of bok choy – Flis and Pip put the finishing touches to the exam paper. Pip was quite pleased with how it had turned out. She'd certainly learned a lot. For instance, Liechtenstein had competed in the most Summer Olympics (sixteen) without winning any medals. Who knew?

'Now what?' asked Flis.

'Well, I've added in enough unusual facts that anyone who gets most of them right will definitely be a suspect. They'd have stolen it, or copied someone, or googled it. I did tell two of the main suspects where I keep my papers…'

Pip's voice tailed off. It didn't sound like quite such a good plan now. How would she prove which of them had taken the paper?

'I need evidence of them taking it, if they try, though. Maybe I should hide in the lockers… or get a CCTV camera.'

'Hang on a mo,' said Flis, jumping to her feet. 'I've got just the thing.'

CHAPTER 9

The girls grumbled a bit at the idea of musical chairs, but within minutes they were laughing and shrieking like seven-year-olds. By the end, after much hilarity, only Grace Faith, Chanel and Rizwana were left, hurtling round and round the last two chairs, a gleaming blonde ponytail chasing a glossy black one, followed by Chanel with her two golden braids, the class shouting and cheering them on.

Pip hit the stop button on her ancient ghetto blaster. Chanel was well placed and sat down. Rizwana slid neatly onto the remaining chair. Grace Faith flew at her, her shoulder connecting with the slighter girl, knocking her and the chair to the ground.

'My bad,' she said, unconvincingly. 'Didn't mean to.'

A few girls helped Rizwana to her feet. Amazingly, she seemed uninjured. Gosh, being a sports mistress was tense. Pip was keen to get out of there before someone did themselves a real injury.

'That was fun, miss,' said Claire, panting with exertion, her cheeks on fire. 'Good exercise too.'

'Very good. And it has a practical application. One day you'll be working in the City and you will have to travel on the Tube at rush hour, and then you'll think of your PE lessons and thank me.'

There was a grudging laugh from the crowd, and a question from Grace Faith: 'But why would anyone go on the Tube, actually? I mean, the car is so much more convenient? And comfortable?'

Either she had a gift for deadpan, or she was deadly serious. Her expression of mild perplexity seemed genuine.

Pip ignored her questions and turned to the class, which was starting to disperse. 'Now, girls, don't forget the exam is tomorrow. I've got the exam all prepared and waiting for you in my office. I think you'll find it fun and challenging. And remember, it *is* for marks. Amelia, can you take the chairs in, please? Put them in the storeroom next to my office.'

Ruby and Claire were helping Amelia stack the chairs slowly when Pip went back to her office to get her bag. 'Thanks, girls,' she said, passing them on her way through the door.

'That's a cute teddy,' Ruby said, nodding towards the fluffy brown teddy bear on Pip's desk.

Pip patted the Teddy Cam she had borrowed from Flis. 'Isn't he? He belongs to my niece. She lent him to me to keep me company at work.'

Ruby gave her a weak smile.

'Right, I'd better get going,' Pip said, picking up her laptop bag. 'Don't want to hit the traffic. Will you pull the door closed behind you? See you tomorrow for the exam.'

Pip was keen to get home and put her feet up. She'd been up until midnight getting the test paper finished so she could save it on the shared drive and email it to Mrs Jenkins, who would print it out and have it ready for Pip to collect in the morning. Teaching was a lot harder than it looked, with all these strange processes and shared folders and needing to know who to email for what. Pip had had loads of jobs, and one thing that struck her quite consistently was that most jobs were harder than they looked. Cheesemaking, for example, was an absolute nightmare, she'd discovered that summer in Switzerland. Backbreaking. The soft cheeses in particular.

She desperately wanted to check her phone, and access the app that Tim had helped her install which would show her the action on the Teddy Cam. But she didn't want to be caught looking, and the corridors of the school seemed unusually full of staff and girls, milling around with tennis racquets and violins and other frightening paraphernalia.

Finally, she found herself alone in the car park. She couldn't wait to see what was on the Teddy Cam. Had someone come into the office to look for the exam paper? If so, the motion sensor would have picked them up and set the thing recording, and a message would come through to her phone. Pip folded her long self into the little yellow Mini and pulled out her phone with a flutter of excitement. It soon gave way to disappointment. No alert. It had only been an hour, she told herself. Perhaps the exam thief had decided to wait until the school was emptier and the chances of detection lower.

Pip didn't entirely convince herself with this line of reasoning. It seemed quite possible that there was no exam thief. Or, if there was, that she wasn't going to come and get the sports test paper. Maybe the girls had realised that sports exams are not exactly important. Or real. Either way, Pip would be no closer to solving the case, no closer to clearing Claire's name and her all-important school record, and no closer to earning her rent money. She sighed, and turned the key in the ignition, sending the engine sputtering weakly to life.

The whole way home she felt the phone burning a hole in her handbag, but she resisted the urge to check it at a traffic light. After that tricky incident on the M3 with the double-decker coach and the rabbit, she'd been a lot more careful.

Pip opened the front door to the flat, for once ignoring the cats who were mewing pathetically as if they'd been shut in a cardboard box without food or water for a week, threading themselves through her legs like some manic feline French knitting. They would have to wait a mo. She rummaged in her bag for her phone and brought it up to her face, holding her breath in anticipation. *Yes!* An alert from the camera app. She exhaled with a 'phew' and clicked on the image, waiting to see the face of the would-be exam paper thief.

No! No, no, no, no, no.

Instead of capturing the image of the thief coming through the door, the camera showed a corner of desk and a small slice of linoleum floor with the toe of a white trainer. An arm came into frame, reaching for the desk drawer. Then a blur. The perpetrator's shoulder was blocking her view. Pip's heart sank. She had been so close to solving the mystery, and now she had nothing. Failure again. Really, she should be used to it by now. But still, it was a blow.

And then, as the thief stood up, something swished across the white sports shirt and briefly filled the screen. Pip knew that swish. It was a ponytail. And she knew just who it belonged to.

CHAPTER 10

The teddy was on his side, as suspected. It must have fallen, or been knocked over. No matter. Pip was fairly certain she knew who had made a fleeting appearance in those last few frames of the recording on the app. She recognised that glossy black ponytail as belonging to the girl Grace Faith had shouldered from her rightful win at musical chairs. Rizwana.

Pip had woken up eager to confront the girl, but on the drive to school she began to wonder if that was her best strategy. By the time she got to her office, she had decided it would be better to let the girls take the test first. That way, she could see who had been given – or, more likely, bought – the stolen paper. The perpetrator might have passed it around.

There was a fair amount of low-key eye-rolling when the paper was handed out. It escalated to a low murmur when the girls turned over the paper.

'But, miss, how can we—'

'No talking, please.'

The murmuring had escalated to muttering and Pip wondered if she'd have a mutiny on her hands, but she gave them her newly acquired Teacher's Glare and obedience prevailed. Amazing how schools manage to achieve that. The girls lowered their heads and tackled the test.

She watched the group – the heavenward glances for inspiration, the sucking and chewing of writing implements, the click of tongues, the hard scrawls on the paper. She remembered the gestures from her own school days. She hadn't been a top-notch student, it had to be said. She was above average in smarts, and really quite willing and pleasant, but things happened to upset what should, by rights, have been a smooth and successful school career. A poor choice, a moment of weakness, a misunderstanding, that inexplicable appearance of a goat in the staffroom – and things went oddly wrong.

The alarm on her mobile phone alerted her that the half-hour was up. Unfortunately, it alerted her with a blast of lyrics telling her to get up, stand up and strut her funky stuff, which Pip had recently set as her morning alarm. For a joke, mostly. Again, a lesson that should have been learned by now. The class erupted into laughter, girls pounding the rhythm out on their desks.

Pip turned off the alarm and gathered up the papers, moving briskly up the rows – 'Time's up. Thank you… I'll take that… Thank you…' – ignoring the smirks and the sighs and the questions and the bitter glances in her direction.

Grace Faith led the way out of the classroom, with Chanel as first lieutenant and her crew gleaming and bobbing in her wake. Ruby and Amelia, the eternal pair, shuffled out, dragging their feet despondently. Pip kept a keen eye on Rizwana, who displayed no sign of either the anxiety of a cheat or the confidence of a girl expecting an A+. Pip had to admire her cool.

'Rizwana, do you have a moment?' she asked. 'There's something I'd like to chat about.'

The girl looked like a deer in the headlights. 'I've got violin now, miss. Shall I come back after? In half an hour?'

'Yes, please.'

When the girls had cleared the room, Pip skimmed the papers.

Most of them got a fair smattering of the regular questions correct – the individual medley order in swimming, and yes, even the offside rule. Or possibly not. Pip still wasn't clear that she understood it herself.

Surprisingly, nearly everyone got the answer to 'Which sport features equipment named after household cleaning equipment and geological artefacts?' Curling, obviously. Brooms and stones. Pip laughed. As one must whenever curling is mentioned.

And then there were the planted questions:

Q2: Which top tennis player's name can be typed entirely with the left hand? (Federer)
Q7: How many dimples are on the average golf ball? (336)
Q10: What is the biggest participant sport in the world? (Fishing)

Pip reckoned that one correct answer out of three could be genuine knowledge, a good guess, or fluke. More than that was suspicious. Three correct would be a dead cert.

It was clear from Ruby's answers to the planted questions – 'Fred, 17, skipping rope' – and Amelia's – 'Joccovitz, 1,000, ????' – that the alleged science geniuses had not hacked the system on this one. And that Amelia was a terrible speller.

She moved on through the pack. Grace Faith and one or two others got two correct. Well, looky here! Only one girl got three of the red flag questions correct. Chanel.

The odd thing was that Rizwana had only got one of them correct – Federer. Why would she steal the paper and not ace the test? Putting her detecting brain into gear, Pip figured it out – if Rizwana was the mastermind behind the exam scam, she must have decided that it wasn't worth the risk to get an A for a mythical sports test.

As Pip was contemplating her cleverness – she'd been at the school less than a week and it seemed that already she had found the perpetrator of the exam paper scam, plus one of its customers – Rizwana herself appeared at the door. Pip had to admit she didn't look like a criminal mastermind. But you couldn't always tell; criminal masterminds could be surprisingly mild and unprepossessing. Not those Russians she'd met in Marbella, though; they might as well have worn big signs saying 'MOBSTER'. Pip beckoned the girl in and got straight down to it.

'Rizwana, did you go into my office yesterday afternoon, after school?'

'I did, miss. I'm sorry,' the girl said, wringing her hands. 'I know I shouldn't have.'

'The thing is, we now have a bit of a situation to manage,' said Pip, who was quite surprised how easy it had been to get a confession out of the girl. Kids these days – no staying power. 'You know that the school takes a very dim view of this sort of thing.'

'I know! I won't do it again, I promise. It's just… I was desperate.'

'That's no excuse, I'm afraid. Anyway, you will have to take it up with Ms Peters.'

'Please don't tell her!'

The girl was pale and shaken, her eyes wide and teary. Pip felt sorry for her, but steeled her heart.

'I'm afraid I'm going to have to. This is a serious business. The school might even have to get the police involved.'

'The police? Please, no!' She started to weep. 'I'll replace it, I promise. It was only one plaster and a bit of arnica gel.'

'It was what?'

'I took a plaster for the graze on my knee,' she said, lifting the hem of her skirt to show a plaster and a bruise surrounding it.

'A plaster?'

'Yes, and some arnica gel for my ankle. I twisted my ankle in the fall,' she continued, rolling her foot and wincing. 'Musical chairs, remember? Grace Faith slammed into me.'

'You're saying you went into my office yesterday and took a plaster and arnica?' Pip said in disbelief.

'Yes. I put it back though,' she said, opening the drawer below the one that had held the exam paper. 'See?'

Pip looked at the tube with the dent of a squeeze, and sighed.

'I know I shouldn't have gone into your office without permission, and I shouldn't have taken anything without asking, but—'

'OK, Rizwana. If that's all, I think we can keep it between the two of us. No need to tell Ms Peters.'

It was back to square one for Pip.

CHAPTER 11

Ms Peters had flat out refused Pip permission to directly question Chanel on her surprising knowledge about sports.

'As I said, we cannot be seen to be accusing our students of anything untoward until we have absolute proof. Especially Chanel. Her parents are… well… they're very… Let's just say that we could expect a *lot* of pushback. Possibly with lawyers involved.'

Pip did not like the sound of that.

'Doing well in a sports-related test that you invented the need for isn't sufficient grounds to make an official accusation, I'm afraid. Especially not with these parents. You need to keep working below the radar and find more proof before we take this any further.'

Pip was a bit taken aback by this. Hadn't Ms Peters herself approved the plan? As if reading her mind, Ms Peters sighed.

'I know that I said it was a good plan. And it was. But I'd like us to have more.'

Pip thought for a moment. 'Could I look at her marks in other subjects?' she asked. 'See if there's a pattern?'

'I don't see why not. I'll ask my secretary, Mrs Jenkins, to give you access to the mark order programme on the network. Needless to say, absolute discretion is required, complete confidentiality.'

'Of course.'

'And Pip, you must come to me before you go to any student with any whiff of an accusation.'

'Noted.'

Mrs Jenkins soon allocated Pip a username and password for the programme that tracked each student's progress. Pip headed home, intending to stop by the shops for supplies and then peruse the sorry state of her students' academic careers over a glass of wine at the kitchen table.

Pip fed the cats and unpacked her shopping. She wasn't much of a cook. She blamed her mother, who was a brilliant cook if there were eighteen interesting people coming for dinner, but didn't waste her talents on her two children. She often said she had no idea why anyone with a brain would spend more than ten minutes making something that would be eaten by a child in five. 'Do you need to eat *again*?' she'd say to the girls in exasperation and surprise, three times a day. Then she would fling herself around the kitchen, pulling random items from the pantry or the freezer, cobbling together something half edible and leaving them to eat it while she went outside to smoke and talk to the Irish wolfhounds, which she found much easier company than children.

As a result, Pip had never really learned to cook, but was very good at putting bought things together. For tonight's dinner, she had procured a jar of pesto, some fancy handmade fettuccine, a block of Parmesan, and a variety of red and yellow tomatoes of different sizes. And a bottle of wine, of course. She was going to make pesto pasta and a tomato salad for herself and Tim, but first she wanted to check the marks.

She had only just plonked her laptop onto the kitchen table when she heard Tim's key in the door and smiled to herself. 'Daddy's home,' she said to the grey kitten at her feet. 'Go say hello.'

He skittered off to the door, but Pip knew enough about cats to know that it wasn't in response to any instruction from her.

Tim looked drawn and tired. 'A hard day hacking?' she asked.

'Backbreaking,' he said, stretching his shoulders and rolling his neck with an audible click. 'I've been at it for twelve hours straight.'

'Dinner and wine awaits,' she said.

'Sounds perfect. How was the busy day of an in-school detective? Have you cleared my sister's name yet?'

She filled him in on her unsuccessful sting operation, making him laugh at the ridiculous exam questions and the trembling arnica thief.

'So you reckon Ms Arnica was telling the truth then? She's not the thief?'

'Definitely. She had the bruise; she knew where the arnica was. I'm sure she was telling the truth. But I'm pretty sure someone saw that paper. It was too much of a coincidence, that girl Chanel getting those questions right.'

'What did she say?'

'I haven't spoken to her. The tricky thing is, I'm not allowed to interview the girls. Ms Peters seems terrified of the parents getting wind of an "accusation" and bringing in the lawyers. Lawyers! Over a test?'

'You'd be surprised. Perfectly sane people go mad when they think their children are under threat.'

'True. What do you know about the school?' she asked Tim. 'What's its angle?'

Tim explained that the school was breathtakingly pricey, and with good reason. 'You are practically guaranteed good results and entry into the top universities. That's its selling point. It gets the best possible results from the, er, you could say, not always the *very* top, top students... Not the superstars...' He stumbled over the words, not wanting to seem disloyal. 'I mean, Claire is very smart, very sparky as you know.'

Pip nodded. 'Absolutely. I can see that, of course.'

'That's why Claire's there. They get those marks come hell or high water, according to my mum. It's an open secret that the teachers get a fat bonus for each A they achieve in the exams.'

'That seems quite…' Pip struggled for the right word. 'Mercenary? And what sort of people go there? Ms Peters seemed positively terrified of the parents.'

'Have you met any parents? I mean, in the flesh? Spoken to them about their children? Or education? They're all insane, as far as their children are concerned.'

Pip did wonder what exactly this said about Tim's own parents, but didn't let herself get sidetracked. 'Granted, but what particular brand of insane are these ones?'

'The kind of insane that spends a fortune on a sort of hybrid hothouse/upper class crammer and expects to get their money's worth. And also, well, Mum can be a bit judgemental, granted, but she does seem to think that there are some families who are… um… not quite…'

'Spit it out.'

'Some rather dodgy, rich, demanding people. Jeez, you saw the car park. Aston Martins. Ferraris. Mum says there are a lot of very pushy parents. A bit nouveau. Competitive. Someone had an American-style Sweet Sixteen party. There was a car with a big bow… That sort of thing. And they expect a lot from their children.'

'They do sound rather terrifying.'

'Oh, they are.'

Pip mulled this over while they started dinner prep. Tim got the pasta water going; Pip opened the wine.

She took a sip. 'Anyway, I've got access to the girls' marks now, so I'll see if I can detect a pattern, or red flags.'

'Well, let's look. Get your computer.'

Pip logged in and up it came, just like that.

'I'm going to look up Chanel. She did surprisingly well on the planted questions in the sports test.'

She looked at Chanel's marks. They showed an improvement since the beginning of the year, but nothing too dramatic. Steady progression, a few more impressive results, but nothing over seventy-eight per cent.

'Inconclusive,' she said. 'Nothing to spark suspicion.' Pip mulled over the idea of the school's computer programme. 'So Tim, how would this network work?' she asked. 'Like, I guess all the teachers could access this information, right? Maybe some of the admin staff?'

'Depends how it's set up. Different people have different access. It's probably not very secure though. You often find that in this kind of system lots of people can get all sorts of information – discipline records, university applications, that sort of thing.'

'Really?'

'Oh yes – once everything's linked up, anything that's on the system is vulnerable. School networks are generally pretty lax.'

A little alarm bell went off and Pip started to wonder if anyone else had accessed the school's network. 'What about email? Is that easy to get into?'

'Email? Half the time you don't even have to hack anything. Most people have it up on their phone, or leave it open on their desktop.'

Pip had saved her own test paper on the shared drive. Maybe no one had been into the drawer after all. Maybe whoever had stolen the paper got it from the school's computer network.

CHAPTER 12

Pip wished with all her heart that she'd gone undercover as a food tech teacher (good snacks) or an art teacher (a bit of light doodling to pass the time). Instead, she was running about the neighbourhood like an idiot, trailing after schoolgirls half her age.

Pip hadn't realised she had to actually *run* with them. She had waved the girls off and was just about to settle down to a nice quiet game of Solitaire on the computer when Ms Peters came by and asked, 'Where are the girls off to?'

'I sent them on a cross-country run. It's a sport, so…'

'Oh gosh, no. You can't send them on their own. Liability issues. Duty of care. All that. You'd better go after them.'

She hadn't even got her bum in the chair! And so off she had sprinted – well, jogged – to try and catch them.

After a few hundred metres of very hard jogging, she caught up with the stragglers. Who else but Ruby and Amelia? They were practically *ambling*. They turned in surprise, alerted, no doubt, by the sound of Pip rasping for breath.

'Wait up,' Pip gasped, clutching onto a 'SOLD' sign outside a large red-brick house encircled by a box hedge.

The girls stopped.

'You all right, miss?' asked Amelia.

'Fine, fine,' said Pip. 'I set off a bit fast is all. Pace yourself, I say.'

'Yeah,' said Ruby. 'That's what we're doing.'

The three of them started to move off at a comfortable walking pace.

'Let's step it up, shall we?' said Pip, breaking into a trot. 'I need to catch up with the rest of the girls.'

'That's not going to happen, I don't think,' said Amelia, increasing her pace by the barest whisper. 'Some of those girls are fast.'

Ruby thought for a minute, gave Amelia a glance which was met with a tiny nod, and said, 'There's a shortcut though. We could show you.'

'Well, that's hardly in the spirit of the cross-country now, is it?'

'A field is the country and we'd be crossing it, so to speak. Anyway, I just thought, if you need to get to the front of the pack…' Ruby flicked her wrist languidly to indicate that it was all the same to her.

'Good point,' said Pip. 'We'll take the shortcut, but I want to see a bit more pace.'

Within minutes, they turned left into a field that was being levelled for development. A huge hoarding advertised an Executive Lifestyle Estate. Was there ever a more dispiriting descriptor? In fact, yes – the name of the property company: Betterworld Developers. Earth-moving equipment was working the far right edge of the field, and in the distance was a small wooden structure – presumably not an Executive Lifestyle Home; more likely the site office.

'Keep to the edge here, along the trees,' said Amelia, setting off at a comfortable walking pace under an avenue of oaks along the left boundary. 'At least they left the trees.' She sniffed disapprovingly. 'Trashed the rest of it. My dad says the whole area will be destroyed by the greedy buggers.'

Pip felt sure a proper teacher would have called her out on her inappropriate language, but Pip had no interest in being a disciplinarian.

'Your dad's right,' said Ruby. 'Where will the animals live if people build all over everything?'

'I guess these ones will move to the Marsh Field. At least that's still there,' said Amelia, gesturing across the gutted landscape to a big wild area beyond. It was the picture of unspoilt English countryside, a green field dotted with meadow flowers and big shady trees, and on the far side marshland and a pretty pond.

'So they're not building there, then?' said Pip.

'Oooh, no,' said Amelia. 'They can't build on the Marsh Field. It belongs to the school. Some old lady left it to the school years ago so the girls could enjoy it.'

'That's a lovely thing to do.'

'We have picnics there sometimes,' said Ruby. 'I saw a hedgehog last time, remember, Amelia?'

The shortcut was a win. Pip and the lazy girls popped out on a narrow road not far from the school, just ahead of the cross-country runners. A clutch of sweating, panting girls came up the hill towards them. Pip went ahead to await them at the sports pavilion.

Surprisingly, Chanel was already there, tucked around the corner almost out of sight, along with the young Gothic-looking man Pip had seen in the staffroom. His name was Adam or Alan or some such – Mr Geoffrey, officially – and he was the Computer Science teacher. He had the thinness and pallor of a person who spent all day behind a screen, and all night too. His hair was jet black – dyed, presumably – and he had a stud in the hard thin bit of his ear. Chanel was in deep conversation with him. Odd, thought Pip. Chanel didn't strike her as the type to suck up to teachers, especially not nerdy ones.

'You made good time,' Pip said loudly, making the girl jump.

'Just got here, miss,' said Chanel, kicking her left foot up behind her with her left hand and pulling back, making a show of stretching her quads. 'It was a good run.' She leaned forward, heel on the ground, toes up to stretch her hamstring.

When she straightened up, Pip noted that the girl was not puffed at all and had not the slightest sheen. The others, who were now streaming in, were positively red and sweating. Pip said pleasantly, 'Chanel, would you come to my office, please? There's something I'd like your help with.'

Pip had been told not to speak to Chanel about the exam papers, but she hadn't been told not to speak to her at all. She saw no reason why she shouldn't discuss more general sporty matters, seeing as she was, after all, the sports mistress. She'd have to be a bit sneaky in her investigations.

The girl trailed after her to the office, looking shifty. 'What's it about, Ms Bloom?'

Pip didn't answer, but took a seat at her desk, gesturing Chanel towards the other one.

'A good run, you say?' Pip said in a neutral tone, and then fell silent, waiting.

She had to give Chanel credit for cool. 'Oh yes,' she said with a smile. 'Very good. My best time yet.'

'That's good. By how many minutes?'

The girl was barely flustered by the question. 'Er, I forgot to set my Apple Watch, so I was estimating. I mean, it felt fast…'

'And you were here quite some minutes before the others, I noticed.'

Chanel paused a moment and decided to come clean. 'Miss, I didn't run. I had a stomach ache. I just walked around a bit and then came back. I should have said. I'm truly sorry.'

She turned her great big innocent blue eyes on Pip.

'A stomach ache. Well, I suppose that explains it.'

'Thank you, miss.' Chanel smiled her dazzling smile, delighted to be off the hook.

Pip fixed her with her Teacher's Glare. 'And tell me, are you a golfer, Chanel?'

'No, miss, not a golfer.'

'Tennis?'

'I play on holiday, sometimes. There's a club near the house in the South of Fr—'

'I like Federer myself. F, E, D…' Pip spelled his name out with her left hand tapping a finger down on the desk with each letter.

'Yes, he's very—'

Pip cut her off. 'Chanel, do you fish at all? Participate in fishing? The most popular participation sport?'

Light dawned on Chanel's face, and all the breezy confidence went out of her.

'The test,' she said glumly.

'Well, since you brought it up, let's talk about that, shall we?' Pip said, folding her arms and waiting. 'You seem to know a surprising number of odd sporting facts.'

'Yes, I do. It's a hobby. Sports facts. Can't get enough of them,' she said gamely.

'Well, it's amazing what you can find on the web these days, isn't it? If you have a computer. Speaking of computers, I see you were speaking to Mr Geoffrey.'

Chanel didn't know which issue to address first – her surprising success, her alleged hobby, or Mr Geoffrey. She stuttered a bit and fell silent.

'He's the IT teacher. He's OK. I talk to him sometimes.'

'Does he like sports facts? Did he help you with your… research?'

The girl blanched.

'Chanel, did Mr Geoffrey help you with the test?'

'What? No!'

'Did he give you any, let's say, inside information?'

'He had nothing to do with it!'

'With what?'

'With me getting the test paper…' Chanel realised that she'd all but confessed. She sighed.

'Why don't you tell me what happened,' Pip continued, keeping her tone light. 'Or maybe I should ask him to come in and explain?'

'No! OK, OK. I'll tell you. I got the test paper. It was all me. Alan, Mr Geoffrey, is innocent! Please don't get him into trouble. I'm the cheat, it was me!'

CHAPTER 13

Chanel spilled the beans. As Pip suspected, she had bought the test paper. She swore it was the first time she'd ever cheated. Funny how often the first time a criminal was busted was allegedly the first time they'd ever committed a crime.

'I shouldn't have done it, I know,' she said. 'But Mrs Stone only lets us take Geography A levels if we get a seventy-five per cent average for everything. And I mean everything, she's really strict about it. My term average was just under seventy-five per cent and we've done our tests in all the other subjects. I worked so hard this term, so hard. It was my best average ever, and if I could get just a few extra marks I'd be over seventy-five per cent. So when you said the test counted for marks, I thought…'

'You thought if you could ace the test, you'd hit that seventy-five per cent. You'd be able to do A level Geography, like you want.'

'Yes. I love Geography and I do really well in it.'

'I get it.'

'And Dave, he's my stepdad, he says if I got a seventy-five per cent average, he'll buy me a horse. Actually, what he said first was, he'd look up for a flock of pigs flying across the croquet lawn; then after my mum told him off, he said he'd buy me a horse. To keep the flying pigs company.'

Dave sounded like a right prince, Pip thought. Way to go with the encouragement, Dave.

'So you cheated.'

Chanel paled visibly. 'You're not going to tell them, are you? Oh no, I couldn't… They wouldn't…'

Pip couldn't help but feel sorry for the girl who had gone from Class Cool Kid chatting up the IT teacher to the trembling wreck hunched across the desk with tears dropping from her chin.

'Let's not get into all of that just yet,' she, handing Chanel a tissue. 'If you tell me everything you know about how you got the paper and who is behind this, we might be able to keep this on the down-low. No promises, but we'll see how we go. But I need total honesty, understood?'

Chanel wiped and sniffed, nodding.

'Tell me, who gave you the paper?'

'I can't tell you.'

'If you're not prepared to come clean, this discussion is over. Total honesty, Chanel. We agreed.'

Pip put her hands on the desk and pushed herself to standing. She was, frankly, jolly irritated with the spoilt, silly girl. Cheating in a sports test to get a pony that her stepdad would probably buy her anyway. Well, Ms Peters could handle it.

'I don't know. I swear! I really don't know!' Chanel was on her feet too by now, clutching at Pip's sleeve. 'Please believe me! I didn't get it from a person. I got it online. There's a website. They send you the paper.'

Now this was interesting. Within twenty-four hours of Pip having set the test, it had found its way onto some mysterious website. She sat down, Chanel following suit, patting at her face with a wadded-up tissue.

'Tell me everything.'

Chanel explained the system. You registered on a website and paid online through a Bitcoin-linked payment service, so the money couldn't be traced. They needed your name, but they never contacted you directly – it all happened through the website. 'So your parents can't find any emails. There's no trail,' explained Chanel earnestly. 'There are rules, though. You can't just crib the whole thing and get one hundred per cent. You mustn't get more than eighty per cent, or a mark that's more than twenty per cent above your term average for that particular subject.'

'How do they know?'

'I don't know, but they do. One time these two girls, Ru—' She stopped herself. 'Some girls got carried away, and they were busted and can never use the site again. Blacklisted. Oh, and another thing, the website people never sell more than three papers for any test. So you don't have, like, ten girls suddenly getting seventy-five per cent for science.'

'A question,' she said to Chanel. 'How did you get the website address? How did you know about this racket?'

'It's very hush hush, but a lot of the girls know. I heard from… a friend. And she heard from this other girl. It's kind of an open secret in a certain group.'

'What group would that be?'

Chanel contemplated how best to answer this. 'Well, you could say, the girls who are not at the top of the class.' She shrugged. 'The ones who don't like to work too hard and who have rich parents, so they can afford the tests. They're really pricey.'

'Who passed it on to you?'

'I can't tell you. Really, miss. If she ever found out, there's no telling what would happen…' Chanel gave a shudder that seemed like real fear.

'Grace Faith?' Pip asked on a hunch. The girl paled and her jaw dropped. She recovered quickly and shook her head – a little too vehemently, perhaps. Pip was certain she'd guessed correctly and that Grace Faith, the ultimate mean girl, had been her source.

'How much?' Pip realised she should probably have asked that earlier.

'Two hundred quid for a test, starting price. More for difficult subjects like maths and science. More for end of year exams.'

A tidy little racket indeed.

'Give me the website address,' she said to Chanel. 'I want to see it for myself.'

'It's www.getyourbestmarks.co.uk.'

Pip snorted, bitterly, while typing the address into her computer. 'OK,' she said. 'I'll take it from here. You can't tell anyone about our conversation, understand? If I find out that you've spoken to anyone about it, our agreement is off. I go straight to Ms Peters. I mean it, Chanel. Tell no one – and that includes Mr Geoffrey. And Grace Faith.'

Chanel couldn't get away fast enough, muttering thanks and apologies and assurances as she dashed for the door, her blonde braids almost horizontal behind her.

It was very clear that one of the schoolgirls must be behind, or at least involved with, this scam. A student could identify possible customers from the correct sector of the Venn diagram of the dishonest/lazy/rich population of the class, and could easily check the mark order and keep tabs on the customers who overreached themselves. Grace Faith had given Chanel the website address. Could she be involved, or was she just a customer herself?

First, Pip would talk to Tim this evening and get his advice. By which she meant his help. By which she meant asking him to hack the site and tell her who exactly was behind it, preferably with their full name, phone number and home address. Mystery solved.

After all, what was the point of having a white hat hacker computer genius for a housemate if you couldn't ask them for a simple favour from time to time? Tim would help her sort this all out pronto.

CHAPTER 14

'Absolutely not possible,' Tim said, once she'd finished describing what she'd found out about the exam scam. He paused while a waitress placed a large plate of chips in front of him. She'd barely removed her hand from the plate when he fell upon them, emptying half a bottle of ketchup onto his chips and tossing two or three into his mouth. Poor man was starving. He'd come on the train straight from a client to the school to see Claire in a piano recital. He watched her play and then, while the rest of the girls plunk-plunked and strummed and beat and blew their way through their various offerings, he had skipped out to meet Pip at a nice pub she had spotted close by.

They'd bagged a table outside, overlooking a river and a few artfully placed weeping willows. Pip mentally drummed her fingers on the table, waiting for him to chew, swallow and continue. Eventually, he did just that.

'There's no way it was dreamed up by a schoolgirl, that's for sure. This is a reasonably sophisticated set-up. You'd need proper skills to hide the IP address and arrange the Bitcoin payment.'

That did all sound rather too technologically advanced for your average sixteen-year-old. But people kept telling her how much cleverer the youth of today are about computers. Maybe Tim was wrong.

'Maybe someone who's clever with computers could figure it out? Or maybe a couple of them put their heads together?'

'I guess it's possible,' said Tim, sounding unconvinced. 'I suppose someone very clever could figure it out for themselves. Much more likely, if you're convinced it was one of the girls, she would have an accomplice, or someone who taught her how to run the tech side of things.'

Taught her? Who would teach a schoolgirl how to hack emails and set up Bitcoin? Pip thought back to Chanel's little tête-à-tête with Alan Geoffrey when she should have been running the cross-country. Was it the two of them behind the exam scam? Who better than the Computer Science teacher to take care of the technical side of things? And his student accomplice keeping an eye on the girls, making sure the rules were observed.

While Tim worked his way through the plate of chips, she told him about Mr Geoffrey and he agreed that it made sense for him or someone like him to be involved. 'He has the computer skills, he has access to the network. From what I know about schools and teachers, he'd probably be the only one who'd have a working understanding of crypto and could figure out the payment and so on.'

Tim swirled a chip around the ketchup, readying it for action while he reduced its predecessor to mash with his molars. Two swans paddled picturesquely in the background. Pip wasn't the biggest fan of swans, so she kept one eye on them, ready for signs of attack. But other than the constant threat of getting her arm broken by a swan, it was very pleasant; all the more so for Tim, who was sipping on a beer. Pip was driving them home, so it was lemonade for her.

What to do next? she pondered. She would have to confront Alan, but she wanted more information – preferably proof – before she did.

Tim interrupted her pondering. 'What else do you know about this Geoffrey guy?'

'He seems to be quite matey with the students. I saw him and Chanel having a chat. It's possible Chanel could get the word out to the right girls, although to be honest, she seems more like a customer than a conspirator, so maybe there's someone else involved. And he'd have access to the school system to check that no one's getting too ambitious with the marks.'

'Does he seem dodgy?' Tim asked, suspiciously. 'With the girls, I mean. A bit too friendly?'

'I've no reason to think anything like that,' said Pip. 'He just looks a bit…'

'A bit what?'

Pip was trying to find the right descriptor for his quasi Goth-nerd persona, when she realised she wouldn't have to.

'Like that,' she said, nodding towards the door. 'There he is.'

Mr Geoffrey sloped across the lawn, carrying a large glass of beer, and looking for an empty table. The summer's evening had drawn the after-work crowd to the pub and an outside table was prime real estate. He came close to Pip without noticing her, his head swivelling side to side, looking for a seat.

Of all the bars in all the world, as that chap said in that movie, he had to walk into mine. Although this place was most likely the local for anyone working at the school.

'Mr Geoffrey. Alan,' she called as he passed, causing him to turn towards her, sloshing the white foam from the beer over his hand and down his wrist. 'You're welcome to join us. We'll be leaving in a minute and then the table's yours.'

He mumbled a bit in indecision and then thanked her, sliding in next to her on the bench. 'Tim, meet Alan,' she said, turning from one to the other. 'In fact, you two have something in common. Both tech guys. Alan's the IT teacher at the school,' she said, as if she hadn't already had a long conversation with Tim about him. 'But he can tell you all about it while I go and powder my nose.'

Tim gave her a questioning look – she was not a nose powderer, nor would she use that awful phrase – and she gave him a hard, meaningful stare back. He looked blankly at her. Microscopic movements of eyeballs and eyebrows are a very ineffective means of communication.

'Yes, you two can get acquainted. Find out all about each other,' she said, idiotically, and saw Tim get the message, a dawning realisation that he was meant to pump Alan for whatever he could. 'Back in a mo.'

She took a slow turn around the garden, checking on the whereabouts and intentions of the swans, and into the pub. She didn't need to powder her nose, actually or metaphorically, but she wanted to give Tim some time to sound out Alan, see whether he had the tech smarts to pull off the exam scam.

She pushed her way to the bar to get another beer and another lemonade. As she waited her turn, she indulged in her favourite pastime – listening in on strangers' conversations.

The woman to the left of her didn't know if her relationship was going anywhere, or whether she should just move on. 'Perhaps I should take it on the chin, y'know? Get out while I've still got my figure?' Pip sneaked a peek at the aforementioned figure and estimated that the magnificent cleavage had a few good years in it. Her companion, perhaps five or ten years older, seemed to disagree.

'It goes just like that,' she said gloomily, snapping her fingers. 'One day they're floating up there by your collarbone, the next, gone. Disappeared! And your options along with them.'

'What can I get you?' the bartender asked, leaning on the bar.

'A lemonade and a half of lager, please,' Pip said, before turning to her right, where she heard a voice that she would recognise anywhere.

'It's fwightfully important that we fwame the environmental wesearch to adequately include the wiver environment…'

Fwog Dude! Pip had met him in her time undercover in the Green Youth for Truth movement when she'd been searching for the missing teenager, Matty Price. She leaned forward and saw him a couple of stools down to her right. He spotted her and raised a hand, giving her a beaming smile behind his spectacles. What the heck was his name? That was the trouble with nicknames, especially secret nicknames based on a speech impediment – you couldn't use them in public, and they tended to wipe out real, usable names in your memory. 'Hey…' she said, hoping that her blank on his name wasn't obvious.

'Hamilton,' he said helpfully. He gestured to the woman between them. 'This is Fwankie, and this is…' He trailed off.

Pip felt better seeing that he'd forgotten her name too. Especially seeing as the name she'd been using at the time was in fact, for various complicated investigatory reasons, her sister's. She remembered now that he was Hamilton Cunningham-Smythe, a nature boff and the brains – or should that be bwains? – behind viral YouTube sensation Cunningham's Cunning Critters.

'Pip,' she said. 'Hi, Frankie.'

The woman smiled as Hamilton carried on. 'Fancy meeting you here. Now there's a coincidence. It's a long way from Hackney.'

'Meeting a friend. Work nearby,' she said vaguely. 'And you?'

'Work,' he said. 'Helping with an enviwomental impact study for a wesidential development nearby. Counting populations and so on.'

'Frogs?'

'Fwogs, newts, toads of course. It is partly wetland. And other animals, non-amphibious. Water wats. Wiver voles. Even birds. Wobins. Wavens. Wens.'

Pip nodded compulsively.

'Fwankie is looking at the flowa – gwasslands, weeds, that sort of thing.'

The bartender came up, pushed two glasses towards her, and said, 'That'll be five pounds.'

Pip thanked him, put the money on the counter and picked up the drinks. 'Nice to see you, Hamilton. Good luck with the assessment. Bye, Frankie.'

Tim should have had enough time to sound out Mr Geoffrey, Pip thought as she made her way through the pub, now buzzing with the after-work punters. Either way, Mr Geoffrey had found his own table by the time Pip arrived with the drinks.

'It's a crush in there,' she said. 'So, what did you learn?'

A big fat nothing, as it turned out. Tim had chatted with Alan Geoffrey and raised a variety of topics – his thoughts on crypto-currency, his experience of web design, general techie matters. As expected, he seemed to have enough skill to make the scam work, but Tim couldn't tell if he had anything to do with it.

'Sorry, Pip, I don't know. He doesn't seem like a criminal master-mind, that's for sure. Bit of a dullard, even if he has the tech skills.'

'Here's an idea,' she said. 'I've got the website address. What if I went onto the site, tried to order and pay for an exam paper? Do you think that would help?'

'I do. There would likely be some information, either on the correspondence or in the metadata, that we could use.'

'Drink up then. Let's get home and go fishing.'

CHAPTER 15

They discussed the plan in the car. Pip would register on the site, 'buy' an exam, see what turned up and take it from there. She would see if the correspondence offered any clues, and Tim would fish around on the technical side (at this point, there was a small side-lecture on IP addresses, which she hummed along to agreeably).

It was the work of moments. She opened up the website while Tim went to feed the cats. The landing page said:

> *To participate in our Hurlingham House exam preparedness programme, please sign up here. Note that while we require your real name, your anonymity is guaranteed!*

Pip clicked on the sign-up link and created a profile for herself. She needed a login name. She couldn't use her own, obviously, but nobody on the site would know she'd made up a name. She was shockingly bad at remembering passwords and logins and the like, so she needed something she'd remember. On a whim, she called herself 'Sally Llama', the actual name of one of Mummy's ridiculous pets.

> *Welcome SALLY. Now, in order to participate in our programme, you simply need to pay £500 in Bitcoin. This will be held as a deposit. Your exam assistance requests will be deducted from this amount. A minimum deposit of £200 must be maintained in the account at all times.*

To convert pounds to Bitcoin and pay, click here. Once funds have been received, you will receive your personal code, and a list of available resources.

'Tim…' Pip called. 'Help!'

Tim came over.

'Five hundred quid,' he said, bending over her shoulder to read the screen. 'That's pretty rich.'

'I know, right? It's a fortune for a schoolgirl. Even at a posh school.'

'You'd be surprised. This is very much the "Daddy, will you buy me a pony" crowd.'

'Funny you should mention,' Pip said with a laugh. 'In my investigations today I talked to one girl, Chanel, whose stepdad is literally going to buy her a pony.'

Tim gave a snort. 'Chanel? I know her. She's quite good friends with Claire. Her stepdad is a bigwig property developer. To him it would be like buying a kitten,' he said, scratching Smokey's tummy. 'So, let's do this,' he said, sitting down next to her.

'Well, yes, except that I don't have a spare five hundred pounds knocking around,' said Pip. 'I can come up with about half of it from what's left of the payment Ms Peters gave me. I'll ask her to reimburse me once this is over.'

Tim said he'd front her the money and help her to navigate the Bitcoin exchange. It was surprisingly simple. The website gave a series of links and instructions, and the next thing she knew, she had a £500 credit for pillaged exam papers. Now she would have to wait for her code and order a paper.

She joined Tim in the kitchen where they scavenged for scraps for dinner. She cut up an apple, sliced some cheddar and dumped a few crackers onto the plate before dashing back to her computer. Nothing from the exam scammers.

Waiting wasn't Pip's strong suit. While she ate, she watched the screen and refreshed her screen compulsively. Full and happy, the cats joined her on the sofa. Smokey was growing up, slim and rangy and full of beans. He was more likely to attack your toes than sit on your knee. If you wanted a cuddle, your best chance was when he was recently fed and sleepy. Like now. Pip popped him on her lap where he stayed contentedly, digesting his supper and purring. His mother, Most, arranged herself on the back of the sofa behind Pip's head. She was covered in cats. It was nice.

Pip looked at her screen. Nothing. She checked her email, in case they'd sent a mail, even though Chanel said they wouldn't. Nothing. Then she checked the junk folder, just in case. There was nothing from getyourbestmarks.co.uk, but she did see an All Staff email from Ms Peters, sent a couple of days before.

The subject line was 'Get Ready for our Fun Day'. This was exactly the kind of sentence that had made Pip's heart sink when she was at school. She had the same response now.

She opened it with trepidation. It was as she feared. A reminder that a school fete was to take place on Saturday, with activities and good cheer. 'Get ready for a PURRfectly fun day out at Hurlingham House. Don't forget! All the money raised goes to Paws with a Cause!' And so on.

It was forwarded with a covering note from Ms Peters which read:

I hope you don't mind doing this – each of the teachers is responsible for a stall or activity, so authenticity demands! I've given you bingo, it's the easiest. You can just print off some cards – the ever-efficient Mrs Jenkins will give you a code for the printer and any help you need. You can ask some of the girls to help with the stand.

Pip rather liked bingo, actually, and organising a bingo game would be a lot less trouble than organising pony rides or a tombola stall or something. Pip googled bingo cards and downloaded a set. No time like the present, and it would take her mind off the wait for a response from the website. She felt quite pleased with herself for her preparedness.

Once she had sorted that out, she realised she would have to actually call the games. She fell down a rabbit hole looking up the bingo lingo that always made her laugh. 'Two fat ladies, eighty-eight!' and so on. She was just wondering whether the term 'Gandhi's breakfast' for the number eighty – 'ate nothing' – was insensitive and politically incorrect, when a ping alerted her to an incoming message.

'Tim, we've got a live one!' she shouted, sending Smokey off her lap, all fluffed up like a bottle brush.

Tim came over, wiping his damp hands on a dish cloth. In addition to being cute and a tech whizz, he did the washing up. She took a nanosecond to reflect on her good fortune, and patted the sofa next to her. They turned their attention to the screen:

Sally Llama. Your application has been received and is being processed. Soon you'll join the many students benefitting from our services.

Things were hotting up.

CHAPTER 16

The word 'Mummy' pulsed on Pip's phone screen, bright with foreboding. Mummy's calls generally came with some sort of complication. At the moment, most of Mummy's complications derived from the new business she was trying to start – a llama farm, of all things.

The last thing Pip wanted right now was a further complication. She had her hands full with impersonating a sports teacher, impersonating an investigator, and impersonating a cheating schoolgirl. It did seem like rather a lot of impersonation for one person to keep a handle on, even a person like Pip who quite often found herself in this particular situation. And now she had the school Fun Day to worry about too. In fact, Mummy's call had interrupted her just as she was photocopying the bingo cards.

Pip hit the little green button on her phone. If she didn't take the call now, she'd have to take it later. Mummy would just call and call until she did.

'Epiphany,' said Mummy, without so much as a greeting. 'Do you remember that marketing course I paid for? When you thought you might want to be in advertising?'

'Ye-es,' said Pip, warily. It was true that Mummy had coughed up for a number of courses over the years as Pip tried, increasingly desperately, to find her niche in life. She's refused Pip's more unusual requests – Aerial Silk Dance, for instance, and Haiku for Fun and Profit, had both got the thumbs down. Pip could right now be suspended acrobatically from fabric ribbons whilst spouting profundities in seventeen syllables and raking in the cash, if only Mummy weren't so narrow-minded in her funding. Instead, Pip was photocopying bingo cards in the little printer room off the secretary's office.

'Well, it's time to put it to good use,' said Mummy.

'What?' Pip asked. It was hard to hear over the swoosh-swoosh noise of the photocopier, and Mummy seldom made perfect sense. 'Put what to use?' Was Mummy asking her to write a haiku?

'Your marketing nous.'

'Nous? I'm not sure I have mar—'

'I need you, Epiphany. The llamas need you. Henry and I have got them all settled and shipshape…' Pip had no idea what the shipshaping of a llama would entail, nor why Henry – the father of her ex-boss at the museum – was involved… 'and I need to start getting the visitors in. The paying punters, Epiphany. I didn't become a llama farmer for fun, you know. This is my business.'

'I'm glad the llamas are shipshape and I don't mean to rush you, Mummy, but I'm rather busy. I think I mentioned I'm working at a school.'

'Yes, you did. I was saying to Henry that it's quite a turn-up for the books given your own school record.'

'OK, Mummy, so I'm really very busy right now with the girls and the sport and some bingo.'

Mummy, as usual, proceeded like a ship in full sail ploughing over some poor windsurfer. 'I still have a cupboard full of uniforms. Some of them hardly worn. My Lord, now I think about it, how *did* you manage to poison the Domestic Science teacher…'

'Mummy—'

'And I still don't know how that swimming pool incident occurred. It's not as if it had a plug.'

'It was a freak accident. It could have happened to anyone. But Mummy, I really have to go.'

Her mother, thankfully, stopped reminiscing about Pip's many educational escapades and remembered the point of her call. 'I need you to help me put a marketing plan together. I need to draw visitors to the llama farm. I was thinking of birthday parties? I mean, what's more festive than South American ungulates?'

Pip assumed – no, prayed – that this was a rhetorical question, and let her mother babble on.

'Especially with the hats. Did I tell you about the hats? So very festive. Henry and I had them made. The llamas look just charming in them. Oh, and Henry has had a little llama box built. It's like a horse box, but for llamas. You attach it to the car. So we can travel around with them, to shows and parties and what have you. To show them off. They are their own best advertisements, really. You should build that into your plan.'

Pip felt sure her head would explode at any moment. It was all so mad – the hats, the llamas. And then there was the sudden appearance of Henry in every second sentence. 'Henry and I' this, 'Henry and I' that. What was actually going on between her mother and dear sweet Henry? Henry might be the father of the very woman who had recently fired her, but Pip wouldn't hold that against him. He was the dearest man she had ever met, and had helped Pip out tremendously when her mother had saddled her with the llamas. She hoped Mummy wouldn't hurt him, or drive him insane. Mummy's previous beau, Andrew, had elected to stay on in South America, allegedly to commune with the blue-footed boobies, but Pip suspected it was to get a break from Mummy. Pip decided to park her Henry concerns for the moment, and concentrate on the llamas.

'Excellent ideas, Mummy. I'll give some thought to promoting the llamas. Yes. Shows. Parties. Let me think about it. I'll get back to you.'

'Good,' said Mummy. 'I'll tell Henry you're on board.'

'I wouldn't say on board exactly, I said I'd—'

'Goodbye, Epiphany.'

Mummy ended the call. Pip groaned and took a moment – a conversation with Mummy was exhausting – then picked up the thick sheaf of photocopies from the tray. Turning to go, she found Mrs Jenkins behind her. She gave a little shriek of alarm and nearly dropped the pages.

'I'm sorry, didn't mean to startle,' said Mrs Jenkins with an apologetic smile. 'Just popping in to see if you managed to work the copier all right.'

'Thank you, yes. All good,' said Pip, and held up the copies.

'Anything else I can help you with?'

'I'm fine, thank you. Unless you can get my mother off my case,' she said, trying for a laugh.

'Well, I don't know about that,' the woman said, a concerned frown wrinkling her powdered forehead. 'Mothers aren't really my remit.'

'Just joking, sorry. I shouldn't have. It's just that she phoned while I was copying and she does have a knack of stressing me out.'

'Oh dear, that sounds tricky,' said Mrs Jenkins sympathetically. 'Would you like to sit down for a moment? I could make you a cuppa?'

Pip accepted the offer and was soon ensconced in Mrs Jenkins's office, a cup of tea on her lap and two shortbread biscuits resting in the saucer.

'This is so kind of you,' she said. 'I hope I'm not keeping you from anything.'

'Oh no, nothing I can't do later. Keeping the girls and the staff happy is part of my job too.'

Pip could see why Ms Peters sang the school secretary's praises. She had a calm, unflappable manner. You just knew nothing could go wrong with Mrs Jenkins in your corner. Pip wished Mummy had the same quality.

'Everyone does seem very happy. It's nothing to do with the school. Just that my mother's a bit, um, eccentric and there's always something. Right now it's llamas.'

'Llamas?' asked Mrs Jenkins, in wide-eyed surprise.

'Yes, she's recently bought some llamas and she's starting a llama farm.'

'Gosh, that's unusual, isn't it? Llamas. You don't come across them very often.'

'No,' said Pip. 'Maybe in South America you do, but not in Kent, no.'

Ms Peters came out of her office and greeted them warmly. 'Everything all right, Pip? Is Mrs Jenkins helping you get the hang of things?'

'Oh yes, all good, thank you.'

Ms Peters turned to her secretary. 'I don't know what I'm going to do without you when you retire at the end of the year.'

'Oh, well now…' Mrs Jenkins blushed modestly and fussed a bit with her pearls.

'Now, what are you two nattering about over tea?'

'Llamas, if you can believe it,' Pip said with a laugh.

'Aren't they just so funny?' said Ms Peters, clasping her hands together in delight. 'I do love them. I even considered getting a couple for the school – we could keep them down by the Marsh Field. I thought the girls would like them, they're so cheering.'

Why did people keep saying that? Why did everyone just llove those llousy llamas? Pip had never found the beasts anything other than an aggravation from the day her mother had shipped them back from Peru, with Pip as the recipient.

'Well, my mother likes them too. She has a small llama farm – it's not far from here, actually. She's going to do birthday parties and other things, honestly I don't know what. They have the most ridiculous names.'

'Oh, do tell,' said Alexandra Peters eagerly.

'They all have names with a double L. Llewelyn, Sally…'

Ms Peters looked delighted at the notion. 'I've got an idea,' she said. 'Why don't you ask your mother if she can bring the llamas to the Fun Day? We'd pay the necessary, of course. It would be such fun to have them. They're so festive, don't you think?'

CHAPTER 17

Pip and her Year 11s were allocated to help with the final bits of set-up on Saturday morning. The activities would take place on the grassy area of the Marsh Field and in the shade of the ancient oaks. It really was a magnificent setting, like a vast country estate from a Jane Austen movie. Pip half expected to see Colin Firth striding across it in breeches and a top hat. Beyond the oaks was the site of the Executive Lifestyle Estate, where Ruby and Amelia had taken Pip as a shortcut on cross-country day.

The central area had been demarcated into sections, for the tombola, the target and throwing games, the bouncy castle, and the seated area where Pip would host the bingo, which would be used for a magic show in the morning and a fun quiz later. And then of course there were the llamas off to one side.

The girls were busy with signage, paper chains and other decorations, prettying things up.

A few more were bringing in extra pieces of furniture. There was a fair amount of joshing and laughing as they struggled across the rather uneven field lugging unwieldy items. 'Bend at the knees, there you go,' Pip said, hamming up her sports mistress persona. 'Wow, look at that upper body strength.'

Aside from the actual sports side of things, Pip had started to enjoy being a sports teacher. She liked the girls. At least you could have a bit of a laugh with them. Not like some of the colleagues she'd had over the years – the Amish milliners were particularly humourless, but fortunately that job was short-lived, after the incident with the pickling brine. Pip wondered again if it was too late to retrain as a teacher. She felt that this was, at last, something she might be good at.

Her pondering was interrupted by Grace Faith and Chanel walking by with a table, Grace holding her side up rather lightly, Chanel struggling under more than her share of the weight. 'Straighten it up, girls, it'll be easier.'

Instead of pulling her weight, Grace Faith dropped her side with a groan. 'You'd think with what our parents pay for this school they could pay some labourers to move all this stuff,' she said grumpily, checking her fingernails for damage.

'You should go tell your dad,' said Amelia, who was passing with a box full of paints and brushes and markers. 'Go tell the chairman of the board you don't want to carry a table cos it'll ruin your nails.'

Grace Faith looked at her coldly and said, 'It's different for you, Amelia, you've got the build for furniture moving.'

There followed the sound of girls inhaling sharply. Before anyone else got involved and upped the drama, Ruby said soothingly, 'The set-up isn't so bad. It's all part of the fun.'

'Yes, and it is for charity,' said Chanel. Grace Faith shot her a withering look and Chanel shrank into herself. 'You're right though, Grace Faith, it's a drag,' she said, back-pedalling. 'I just meant, you know, it's good about the animals, isn't it?' She looked unsure.

'You make a good point, Chanel. We're doing it for the animals,' said Pip, turning her back to Grace Faith. She had been on the receiving end of mean Queen Bees at school, and she knew it was best to ignore them.

'I'm going to the bathroom,' Grace Faith said and stalked off, leaving Chanel looking miserable and holding on to one end of the table. Pip picked up the other end.

'I'll give you a hand, not far to go. Oh, and Chanel, I wanted to ask, can you help me at the bingo stand? I need someone to hand out the cards, that sort of thing.'

She looked as if she'd been invited to join Pip in dissecting a frog. 'Bingo? Oh, I don't know…' Pip could see her brain whirring, looking for an out. 'My stepdad said he'd take me for lunch. Like that's something to look forward to, but still.'

'Perfect. It's just an hour between eleven and twelve. Come at quarter to eleven to set up, and you can be out and ready for lunch by twelve fifteen.'

'I guess I could…' she said. 'I'll see.'

'Good, I'll expect you then.'

Across the field she saw Mummy with Henry beside her, consulting with Amelia about the signage. Even from a distance, Pip could see that Mummy was at her most charming, smiling warmly and tapping Amelia gently on the arm.

Pip helped Chanel deliver the table to the tombola stand and then made her way over to Llamageddon, where she heard her mother wittering away. 'Oh, I do like the blue you've used,' she said, beaming at Amelia, and at Ruby who had joined them, a big camera slung around her neck. 'It sets off Sally's colouring so well. And what a nice little stall they've put up for us. Don't you think so, Henry?'

'Oh yes,' said Henry. 'It's a perfectly lovely spot. Nice and shady, and close to the tea garden. Ah, Pip! Dear girl, there you are. How are you?'

'Good, good,' said Pip awkwardly. It was the first time she'd seen him since the fire. He was, after all, part owner of the museum she'd immolated. But he appeared to hold no grudge. In fact, he was in cheerful good humour. She thought she'd clear the air anyway. 'Henry, just to say, I'm so very sorry about the fire.'

'Do not concern yourself, Pip. It could have happened to anyone. Our insurance paid out and we're doing a bit of an upgrade while we're about it, so no hard feelings on that score.'

She mumbled her thanks.

'Isn't this jolly good fun, hey? I hear you're in charge of the bingo. I'll come and have a game. Wouldn't miss it! Your mother can man the stand – or woman the stand, I suppose I should say. Keep an eye on the livestock, anyway.'

'The llama is looking good,' Pip said, mostly to be nice. It looked the same as they always looked: long-legged, fluffy and curiously dim.

'Doesn't she just? I gave her a good brush this morning, and applied my special conditioning lotion. I invented it myself and it works a treat. Gets their coats all glossy.' He leaned in and said conspiratorially, 'Coconut oil, mostly. That's the secret. But don't tell a soul. I'm about to be going into business, marketing it to the broader llama community.'

Ruby took a few pictures of Sally – 'For the school paper,' she said, causing Pip to move swiftly out of frame. Amelia had the sign up and was adjusting it under Mummy's direction – a bit left, no, a bit right, yes, up a bit, now down, and so on – for quite some minutes (or, in Pip's case, a lifetime). Finally, there it was, in all its glory.

Guess the weight of the llama!
Only £1!
Win a llama wool scarf, perfect for trekking in the Andes!

And at the bottom, in smaller writing:

Ask us about farm visits and birthday parties.

There was a little pile of fliers on the table, outlining their services. Another, smaller sign said:

Take a selfie with Sally!
£1 – goes to charity!

Visitors were starting to trickle in. A little boy came barrelling over, dragging his mother by the hand.

'Mama, look!' he said. 'A giant sheep camel!'

Henry laughed merrily, and bent down to explain the subtle difference between a llama and a giant sheep camel.

'Gonna go,' Pip stage whispered. 'See you later.'

'No probllama!' said Henry, laughing his head off at his own joke.

Surveying the scene, Pip decided that her work was done and she could, with clear conscience, hit up the doughnut stand. Her phone vibrated while she waited for her order. A message from Jimmy: *Here. Where are you?*

Pip had invited him when he had expressed his deep and abiding love for bingo, and begged to be allowed to play. Pip was ninety per cent sure he was having her on, but he'd be good for moral support and entertaining company. She had warned him that she'd be busy, what with the bingo and nosing around for anything that might be useful for the exam scam investigation. He had joked that he'd be happy to keep his own slightly crooked nose to the ground. He was, after all, an ex-bouncer, so Pip reckoned he was likely to be better acquainted with criminals.

She was typing *Over by the…* when he came up behind her and lifted her off her feet. She might have been a petite ballerina for all the effort he seemed to put in.

'Jimmy!' she said with a little shriek, as he plonked her back down. 'You nearly gave me a heart attack.'

'It's good for you, a rush of adrenaline.'

She noticed Grace Faith whispering behind her hand to a little gaggle, all eyes on Pip and Jimmy. He was fairly startling in this environment, amongst the soft suburbanites, the pampered wealthy: his lean body, muscled and tattooed. The stubbled head and jaw. The knowing glint in his eyes. She caught the look of the girls – behind the sly laughter, a kind of respect, even envy of Pip being lifted off her feet by this hard man. She put her hand on his arm and, leaning in, murmured huskily into his ear, 'Can I interest you in a doughnut?' That would give Grace Faith something to whisper about.

CHAPTER 18

The bingo seats and tables were filling up nicely, and there was still a queue at the ticket table. It was going to be a full house. Each entrant paid their £5 to Chanel and received a bingo sheet, plus a pencil to cross out the numbers as Pip called them.

Pip felt a flutter of nervousness, which was crazy, seeing as it was just school bingo. She had been anxious about being up on stage ever since she'd accidentally found herself on the London stage playing Cat 13 in the musical *Cats*. Her friend, the real Cat 13, had wanted to meet her boyfriend and asked Pip to stand in for her, just for half an hour, but she'd been delayed by a fire on the Tube and, as they say, the show must go on. And with it, Pip. Pip tried to forget about the dancing, the prancing, the meowing, the arched back and the reaching claws. It could have happened to anyone. Except that it didn't.

Anyway, this was a much simpler affair. She looked out over a sea of faces – Henry and Jimmy amongst them – all smiling up at her in anticipation of a happy round of bingo. Chanel gave her a thumbs up from the back. They were good to go.

Pip welcomed everyone and got started, pulling a number out of a velvet sack provided for the occasion.

'Two fat ladies, eighty-eight,' she said, gaily.

Funnily enough, no one had two fat ladies. *Oh well.*

'Legs eleven,' Pip boomed in her best carnival tout voice. This time, heads went down.

'Thirteen, unlucky for some!'

It turned out to be unlucky for all. Not a single taker.

Chanel looked at her, pale and wide-eyed. Pip gave her a reassuring smile.

'Two little ducks, twenty-two.'

Heads bent. All the heads. All the pencils scratched on all the papers. What a coincidence.

'All the fours, fours,' she called, pulling the next number. All the heads went down again.

All of them.

She and Chanel looked at each other in sudden awful recognition. Pip realised with a sinking heart that in her excitement, she had copied only one bingo sheet. Which meant, of course, that the punters all had the same numbers!

The room got it too, at the exact same moment. People turned to compare sheets with their neighbours. A bristle of hands went up, accompanied by a grumble of voices. She heard Henry's distinctive chuckle.

'Ah, apologies,' Pip said, with as much dignity as she could muster. 'It seems there's been an administrative error. If we could reconvene in half an hour, play can resume.'

She dashed for the door, shouting, 'Hold the fort,' over her shoulder in the direction of Chanel. The girl started about her lunch plans, but Pip was already on the move, jogging across the field to the administration block, dodging the carefree throngs with their ice creams and hot dogs. Out of the corner of her eye she saw there was a long line at the llama enclosure. Maybe Mummy was onto something after all.

Back she went to the print room. She would have to print out a set of (assorted!) bingo cards, but she didn't have her laptop with her. Fortunately Mrs Jenkins was in her office next door. Pip came in panting, explaining between breaths.

'Not to worry, dear, we can sort that out. Lucky you found me, I just came to fetch a cardigan,' said Mrs Jenkins calmly, seemingly unaware of the urgency. 'I'll just turn the computer on.' Pip hopped from foot to foot impatiently.

For all her calm, Mrs Jenkins was marvellously nimble on the computer. Within minutes she'd found a site, downloaded the new cards, sized them and had the printer spitting them out. A quick slice with the guillotine and she was done.

As Pip gathered them up gratefully, men's voices drifted in from the corridor. Something in their tone made Pip stop, despite her great hurry, and wait, her hand on the doorknob.

'We wouldn't want it to get out, now, Charles, would we? It wouldn't do Grace Faith's future any good at all if people knew how she got her great marks,' came a smooth voice.

'Are you threatening me, David? Using my daughter?' The second man, presumably Charles, had an almost unbelievably plummy voice, squeaking with fury.

'Whatever do you mean? That's not it at all,' said David calmly.

'I caution you against it, David. I am not a man to be messed with and besides, it's not as if Chanel is innocent on this score.'

Mrs Jenkins and Pip were both blatantly eavesdropping at this point, both struck still and silent. The men had stopped right outside the door, and the women could hear every word.

'Oh come on, Charles, we both know Chanel's no rocket scientist. She wouldn't have known how to do this without Grace Faith. Besides, I took the screen grabs from her phone – it's clear. It's got the website address. And it's your girl who sent it to Chanel. I really should take it to Alexandra. She'd be able to get an IT expert in and trace the perpetrator, as well as which girls were involved. But do we really want to do that to the girls? Especially given that you and I both know who probably came up with this.'

'I certainly agree we don't want to make trouble for the girls. Blowing up a silly schoolgirl mistake into a big drama is in no one's interests.'

'Speaking of my interests...' Chanel's father let the words hang in the air for a while.

Charles's voice came, filled with understanding and disdain. 'Oh, I see. I know what this is about. It's the vote, isn't it?'

There was a brief silence – perhaps there was a nod or a whisper behind the door – and then she heard Charles say, 'How dare you! I'm chairman of the board of this school. I will not be threatened or blackmailed by an upstart like you.'

Pip was aware of the minutes ticking by, the would-be bingo players waiting for her. She needed to get out of the office. She made a few loud noises – a cough, a slam of the photocopier – and waited a moment, then said loudly to Mrs Jenkins, 'Thank you for your help, I'll be going then.'

When she opened the door, the two men had moved briskly off, heading towards the Marsh Field and the festivities. Although they didn't seem festive at all, heads down, conversing tersely. She followed, heading for the bingo, mouthing her thanks to Mrs Jenkins who was staring after them.

Pip followed at a distance, her papers in hand. She couldn't hear what they were talking about but she caught enough of their conversation to ascertain that the bigger sandy-haired fellow was Charles, Grace's father, and the slighter, darker man was Chanel's stepfather, David.

More importantly, she had a clue! From what she'd just overheard, it seemed that Grace Faith was the one providing girls with the website details. Which made it likely that Grace Faith was the one behind the exam scam and Chanel one of her customers. That's certainly what Chanel's stepfather thought. Now all Pip had to do was get a confession out of Grace Faith and find out who else was involved in setting the whole thing up. With Tim's help investigating the website, she would have the proof she needed to wrap it all up in a bow and deliver it to Ms Peters, thus clearing Claire's name and winning the grateful thanks of Tim. Bingo! But first, bingo!

CHAPTER 19

Round two of the bingo went smoothly. Pip's heart wasn't quite in it second time round, and her mind was occupied with how she would confront Grace Faith without overstepping Ms Peters's instructions, or bringing on the wrath of the chairman of the board. Chanel looked preoccupied too, and rather gloomy in fact, even as she handed over the tin of luxury shortbread to the winner and posed for a picture in the *Hurlingham Herald*.

Pip went over to the girl and patted her shoulder. 'Thanks for all your help today,' she said. 'It was a bit of a muddle and you were great.'

'You're welcome. It was fun,' Chanel said distractedly.

'I can collect the sheets and pencils. You go along and meet your dad.'

'Oh, that. My stepdad. He cancelled,' Chanel said, with studied carelessness. 'He couldn't hang about, said he had to go and meet someone at one of his sites. It's right next door.'

'I'm sorry, I think that's my fault. Everything was delayed because of, you know…'

'Don't worry, he's very busy. Always got a meeting. But it's all cool, I was kind of dreading it. I guess I'll meet up with my friends.'

'Like Grace Faith? Is she here?'

'Yes, I've seen her around.'

'You're friends, right?'

'Oh yes, she's really great. I mean she's, like, cool.'

There was a distinct lack of warmth in her response. Pip wondered if this was one of those teenage friendships held together by fear and status and history rather than real affection.

'Well, thanks again for everything. You did great. I'm going to go and have a look around.'

Chanel perked up a bit. 'You should go see the llama. Everyone says it's really cool, and there's some crazy old lady telling llama facts and llama jokes. Everyone says she's absolutely hilarious.'

'Good info,' said Pip, who intended to give the llama and the hilarious crazy old lady a very wide berth. 'And I think there's a Scottish dancing demonstration starting any minute. That should be fun too. See you Monday.'

When she'd packed up, Pip went to find Jimmy who was hanging around waiting for her.

'Go on, get it over with,' she said.

'What do you mean?' he said, in exaggerated innocence.

'Have your laugh at my expense. I know I messed up the bingo cards.'

'Hey, I think you made a great recovery. Ask any athlete, they'll tell you anyone can dribble an offside half-shot off the pace on a good day, but not everyone can birdie the ace of clubs when they're three under in the outfield.'

Or something like that; Pip wasn't au fait with the terminology, and it didn't quite stick.

'Thanks, I think. Anyway, do you want to walk around with me? I'm looking for a girl.'

'Well, you're in the right place. There's hundreds of them.'

'Someone specific. About yay high, blonde ponytail?' He raised an eyebrow. She was describing about ninety per cent of the girls there. 'Never mind, just wander around with me while I look. Her name's Grace Faith.'

'Why are we looking for her?'

'She's a bit of a cool mean-girl type; her dad is chairman of the school board. I overheard something that makes me think she might be involved with this exam scam.'

'Ah, I know the type. Not personally, mind, I was never at a school like this. But I know that there's a certain sort of person who thinks they're entitled to whatever they want – money, status, marks, in this case.'

'That's her for sure, but I don't reckon she could pull it off.'

'Oh, that sort never does the dirty work. There would be someone else for that.'

'One of the teachers, perhaps…' Pip thought of what Claire had told her about the teachers, and how they would never cheat. If only she could find out *which* teacher might be the exception. Someone without a moral compass, and with more to lose than most.

Pip was interrupted by the Geography teacher Marie Stone, who waved her over to a shady table where she was seated with a group of women – at least two of whom Pip recognised as teachers. They all eyed Jimmy with interest, except for Candice the Maths teacher who was digging around in a voluminous handbag. All teachers seemed to own a voluminous handbag, and Pip made a mental note to buy one of her own.

'Join us for a scone?' Marie asked, pushing a plate of creamy, jammy scones in her direction. 'They're delicious. Plenty for your friend.'

There was an expectant silence as they waited for an introduction.

'This is Jimmy,' she obliged. 'Jimmy, this is Marie, and these are some of my colleagues at the school.'

'Good afternoon, everyone. Lovely day,' said Jimmy, with his sexy crinkly grin.

With the exception of the handbag delver, they stared at the two of them, clearly wondering what kind of a friend this good-looking tough was to Pip. She didn't feel like explaining.

'That's kind of you, Marie, but we're on our way to the Scottish dancing.'

'Oh, don't miss the llamas. They're too cute!' said a teacher whose name Pip could not remember, clasping her hands together in delight. 'We got our photos taken, didn't we, Candice?' She nudged the handbag scratcher, who looked up reluctantly and agreed.

'Yes, lovely photos,' she said. She got up rather abruptly. 'I must go,' she said briskly, moving off towards the admin block.

'We're off too. Nice to meet you all,' said Jimmy. 'Enjoy the scones.'

He took Pip's arm and they moved in the other direction, towards the central area where the entertainment took place. The dancers were milling around, fiddling with their shoes and their hair.

'I know that woman,' Jimmy said, as soon as they were out of earshot.

'Which one?'

'The blonde on the far side of the table.'

'Candice? She's one of the Maths teachers, I think.'

'She's good with numbers, that's for sure.'

'What do you mean?'

'She was a top poker player a few years back. Won all the tournaments.'

'Really?' Pip said incredulously. 'She doesn't look like a professional gambler... Are you sure?'

'Positive. They called her Candy Counter because she counted cards. Got her into trouble.'

Pip nodded. 'I know the casinos are on the lookout and take it very seriously. I worked in one once.'

Jimmy looked mildly surprised, but continued, 'Protecting their profits, the greedy buggers. Still, as you say, it's prohibited and she was banned from all the joints eventually.'

'Interesting,' said Pip. 'She certainly didn't look pleased to see you. Did you notice how she kept looking in her bag? I think she didn't want you to see her face. And then she dashed off.'

A person with the smarts and morals – or lack thereof – to become a card counter might well also arrange an exam scam. And if she was good with numbers, she might be good with computers and Bitcoin too. Jimmy might just have found the answer to which teacher was helping the girls. Pip felt a flutter of excitement. She needed to investigate this Candice. Where had she gone?

But now, Jimmy and Pip had come to a small crowd waiting to watch the Scottish dancing – mostly the eager parents of the dancers, iPhones at the ready, waiting restlessly for them to start. Pip scanned the crowd for Candice, hoping to corner her for a chat.

'Your mum's doing well by the looks of it,' Jimmy said, with a nod towards the little stall. There was indeed quite a crowd gathered for llama weight guessing and the selfie station. 'We should go say hello to our girl Sally, and the 'rents too.'

'Urgh! Please don't call them that! They do seem very friendly with each other though.'

'Their eyes met across the llamas, and they knew instantly that they were meant to be…' Jimmy started in a dreamy voice, like the voice-over in a Hallmark movie. 'Once the furry beasts had brought them together, nothing could tear them apart.'

'Enough, the Scottish dancers are ready to start,' said Pip, batting him on the arm. 'It seems like a lot of bobbing and prancing, but believe me, it's much harder than you'd think.'

Pip reached for her elbow and felt the raised scar she'd got from a bad fall on a sword when she'd given the dancing a try, in the month she'd lived in the Highlands with a Pipe Major. She sighed, but was distracted from reviewing her dubious relationship choices by the sound of Scottish music and the start of the dance.

It was lovely and calming to watch the girls bobbing and weaving, jumping and pointing, in their pretty dresses and laced shoes. Pip tapped her foot to the familiar beat and felt herself relax after the stress of a week of teaching and investigating, not to mention the bingo. She allowed her mind to drift off for a bit, not worrying about bingo or llamas or stolen exams, and just enjoying the dancing and music and sounds of people enjoying themselves. That said, she hadn't expected each dance to go on for quite as long as it did. The same four girls must have been kicking and bobbing for almost a quarter of an hour now – they must be exhausted. Pip was, it must be said, getting slightly bored. And still no sign of Candice the card counter.

Out of the corner of her eye she saw movement in the crowd to her right; a ripple as a clump of people turned from the dancers in the direction of – *Oh no*; Pip's heart sank – in the direction of her mother's stand. There was a commotion of some sort, an indistinct sound of conflict. Pip pushed her way through, pulling Jimmy behind her, hissing in a stage whisper, 'Something's going on with the llama.' As she neared the edge of the dance audience, she heard raised voices. She could see her mother now, her hand on Sally's harness, being shouted at by a woman with two young children in tow.

'Your alpaca *spat* at Savannah,' she was shouting at Mummy, while rubbing fiercely at a dark, damp patch on the head of the older of the two children.

'Actually, alpacas are smaller and their ears are more—' Henry's point of order was obliviated by the woman's rant.

'*Spat!* It is disgusting. I should call the Government Hygiene Services.'

'It's only a bit of saliva, it's perfectly harmless,' said Mummy. 'Spitting is just a natural stress response. Besides, the child started it.'

Pip's heart sank. This was not going to end well.

'The child started it? *Started* it?'

'She did pull Sally's ears.'

'She is *seven*!'

'Old enough to know how to treat an animal, if she's been brought up properly.'

'How dare you? I'll get the lot of you shut down…'

Pip was next to Mummy now, and could see the whites of Sally's eyes. She pulled at her harness – even the idiotic beast had enough nous to want to get far away from Savannah's furious mother. Mummy patted her neck to soothe her, but Sally was having none of it. She lifted her head and aimed a great blob of spit right into the shouting woman's face. The shriek she emitted might have cracked windows across the campus. It was enough to make even Mummy flinch and loosen her grip on Sally, who took the opportunity to slip out of her harness. Henry grabbed for her, but the animal trotted away. Pip made a desperate lunge for the llama, her hand sliding across the glossy, well-conditioned coat, and coming up empty and slippery and smelling of coconut.

Sally was off across the field, trotting in her ridiculous gait at a steady pace. Pip and Jimmy gave chase, but the llama proved difficult to pin down, dodging and ducking between stalls and people, speeding up quite remarkably at some points. She stopped briefly to take a lick of a passing child's candyfloss and then sped up past the tombola and the white elephant stall, narrowly missing Mrs Jenkins who was examining the wares, and gambolling briskly until she arrived at the Scottish dancers. There she stopped momentarily to observe the surprising scene of humans hopping from foot to foot, twirling and circling each other to the sound of music. Who could imagine what strange thoughts went through the little brain in her narrow skull at that moment?

Pip was within striking distance when a great wail of bagpipes shocked the llama from her reverie and she hurtled across the grass, scattering dancers in her wake. Jimmy and Pip set off after her at their respective top speeds. The boxing and the school sports had built up her fitness, but she was still a little behind him.

Mummy and Henry were well behind both of them, following at a much slower pace, and behind them a trickle of curious onlookers. Sally had clearly had enough of humans and was heading for the edge of the field at speed. When she came to the fence separating the Marsh Field from the building site next door, she hesitated momentarily and then jumped, sailing over the fence with a surprising agility that drew an admiring 'Aaaaahhhh' from the ragtag trail of people following her.

Pip climbed over the fence with considerably less grace, landing heavily on the other side and falling onto her side, eliciting a collective 'Oooooohhh'. Struggling up from the muddy ground, she shouted to Henry, who had arrived on the scene, 'Keep everyone out. Sally's just scared. Let's let her calm down a bit without the crowd, and Jimmy and I'll try to catch her.'

'Excellent plan, Epiphany,' cried Henry, who, as usual, seemed to be having a whale of a time. Mummy came up and tossed Pip the harness and a carrot. 'Good luck! Bonne chance! Bon voyage!' she shouted, dramatically and slightly inaccurately.

Now that Sally was no longer being pursued, she slowed to an amble. She stopped to nibble a patch of grass that had yet to be torn up by the diggers or flattened by the rollers parked on the site. Jimmy and Pip approached her carefully, taking care not to startle her. Pip made what she hoped was a soothing clicking noise. 'I'll give her the carrot, you put on the harness, OK?' she said to Jimmy, handing it to him.

Her plan worked. Sally munched the carrot, barely pausing when Jimmy slipped the harness onto her. A small cheer went up from the other side of the fence, and the onlookers started to disperse back to the fete, the drama over. The ground was so boggy that they led Sally home along the perimeter where it was less disturbed and firmer. It was rather pleasant, strolling the oak-fringed edge of the path, leading a llama, as long as she ignored the machinery and muddy mess in the centre.

'We can walk across here,' she said, leading the way to an area behind a yellow steamroller, where the ground had been flattened. Jimmy followed, Sally plodding happily behind him. Then the llama stopped dead.

'What's up?' he asked, turning to the animal. 'Come on then, beastie.'

Jimmy gave the harness a gentle tug. The llama stood firm.

'Probably scared of the earth-moving equipment,' Pip said, nodding towards the yellow roller a few paces downhill from them.

'It's fine, Sally, look,' she said – yes, she too had taken to conversing with llamas – and took a step forward to demonstrate. She felt something give beneath her foot, something firm but yielding. Before she even looked down, her churning stomach told her something her brain didn't yet know. And then she looked, and saw that she was standing on a man. A man, face down in the mud, almost buried, and almost certainly dead.

CHAPTER 20

Pip thought unusually quickly. She carefully stepped off the dead man's shoulders. She'd seen her share of police procedurals, and she knew to disturb the area as little as possible lest she spoil some vital clue.

'Don't move. Stay where you are,' she shouted to Jimmy. 'Jimmy, there's a dead body here. We might be in the middle of a crime scene. This whole place could be full of evidence. We have to be careful.'

Jimmy looked down at her feet and took in the broad back and the tufts of dark hair covered in mud, the edge of a hand curled around something pale. 'Bloody hell. That's why the llama wouldn't move. What should we do?'

Pip did the only thing she could think of – she called the police and tried to quickly explain what was happening. There was a brief confusion, when the chap on the emergency line seemed incapable of understanding her simple story.

'It doesn't matter *why* I was chasing a llama,' yelled Pip into the phone. 'The important part is that there's a dead body in the field. That's why the llama wouldn't move.'

Next, she phoned Ms Peters, who for once seemed flustered and was full of questions Pip couldn't answer: 'But I don't understand. What do you mean? Who died? And why are you on the building site? What do you mean about the llama?'

'Please, Ms Peters – Alexandra – just get here. The police are on their way.' That jolted the headmistress into reality.

She turned to Jimmy. 'Go back the way we came. Don't tell anyone what's happened here. Try to get everyone back to the school. The police will be here any minute.' She hoped this last part was true. Nothing in the phone call had given her great confidence.

Jimmy retraced their steps and handed the llama over to Mummy and Henry at the gate leading to the school. As they made their way back to the Fun Day, the last of the curious onlookers trickled after them.

Pip tried to step as close as she could to Jimmy's footsteps. Picking her way through the mud, she arrived at the gate at the same time as Ms Peters and a big man who Pip recognised as Grace Faith's father, Charles. 'Epiphany Bloom, Charles Eastleigh. Charles is the chairman of the school board,' Ms Peters said. Pip nodded as if all this was news to her.

'What happened?'

Before Pip could answer, a police car pulled up at the gate on the road and two men got out. As in every crime drama Pip had ever seen, one was young, tall, thin and eager; the other older, short, stocky and gruff. Inspectors Goodall and Truman, respectively, in this case.

They skirted the edge of the field, and came over to the huddled group. Pip told them all the same story – the llama chase, the field, the discovery of the body.

Truman asked the questions while Goodall waited, pencil poised above his notebook.

'What can you tell us about the deceased, ma'am?' he asked.

There wasn't much to tell. From the broadness of the back and what she could see from the cut of the hair, she thought the body was probably male, definitely an adult. She hadn't wanted to touch him or turn him over.

'Good thinking,' said Goodall. 'We don't want civilians turning over bodies and trampling all over the evidence, making a mess of things. That's our job.'

Fixing the group with a stern gaze, Truman continued, 'You lot wait here. No one must leave. Let me go and have a look.'

He trudged across the muddy field, bent down and pulled at the dead man's shoulder. It didn't budge. He bent his knees and put his back into it. He raised the shoulder a few inches before the mud sucked it back. 'Goodall, get over here,' he shouted. His colleague trudged in his footprints, notebook in hand.

'Shouldn't there be some sort of crime scene team?' Ms Peters asked Pip, who had presumably seen the same television series as Pip.

'One would think,' said Pip from her perch on a fallen log, where she was trying to scrape the clay-like mud from her shoes with a stick. 'But I suppose they must know what they're doing.'

The two policemen bent down and together took hold of one side of the corpse. They groaned as they hauled the body over, then looked at it a bit, as if hoping it might come back to life. Truman poked it gingerly with the end of his baton. Goodall made notes in his notebook. Then they slogged back through the sticky mud and confirmed that it was indeed a man, probably in his late forties.

'Definitely dead,' said Goodall officiously, as if that had been in any doubt. 'Took a picture of him. Anyone recognise this gentleman?' He held up the phone.

It was a man, but Pip didn't recognise him. The face was dirt-streaked and pale grey from the dampness, the hair dark. He was holding a mobile phone in his right hand.

'Oh my goodness,' said Ms Peters, in shock. 'It's…'

'That's David Cole. He's a parent at the school,' said Charles Eastleigh. 'His daughter – stepdaughter, actually – is friends with my Grace Faith. Her name's Chanel.'

Pip felt suddenly light-headed. The bingo, the chase, the discovery, and now this new piece of information, all came together in a wave of adrenaline.

'Whoa there,' Jimmy said, taking her arm. 'You OK? You're as white as a sheet.'

'I'll be OK. Just shocked. I know Chanel, she was the girl helping me with the bingo this morning. She was meant to meet her stepdad for lunch when we finished, but he had to go to a site meeting.'

'This must be the site,' Ms Peters said. 'He is… was… The housing development they're building here is his. Betterworld Developers.' She gestured across the field to the giant billboard and the computer-generated happy homes.

'What happened to him?' asked Charles. 'Could he have slipped, do you think? A freak accident?'

'That's the million-dollar question,' said Truman, self-importantly. 'Cause of death will be determined by the coroner, but I see no signs of foul play. No obvious wounds. Heart attack maybe.'

Pip couldn't believe her ears. 'Heart attack? How would he end up half buried in the mud from a heart attack?'

No one had a good answer to that question. They all stared glumly at the site of the body surrounded by mud, churned up by the policemen's feet, the yellow roller parked downhill like some great prehistoric beast. Goodall was literally scratching his head.

'The steamroller!' said Pip. 'He was run over by the roller. The ground is so soft he was pushed into the mud. Instead of being crushed, he was drowned or suffocated.'

Jimmy gave a low whistle – of admiration or realisation.

'It's a possibility,' Truman said grudgingly. 'Goodall, put it on the list.'

'Would it have been an accident, then?' Ms Peters asked, hopefully.

'Very likely,' said Truman, nodding wisely. 'He could well have been walking in front of it and the handbrake slipped. Freak accident.'

Goodall, who, it turned out, could speak after all, nodded in agreement, saying, 'That makes sense. He was surveying the land, and in a strange twist of fate it just sort of rolled over him.'

Pip caught Jimmy's eye and saw the look of stark disbelief that he no doubt saw in her own. A freak accident with a steamroller and no driver? Absolutely no way. There were about fifteen things wrong with the scenario. Did the thing even have a handbrake? Alexandra Peters's face held a similar expression.

'Goodall, take down everyone's name and phone number so we can be in touch,' said Truman.

Goodall started with Charles, who had to spell out his surname three times. Pip looked across the fence to the trampled scene where David Cole was slumbering unperturbed in his muddy grave. This was very likely a murder investigation – not for a minute was she buying the tragic accident theory.

Goodall was now laboriously taking down Jimmy's details. She heard him ask, 'Double M, you say?'

Pip had found the man. She wanted to know what happened to him. She hoped these two policemen were up to the job.

CHAPTER 21

Flis's thumb found a spot just below the ball of the big toe of Pip's left foot and pressed firmly. The pain was quick, surprising and horribly intense. Pip squealed and drew her foot back. 'Good God, I thought reflexology was supposed to be pleasant and relaxing.'

'That was your digestive system meridian,' Flis said. 'Looks like you haven't been taking care of that tummy. Have you been getting your omegas?'

'I know you want to practise for your course, but can't you just give me a nice foot rub without dragging my digestive tract into it? Like I said, I did discover an actual body.'

'Yes. I want to hear all about it. Go on, talk. I'll be gentle with your feet.'

Pip explained about the drama of the escaping llama.

'Oh Lord,' said Flis. 'She trampolined someone? How awful. Who was it? Not a child, I hope.'

'What? Trampolined? Oh. No. No trampling. Or trampolining for that matter. Sally didn't kill anyone. I finally cornered her in the building site next to the school, a huge plot of land that's being cleared for building houses.'

'What are they going for?'

'What?'

'The houses. I was thinking of buying a place in the country, getting out of the city. It's got so busy, I feel I'm getting xenophobia.'

'But Flis, you know immigrants are an important part of our rich cultural life?'

'Who said anything about the immigrants? It's everyone. I can't breathe with all the traffic and the people. I feel like I'm in a small space, getting squashed.'

'That's claustrophobia, not xenophobia. And can we park the property discussion, please? I've got enough in my brain as it is.'

Flis shut up and pulled gently at Pip's baby toes.

'Oooh, that feels nice,' said Pip, and explained about David Cole. 'We'll have to wait for the coroner's report. My theory is that he was squashed into the mud by a steamroller and he suffocated.'

'A steamroller? What, by accident?' Flis asked, working her way up through the toes to the biggie. 'Or he was driving it and he fell over the front and somehow ran over himself?' Which would have been a suggestion of unusual lunacy, except that Pip had heard an actual policeman posit something not dissimilar as a legitimate possibility. Flis was massaging those big toes beautifully, and she had put on her 'therapeutic music' too, pan pipes and whales and rain and what might have been robins, if Pip wasn't mistaken. A peculiar combo, but as long as you didn't overthink it, it was very relaxing. If it weren't for the small matter of Dead David, Pip would surely have fallen into a deep and delicious sleep.

'You are so good at this,' she said dreamily.

'It's all those TV crime dramas I watch.'

It took a moment to unravel this. 'The feet, I mean. Wow, it's just wonderful.'

Pip lay her head back and wished she could just drop off. But she couldn't. She needed to get her thoughts straight. 'So, I'll tell you what I think. I suppose someone *might* have run over him accidentally and then got scared, so they gapped it. Or – and I have to say, I think this is more likely – someone ran over him on purpose.'

'No wonder you're so tense. Investigating the scam and now this death.'

'I'm not investigating the death. Just, well, you could say I'm planning to look into it. A bit. Because here's another thing. There's a possibility that David Cole's death might somehow be related to the exam scam I'm investigating.'

'Really?' Flis was rotating the ankles now, smoothing out little clicks. Bliss. Pip breathed in the lavender scent of the candle Flis had lit 'for body–mind connection', and let her breath out with a deep, relaxed sigh. 'It all sounds very notorious.'

'Notorious? Why, who knows about it?'

Flis stopped massaging Pip's feet. 'When did I say anyone knew about it? I said it was notorious. You know, very evil.'

'Nefarious,' said Pip, with a sigh. 'But yes, it could be. Just hours before his death I overheard him arguing about it with another dad at the school, Charles Eastleigh. I suspect Charles's daughter, Grace Faith, is connected with the scam, maybe even the ringleader. David's daughter, Chanel, is also involved somehow. The men seemed to be arguing about their two daughters and who led whom astray. I couldn't hear all of it, but it got quite heated. David was adamant that Grace Faith was the one who got Chanel involved.'

'So Charles ran him over with a steamroller?'

'I'd say he's the most likely suspect at this point. Think about it. If Charles believed that David was going to out Grace Faith as the ringleader of the exam scam, and get her expelled and ruin her life, maybe that would be enough for him to snap and kill David. And he was chairman of the board, so there was his own position and ego to think of too.'

'Really, kids today are so clever. To think two schoolgirls managed to set up a complicated cheating scam with passwords and so on, and I can't even programme the microwave,' said Flis, resuming her massaging. It was true. Flis was the only person Pip knew who could burn things in the microwave. There was that time with the jacket potatoes. That took hours to clean up.

'There's a young IT teacher who seems to hang out with the girls rather a lot; I'm thinking he might be helping them with the technical side of the scam.'

'Oh gosh, but that doesn't sound good.' Dammit, she'd stopped massaging to talk again.

'There's also a Maths teacher, a woman who used to be a card sharp – she's another possible suspect. I need to find out more about her.'

'You've got to be careful with these teachers. I was reading something on one of the blogs – Red Flags for Dodgy Teachers or something. You know, how to spot the signs that some predator is taking advantage of young people. It starts off with the pedagogue being nice, making them feel special…'

'Paedophile,' said Pip, automatically correcting her sister's endless malapropisms.

'No, pedagogue. It means teacher. Anyway, it's very common for the teacher to find an area of interest, help the child with that.'

Flis was alarmist by nature, no doubt about that. But there was a chance that in this case, she might be right. Did this exam paper lark go deeper than anyone expected? Did it somehow involve an inappropriate relationship between a teacher and a girl? And did this somehow lead to murder?

CHAPTER 22

Chanel had the glassy-eyed look of someone whose world had been horribly and unexpectedly shifted overnight. Pip had been surprised to see her at school at all, just two days after her stepfather's death, but there she was leaving the locker room, her bag over her shoulder.

'I'm so sorry,' said Pip, proffering the utterly inadequate words people were always left with in these circumstances. 'I'm so very sorry for your loss. It's all just too awful.'

'Thanks, Ms Bloom. Yeah, awful.'

'Could you come into my office for a minute, I'd really like to talk to you,' Pip said.

The girl looked reluctant. 'It's nearly time for Geography…'

'Just for a minute, please.'

'OK,' she said, and followed Pip into the room. Pip shut the door. Poor Chanel sat slumped in the seat.

'How are you doing? Are you sure you should be at school? You've had a terrible shock.'

'I'd rather be here. It's worse at home. My mum and my little sister crying. And there are journalists calling.'

Pip had summoned the girl to express her sympathies for her loss, but the truth was that there were some questions she'd like answers to, and Chanel might have them. It was a very difficult situation. Firstly, Ms Peters had told her explicitly not to speak to the girls, or make any accusations or suggestions of involvement in the exam scheme. Secondly, this girl had just lost a parent. Pip wasn't actually sure what she was going to say to Chanel, but she knew she would have to be extremely gentle and not put a foot wrong.

'I'm sorry you didn't get to have lunch with your dad after the bingo; it all seems so sad. He went to that site meeting and...' Pip let her sentence drift off in the hope that Chanel would pick it up.

'Stepdad; my real dad died when I was five. Yes, he went to the site meeting. That's when the accident happened.'

'The accident, yes.' Interesting that it was being described as an accident. 'It must be very hard for you.'

'It's awful, to be honest. That he's dead and Mum's so sad.' She started to sniff, rubbing her nose on her sleeve. 'And, miss, I feel so bad. We'd been fighting so much the last few months. It was just that Dave was always on my case about my schoolwork and my marks.'

'Ah yes, the horse.' Pip smiled, remembering the 'buy you a pony' promise that had tempted Chanel to cheat on the silly sports test.

'Yes, the horse. Dave was a big achiever, you know. His family was, like, really poor, and he worked hard and put himself through university and worked in a shop on weekends. Sold stuff door to door. That kind of thing. He made his money from nothing. He just wanted me to do well so I would make something of myself. That's why I... you know... the sports test...'

She was weeping properly now. Pip fetched her a glass of water and some tissues. She fished a Twix out of her drawer, and gave them half each. 'Have some sugar, it helps.'

The girl gulped it down in two bites. 'Sorry, it's just... I haven't really had a chance to talk to anyone. It's such a relief to be able to talk about it. I feel so terrible because we had an awful fight the day before. He was always interfering in my life, trying to make all sorts of silly rules.'

'Phones and friends and curfews.'

Chanel had settled down a bit, and smiled weakly. 'Yes, exactly that.'

'Typical dad stuff, I guess. Protective.'

'Except this time, he went too far – he read my private messages.'

Pip felt a prickle of anticipation. She suspected she was going to hear more about the screen grabs David had mentioned to Charles. The screen grabs that might have led to his murder. Pip knew she had to keep her cool, be the listening ear, the supportive friend, not the inquisitor.

'He looked at your phone? That must have been so maddening. An invasion of privacy.'

'Exactly! He was completely out of line. I put my phone down to go and answer the door, and he picked it up before it locked. He looked at my messages. I freaked out! And, to make it worse, he totally got the wrong end of the stick.'

This was interesting. What did Chanel mean? What had he misinterpreted about the exam paper situation? Pip put her most successful investigator's trick into practice. Instead of asking questions, she nodded calmly, a gently expectant look on her face, waiting for the girl to continue.

Which she did, after a small symphony of sniffs and sighs.

'He found messages from Alan – Mr Geoffrey. They were completely innocent,' she said, with some anger now. This was not at all where Pip expected the conversation to go.

'We were planning to meet up about a thing we're working on. But when David saw the messages he went completely nuts, and threatened to go to the school, to get him fired. "Inappropriate," he called it. I told him that Alan and me, we're just friends. There's nothing going on, he's not like some dodgy pervy teacher. But he wouldn't listen, and that's when I told him he should get out of my life, that he wasn't my real dad. He was ruining my life. And he was going to ruin Alan's too if he complained to the school.'

Pip nodded sympathetically. 'Oh dear, that sounds like a horrible row…'

Chanel continued, 'And then he started on Grace Faith. He'd read our private messages too. She was a bad influence, he said. She would land me in no end of trouble at school. That's when I told him I wished he'd go away forever.' And she dissolved in a fit of sobbing that even a Twix couldn't fix.

Once again Pip tried to soothe the girl with pats and there-theres. Chanel calmed down, and when she went to the bathroom to splash water on her face and clean herself up, Pip tried to work through what she'd heard. David had got into Chanel's phone and seen her messages to Grace Faith and Alan Geoffrey. He was understandably concerned about a male teacher texting his stepdaughter. And as for the exam situation, Pip already knew from the fight she had overheard that he'd worked out exactly what was going on. Chanel and Grace Faith were involved in the exam scam – with Grace Faith as the ringleader.

Chanel came back looking somewhat better, although her eyes were still puffy and her nose red. 'Feeling better?' asked Pip kindly.

She nodded.

'It helps to get things off your chest, doesn't it? And you know, Chanel, that fight you had with David, it was just one incident in a long relationship. It would have blown over. If he hadn't died, it would have been forgotten by next week. Try to let it go.'

'Thank you, miss.'

'Call me Pip – at least when we're not in class.'

Chanel smiled. 'Thank you… Pip.'

'Oh – Chanel?'

'Yes, Pip?'

'That conversation with Grace Faith, the one David saw. Was it about the exam papers?'

Chanel reddened.

'It's OK, I won't let on that we spoke. Grace Faith sent you the web link, didn't she?'

There was a pause, and Chanel nodded. 'Yes. She gave me the link – the one that I… I used it… the sports test… you know – and he worked out what it was and he completely freaked out about that. But please don't tell her I told you, Pip. She'll be so angry if she finds out. And when Grace Faith gets it in for you…'

'I understand. And I'd like to ask you the same – let's keep this conversation between us.'

'OK. I'd better get going though,' said Chanel, looking at her watch. 'Geography has started already. Thank you for the talk, Pip. I do feel better.'

'You look after yourself, Chanel,' Pip said. 'Oh, and one last thing. Do you happen to know who David was meeting at the site?'

'No, sorry. With David it was always a hundred meetings and plans. You never really knew who with.'

Pip put that one onto her to-do list – find out who the meeting was with. Another unknown. On a more positive note, she was fairly certain that she was well on the way to solving the mystery of the exam scam. She needed to update Ms Peters, and get her permission to take the next step – break her cover and interview her suspects. She popped by her office.

'Could I have a moment with the boss?' she asked Mrs Jenkins. 'I haven't got an appointment but I just need a minute. She'll know what it's about.'

Mrs Jenkins looked at the calendar on her screen and at the door. 'It's a busy day, but I'll see if she will see you.'

She picked up the phone on her desk and pushed a couple of buttons.

'The substitute sports teacher wants to see you, Ms Peters, says you'll know what it's about.' Mrs Jenkins smiled and nodded. 'She'll be out for you now, dear,' she said to Pip.

Ms Peters opened the door and invited her in, shutting the door behind her. She looked strained, her eyes dull as if from lack of sleep.

'I've made some progress and have an update for you on the exam paper leak,' Pip began.

'The exam paper leak. Of course. The David Cole matter has taken all my attention, but I do want to know what you've found.' Frankly, she didn't sound that interested, but Pip was used to that in an employer.

Pip explained her discovery – that the scam was run online, via a website – and a possible theory: that Grace Faith was the 'frontman' and Mr Geoffrey might be the tech muscle. She left Chanel out of it for now.

'Honestly, I find that hard to believe.'

Clearly, David Cole hadn't mentioned his suspicions to Ms Peters.

'I would like your permission to interview both of them, separately.'

Ms Peters ran her hand over her braids and thought about Pip's request. Pip felt sorry for the poor woman. What a lot of troubles and problems she had on her plate.

'You can only speak to Mr Geoffrey as long as I'm with you. It's an HR nightmare. Set up something with Mrs Jenkins. It will have to wait a few days though, I'm swamped with the David Cole incident.'

'I'd like to do it sooner rather than later. How about tomorrow?'

'No, really. I know this is important but it's not my priority right now. Thursday or Friday. But you can't speak to Grace Faith. You are here to find information on the quiet. Sitting a student down for a formal interview is quite a different matter.'

'But if I—'

'Have you had much interaction with Grace Faith?' she asked, unusually brusque. 'Because I have. That young woman is… Let's just say, she was inappropriately named. Between you and me, she is sly, entitled and a bully. Cut from the same cloth as her father.' She swallowed that last remark, as if realising she'd said too much.

'Could I just—'

'No, Pip, I've made my decision. I can't risk any more trouble.'

The woman looked at the end of her rope, poor thing. Pip said, 'So, about David Cole – I've been thinking.'

'Pip, you need to leave this to the police. They know what they're doing.'

'Yes, but—'

Ms Peters's mobile phone rang. She looked at it and sighed, her hand to her throat. 'The police. Sorry, I have to go. And, Pip – I don't want you involved in this murder investigation. Please. Let the authorities do their job.'

CHAPTER 23

Pip knew enough about schools and enough about offices to know that the staffroom would be abuzz with the weekend's drama. She wasn't going to interfere in the murder investigation – Ms Peters had been very clear, and besides, Pip had her work cut out for her on the exam scam – but she was keen to hear what the staff had to say about David Cole's death. She'd go over there and see if she could pick up some local intel, aka office gossip, and while she was there, she'd keep an eye out for Candice and hopefully corner her for a little chat about her gambling days.

The staffroom was almost empty, as morning classes were in session. Three women huddled around a small table, heads together and voices low, a coffee cup before each of them. Classic gossip pose. Pip smiled a hello and moved over to the tea area, ears straining as she quietly poured a cuppa. There she lurked as unobtrusively as she was able, given her height. She imagined herself as a tree. A big, tall quiet tree, a fir perhaps, unnoticed, almost invisible in the forest. They would forget she was even there.

'Excuse me, miss, um…' called a pretty young woman with a stylish razor cut, who Pip hadn't yet met but knew to be a Biology teacher.

'Bloom. You can call me Pip,' spoke the tree.

'Amy King. I heard you were there when the body was found?'

So much for their discretion. The other two struggled between looking embarrassed by her boldness and eager for the gossip that might result from it.

'Yes, I was there on Saturday.'

Their eyes gleamed, and they made a space for her at the table. Pip had hoped that they would share information with her, not the other way round. But perhaps if she gave them a little something to get the ball rolling, she'd get something back.

'I actually found the body.'

There was a sharp intake of breath and the women huddled closer with an almost unseemly glee.

'How awful for you. And so tragic, poor Mr Cole,' said Amy, in a rather perfunctory display of concern, before continuing her interrogation. 'What was it like? How did he look? I heard that he was run over?'

'Yes, that's what seems to have happened. Run over by earth-moving equipment.'

A chill – or thrill – went through the audience.

'Murder then, was it?' The eldest of the three, the English teacher called Janice who Pip had met before, cut to the chase. 'No one seems to know. Or they won't tell.'

Pip could see no other explanation, but she said: 'I don't know for sure how it happened. No one does, yet. There will be an autopsy and the police will have to look into it. I didn't know poor Mr Cole, although I've taught Chanel, but it's hard to imagine anyone wanting to kill a dad at the school.'

Pip looked at them expectantly, hoping that someone would come up with something.

'I've wanted to kill a few,' said Amy, laughing. 'Mums too. I've got a list.'

Janice sniggered and then turned to Pip, saying knowingly, 'You'd be surprised. There's all sorts at this school. I've no doubt there are some dodgy dealings – extramarital affairs, financial shenanigans, business deals gone sour. Oh, there's all kinds of nonsense going on.'

'And some of those parents, heaven help us,' Amy said, rolling her eyes. 'Talk about competitive. I know a few who would steamroll you if they thought it would help their daughter get the lead role in the play.'

She and Janice had a good laugh at that one. It was pretty funny, although hopefully apocryphal.

The third member of the trio, a tiny bird of a woman who had hitherto been silent, put down her cup and spoke up at last. 'He was a property developer, Mr Cole. That's a dirty business. His company has been buying up land all over. You never know, he might have ripped someone off or perhaps sold someone a badly made house and made an enemy. Also, there's a lot of resistance to that development.'

Did people kill over property deals? Perhaps, but Pip thought it unlikely, at least in Kent.

Janice didn't agree, clearly. She nodded and leaned forward, eager to add her two pennies' worth. 'Good point, Ling. Any one of those could be a motive.'

Ling continued, 'The locals feel that greedy people from outside are tearing up the countryside to make money, and that bringing in all those new people, and that traffic, will destroy the area. Someone might have wanted to stop them.'

Amy hesitated for a moment, before deciding to throw her ace onto the table in the poker game that was work gossip: 'My brother-in-law writes about property for the papers and he told me that Cole's company was trying to buy the Marsh Field. If they had the field, they could put up more units and make more money.'

'So they want to buy the field from the school?' Pip asked. 'The field that the fete was held on?'

'Yes, the same one. Apart from having more land to build on, it would give them easy entry from the main road and they wouldn't have to build an access road to their other property, the one where he died. It would save them hundreds of thousands, apparently. I'm sure they made the school a very good offer.'

Pip felt the strange tip-of-your-tongue feeling that she got when some important piece of information was trying to worm its way out of her subconscious and into her thinking mind. Before she could grab it, the bell rang, and almost immediately the room started to fill with teachers returning wearily from battle.

They queued for tea and coffee, and swooped like gulls on the plate of chocolate digestives (Pip wasn't judging, she'd already had three). As the rush died down, and the teachers settled into the sofas and around the tables, Pip spotted Candy Counter come in and take a seat at the far side of the room. The small and rather mousy blonde in a modest button-through dress printed in a faded floral didn't look like a professional card sharp who had been banned from the casinos of London. But then again, Pip herself had briefly been on a No Fly list, due to a strange set of circumstances she preferred not to think about, and you couldn't tell that from looking at her. Or at least, she didn't think you could.

Pip manoeuvred her way over to Candice, not sure what she would say when she got there.

'Hi – Candice, isn't it?' she asked casually.

'Yes, hello,' she answered, and turned away, discouraging further conversation.

'I'm the substitute sports teacher. Pip. We met briefly at the Fun Day,' said Pip. 'Jimmy was with me. I think you two know each other?'

'A bit. A long time ago.'

'Yes, he mentioned it was a while since he's seen you. So how long have you been at Hurlingham House?' Pip tried for a casual and friendly manner, but somehow her question came off as interrogative, and Candice responded accordingly.

'A year and a half,' she said, stonily.

'Enjoying it? The Maths teaching?'

'Look, I don't know what Jimmy told you…'

'Nothing. Just that he knew you from the casino scene.'

Candice took her arm, pulled her close and said quietly, 'No one here knows about that, and I want to keep it that way. I left that world behind. My gambling days are in the past.'

The poor woman looked desperate, and said, 'I'm a good teacher. A very good teacher. This school is my life now. Don't ruin this for me, please.'

At that moment, Ms Peters came in and called for their attention, and Candice dropped Pip's arm. The poor woman looked even more exhausted than she had an hour ago, her pretty and usually cheerful face drawn.

'Good morning, all. I have an announcement to make.' The room quietened instantly. 'I'm sorry for the imposition on your teatime; I would have called an official staff meeting, but I'm afraid this is urgent. As you know, one of the parents at the school died on Saturday. It is my unpleasant duty to inform you that the police are treating Mr Cole's death as murder.'

Teacups clattered in hands, and small gasps and exclamations escaped from the assembled throats. Pip, herself, was not surprised. There hardly seemed any other explanation. The only question was who and why? And Pip thought she knew the answer. She would have to tell Ms Peters.

Ms Peters continued, 'This is, of course, a great sadness for our school community. While this incident did not happen on school grounds, it was on the adjacent field, and Mr Cole had been at our Fun Day immediately prior to the incident. The press is aware of the situation and the connection to the school, and we anticipate a lot of media attention over the next few days. I ask you all to please be very discreet. Please do not speak to the media, but direct any enquiries to my office, via Mrs Jenkins. I must reiterate the seriousness of this instruction – no comments, no gossip, no conjecture.'

There was some nodding, and Ms Peters went on, 'Our priority right now is the emotional support of our students. We are making specialised resources available, and you will get the details via email shortly. I thank you for your support.'

As the teachers turned to each other to discuss this bombshell, Pip approached Ms Peters. 'I need to talk to you.'

The headmistress hesitated.

'It's important. I've got something to tell you.'

Ms Peters gestured towards a door that led into a pretty walled garden with roses and a bench. 'There are a lot of ears in a staffroom,' the head said with a smile. 'Probably best to talk out here. I'm sorry but I've only got five minutes. The police are on their way.'

'It's about the murder. There's something you need to know.'

'I thought we agreed that you wouldn't interfere…'

'I wasn't. Ms Peters, I overheard David Cole and Grace Faith's father, Charles, arguing on Saturday morning. David Cole had found out about the exam scam and was furious that Grace Faith had involved Chanel by sending her the link to the website. He threatened Charles. Said he was going to expose the scam. Charles would know that that would likely end in Grace Faith's expulsion.'

A small storm of emotions passed over the headmistress's face – confusion, shock, disbelief.

Pip spelled it out for her. 'And two hours later, Mr Cole turns up dead. I think Charles Eastleigh might have killed David to protect his daughter.'

CHAPTER 24

'Charles Eastleigh? The chairman of the board? Oh, no. No no no no.' Ms Peters gave a brittle laugh that seemed to border on hysterical. 'That is just absurd! Unimaginable!'

Pip was silent for a long minute, then said, 'OK, you might be right. Tell me, you said that Grace Faith was cut from the same cloth as her father. What cloth would that be? What is he like?'

Ms Peters sighed and gave the appearance of someone deflating. 'Arrogant, entitled, bullying, highly status-conscious.'

'Then why would he not be a suspect?'

'Because it's insane, that's why. There's a big difference between being an arrogant ass and being a murderer.'

'You said yourself that parents can be irrational where their children are concerned. You are so fearful of them that you won't even let me interview the girls.'

'I'm fearful of litigation, and bad press, and hysteria. Not murder.'

'But don't you see? It's part of the same thing. People will stop at nothing to protect their children.'

'People do not murder each other over the antics of schoolgirls.'

'Think about it. He wasn't only protecting his daughter's future. He was protecting his own reputation. Imagine, the chairman of the board's daughter involved in a cheating scandal. It would be in the press. His business associates would hear about it. Everyone at the school.'

Pip had another idea. 'He might have been protecting the school, too, in some weird way. Imagine the scandal. Hurlingham

House, famous for its excellent marks and academic success, all built on a scam.'

'Don't think I haven't considered the very dire consequences this exam business could have for the school.' The blood drained from Ms Peters's face at the thought. 'But a steamroller, Pip?' she asked weakly.

'I know. I know. It's crazy. But right now it's the only thing that makes sense.'

Mrs Jenkins's head appeared round the door from the staffroom. 'Sorry to interrupt,' she said in a stage whisper. 'But the police are here. I've given them tea and they're waiting for you outside your office.'

'Thank you. Pip, walk with me.'

They followed in Mrs Jenkins's footsteps across the campus to the admin block. 'Let's keep this between us for now, Pip. I just need a moment to think it over before I tell the police. The fallout… I don't suppose it will make a difference to poor David Cole if I tell them later this afternoon.'

'Of course, I understand.'

'Thank you.'

They arrived at the office to find Truman and Goodall sitting in the chairs Pip and Tim had occupied a mere week ago, when their only concern was to clear Claire's name. Things had certainly escalated fast. Ms Peters took the two men into her office, leaving Pip with Mrs Jenkins. 'A sorry state of affairs,' said Mrs Jenkins. 'I've been at this school for over thirty years. Never seen anything like it.'

She reached into the drawer by her desk and pulled out a tin of biscuits. 'Bicky, dear?' Pip feared she was rapidly adopting an all-biscuit diet, but she took one anyway.

'Thank you. Yes, horrible situation. It's a lovely school. I've enjoyed being a substitute here.'

'Where did you teach before?'

Pip's brain went into the stress-induced gridlock she always got when forced to make something up on the spot. Fortunately, Ruby and Amelia came in at just that moment; Ruby with a laptop, Amelia with a sheaf of papers.

'Morning, ma'am, morning, Mrs Jenkins,' they said in unison.

'Mrs Jenkins,' said Amelia. 'Can you help us with the layout for the school paper? We've got so many good pictures from the Fun Day, we can't get them all in.'

'Of course, girls. You get set up. I need to go and fetch more printer ink from the storeroom. Give me a minute,' she said, picking up a large bunch of keys.

'Mrs Jenkins is a whizz at the layout programme,' Ruby told Pip. 'Oh, and Ms Bloom, there are some pictures of you and the llama.' She sat down next to Pip and opened the laptop.

'Here's my favourite. I'm quite proud of it actually.'

It was a great shot: the beast's silly face foregrounded, teeth bared in a manic grin, half filling the frame; Pip in the background, running full pelt after him, arms outstretched. Pip couldn't help but laugh.

'Let's see some of the others,' she said. The girl clicked through them at pace. There were a few more of Sally's path of destruction – Pip flipped quickly past those – and lots of lovely crowd shots. People eating ice creams and tossing pennies. Toddlers on the bouncy castle. The Scottish dancers.

'These are wonderful, Ruby. You're really talented. You've got the eye.'

The girl blushed. 'I love photography. Amelia is a writer, so it's nice – we work together.'

Pip took over the clicking, enjoying the cheerful pictures washing over her. There was Charles Eastleigh, handing over a prize to a beaming adolescent with a mouth full of braces. Then another picture; Charles with another kid. A whole series of them. 'What's happening in this lot?' she asked, with studied casualness.

Amelia leaned in, pushing her glasses up her nose for a better look. 'Oh, those aren't very interesting. Just the prizes for all the competitions that happened in the morning. The dress-up competition. Handstands – this girl is amazing, stayed up for seven minutes and twenty-three seconds, can you believe it? Anyway, there are loads of different competitions for the younger girls and the chairman gives out the prizes. Went on forever.'

While Amelia rattled on, flipping through the many pictures of Charles smiling and shaking hands with little girls, Pip's brain was whirring. The timeline. She needed to work out the timeline, prove to Ms Peters that it was at least possible that Charles had killed David. What time had she seen Charles and David's altercation? David was found dead at two o'clock.

'What time was this taken, do you know?' she asked of one of the last in the Charles-shaking-hands series.

Ruby clicked a few times, and brought up the metadata. 'Twelve twenty-five.'

'Interesting. Just wondering about the light, you know, the sun. Always looking for tips in the photographic department. I'm useless. Twelve twenty-five, you say. Anyway, good work, girls, your pictures look great. I look forward to seeing the paper.'

Pip headed for the door, almost running into Mrs Jenkins returning with her armful of toner. 'Bye, all,' she said.

'Bye. I'll print you the llama one,' Ruby called after her, sweetly. 'For a keepsake.'

CHAPTER 25

Pip took out her lurid notebook with its disconcerting blue holo-gram eye and its helpful – hopefully prophetic – message, 'See the Light', scrawled on the cover. She took a pencil and drew a line from top to bottom. On the left, she would put the times; on the right, the activities.

First, the altercation. Pip had been reprinting the bingo cards. If the bingo had started – the false start – at 11.00, it must have been at about 11.30 that she overheard David and Charles arguing. She wrote that down.

One possibility was that Charles had either walked with David or followed him from the admin block, where the altercation took place, to the site where he was killed. She knew from the photograph that Charles was back at the Fun Day in time to hand out that prize at 12.25, when Ruby took the picture. Could he have walked to the field, killed David, and walked back in that interval of about forty minutes?

The other possibility was that Charles had killed David after the prize-giving. He had had lots more prizes to hand out – Ruby said it took 'forever' – so he couldn't have left before about 12.40 at the very earliest. But the Scottish dancing had started at 12.30, so the llama drama must have started at about 12.45. If Charles murdered David after handing out the prizes, he would have had to sprint down to the field, find the steamroller, run over David and sprint back, as there was no sign of him when Pip and Jimmy arrived on the scene, unless he was hiding in the bushes. But that wasn't possible, because he'd come sauntering down with Ms Peters when she arrived at the scene. No, if Charles murdered David, it was in the forty minutes before he started handing out the prizes. Now all Pip had to do was work out if that was possible.

She would walk the route from the admin block to the building site and estimate how long it would have taken Charles to do it on Saturday. She was glad to be wearing her all-purpose, not-too-expensive sports shoes – she knew first-hand how muddy the site was.

With the notebook in one hand and her iPhone in the other, Pip set out to determine whether Charles had time to kill David.

She set the time when she left the admin block, and wound her way through the school at a middling pace. It took Pip thirteen minutes to get to the site. Of course, on the Fun Day, Charles would have had to make his way through the throng, skirting past stalls, dodging crowds, getting away from people keen to greet him. She reckoned she could easily add another five minutes for that. He was likely a bit slower than Pip, being older and rather large and not particularly fit-looking. Let's say the whole journey, from the admin block to the Marsh Field to the building site, took twenty minutes.

Pip leaned against the fence, surveying the site. Construction had stopped. The steamroller was still there where she'd last seen it; the body, of course, was not. There was crime scene tape around a large area to protect any evidence – uselessly, thought Pip, seeing as she and Jimmy, a llama and two gormless policemen had already tramped all over it days ago.

What had happened when Charles got there? Was there an altercation? There must have been some sort of argument at the very least, she thought. You wouldn't just run a chap over without so much as a conversation. So, the two men had their argument.

And then? Did he chase him around with the steamroller? There was no evidence of that from the marks on the field. Besides, David wouldn't have just let himself get run over. It didn't make sense.

Pip's timeline processing was interrupted by another problem. How did Charles get that steamroller moving? He wouldn't have had a key. There was a small wooden office at the top end of the construction site, with one lone workman sitting outside it on a chair, his back to the sun, reading a newspaper. Pip skirted the muddy bog as best she could, and approached him.

'Hi there. Excuse me,' she said, startling the man out of his morning read.

'Private property, lady, and a crime scene. You can't be here.'

'Yes, I know. I'm here on a… you could say a pilgrimage, a journey of, um, self-healing.'

He raised an impressively hairy eyebrow and looked at her as if she was quite mad.

'You're on a what?'

'I found him…' she said, her voice low. 'I was the one who found the body.'

'You found the dead guy? Squashed flat in the mud?' he said, rather indelicately, Pip thought.

'Yes, it was awful. I'm traumatised. Can't sleep. I finally came in search of closure, to see if perhaps being here would help me make sense of it all.'

'Christ, lady, I'm sorry. That must have been horrible. You take all the time you need. Just don't muck up the crime scene. Anything I can help with, you let me know.'

'There is one thing I've been wondering,' said Pip. 'The steamroller. How would the, um, perpetrator, have got it moving? Surely there's a key?'

'Yeah, bit of a mystery, now you mention it. There's no key. It's a keyless system, this is. For safety and security. Anyone who's licensed to drive the thing would have the code to start it. You can't turn it on without it.'

'Ah. Well, that is a mystery. Do you know the code?' she asked.

'I'm the assistant foreman, 'course I know the code,' he said, self-importantly. 'Me and about four other people, but none of them was here. They don't work Saturdays.'

'What is it? Just as a matter of interest. For closure, you know. What's the code?'

He blushed, cleared his throat and stammered, 'Well, I can't be telling you...'

'It's 1-2-3-4, isn't it?' she said, in a sudden flash of brilliance.

He reddened even more deeply. She'd got it in one!

'How did you...?'

'Oh, don't worry,' she said, dismissing his embarrassment with a flick of her hand. 'All my passwords are 1-2-3-4. Except some, which are 1-2-3-4-5.'

Pip went back to her musings. So, assuming Charles climbed up on the steamroller on a whim, and just put in the obvious silly code. Then what?

This was yet another mystery. David had been run over from behind, as evidenced by the fact that he was face down in the mud. Had Charles knocked him out, perhaps? Or surprised him? It seemed unlikely that you could surprise someone with a steamroller.

'Is it noisy, the steamroller?'

'Not as loud as you'd expect. The new ones are quite quiet,' said the foreman, pleased to have moved on from the subject of the code.

'But still, you'd think he would have heard it.'

'I would say so.'

'But hang on, there was all that noise from the Fun Day. The bands, the announcements. The bagpipers for the Scottish dancing. Those bagpipes were ear-splitting. If the wind was blowing the right way, down from the school towards the site, maybe it drowned out the noise.'

'That's true. It was a right racket.'

'And he was on the phone,' said Pip. 'When I found him, he had a phone in his hand. He might have been talking or listening to someone.'

'You know, I was here that day,' said the foreman suddenly. 'David Cole called and said he was going to come down and fetch some plans from the office. Was going to meet me here. I was late – problem with the trains – and I missed him. By the time I got back, the whole place was cordoned off.'

'So it was you he was meeting at the site office?' she asked.

'Yes. He phoned me when he got here and saw I wasn't there. When I arrived, there was a missed call from him and a voice message, telling me he'd been and missed me. Giving me a few instructions.'

'It must have been you he was phoning!' said Pip. 'That's why he didn't hear the steamroller.'

The foreman went pale. 'He was talking to me when he was… When he was run over…'

'It sounds like it. Do you remember hearing anything strange when you listened to the message?'

'I remember that it was a bad line and there was the noise of the Fun Day. Actually, I couldn't hear the end of the message, he seemed to be cut off…'

The gory realisation hit him.

Pip was ahead of him. She was excited, despite herself. 'He was talking to you. Distracted. And someone got into the steamroller right behind him, drove slowly forward, and killed him.'

'Not to be rude, but who did you say you are?' he said, growing suspicious of her endless steamroller questions and her suppositions.

'My name's Pip. Like I said, I found him, just coincidentally. I didn't know him at all. Just trying to sort it out in my head.' She tapped her forehead, for illustration, and went on. 'I was just wondering, as a construction professional, can you think of any way this steamroller rolled over him by mistake? Is there any possibility it could be an accident?'

He looked at her in astonishment. 'Well, I could be Prince Charles, I suppose. In fact, it's more likely.' More kindly, he added, 'Look, Pip. Sorry for your troubles. Horrible business. Horrible. But if you want my opinion, it wasn't an accident. Someone drove over that poor fella.'

In a truly remarkable act of persuasion, Pip got the assistant foreman – his name was Brian, it turned out – to let her see the roller up close. Pip had once talked her way into one of the confession booths at the Vatican on a dare – the priest's side of the screen, mind you – but this had to be a close second in the rankings of improbable access.

'Very quick,' said Brian, leading her to a line of planks that had been laid out over the mud, presumably where the police and the forensics chaps had gone back and forth. 'For your closure. One peek, then we're out of here.'

Up close, it was surprisingly neat and compact, not like the ones you saw constructing highways and such. It was not much bigger than a Range Rover. Pip had driven bigger vehicles than this herself – that time she'd worked on the farm, and then there was the bin lorry. She shuddered. She preferred not to think about the bin lorry. She could still hear the sound of the priceless piano splintering.

She climbed inside and sat on the bucket seat. She saw the keypad where the code was entered, the numbers 1, 2, 3 and 4 dirtied from many fingers over many years. That answered that question. The dials and switches looked simple enough. You wouldn't need special skills to operate it.

She imagined herself as Charles, bearing down on the man who was putting his daughter's future in jeopardy. It seemed unreal, impossible, coming up behind a man and squashing him in cold blood, but of course people did awful, violent things all the time. Time to get off the site. She had established that Charles could have accessed and operated the steamroller, but did he have the time? She needed to get back to her timeline.

She stepped out of the roller onto the little step. As she reached her foot down to the ground, she saw a flash of white under the seat. A folded piece of paper. Looking over her shoulder to Brian, she saw that he was surveying his watch anxiously. She took that moment to slip her hand into the darkness, pulled out the piece of paper, and stuffed it into the pocket of her denim jacket.

As she did so, her phone rang.

'Pip,' said Ms Peters. 'Where are you? We need you at the staffroom now.'

CHAPTER 26

It had just been a staff meeting. Which, of course, Pip had forgotten all about, if she'd ever known in the first place. Honestly, she wasn't even a real teacher. She'd be out of here any day now. She certainly didn't need to attend a meeting on how to complete the registration form for exam sessions, although as Ms Peters had said, she had to act like a normal member of staff or people would get suspicious.

Finally alone, and sitting on a well-placed log under a tree in the Marsh Field – now cleared of the detritus of the Fun Day and looking green and peaceful – Pip took out her notebook, and considered the timeline.

The altercation, the walk across the campus to the building site, the second altercation, enough time to get to the steamroller, work out the code, run the man over, and walk back, and then present prizes, looking clean, presentable and not at all flustered… There was no way Charles Eastleigh could have killed David Cole.

It was pretty devastating. Pip had thought she had it all worked out. Thought she had solved the mystery of the exam leak and the death of David Cole in one go, but now she was back to square one. Admittedly, the world did seem a slightly better place now she knew that a school dad hadn't run over another school dad with a steamroller. Still, the fact remained that *someone* had run over David Cole with a steamroller – but who?

She turned her attention to what she knew about the dead man. It seemed he had put people's backs up. He was just that kind of guy. Chanel was furious with him for going into her phone – not that Pip had her pegged as a killer. He'd pissed off Charles – but not enough to kill him, it seemed. As a property developer, he had detractors and even, perhaps, enemies.

A thought occurred to Pip, bringing with it that little tingle of recognition that she might be onto something. What about Alan Geoffrey? Granted, he looked rather weedy for a murderer, but he did have a motive. David had seen the phone messages and suspected there was something between him and Chanel. He had threatened to report him to the school. Alan knew he would be fired if there was any hint that he was having any kind of relationship with a student. He might even be in trouble with the law, depending on how old Chanel was and when this whole thing started. Yes, he certainly had a motive, and who needs muscle when you have a steamroller?

Pip needed to speak to Mr Geoffrey. Ms Peters had, after all, agreed to it. Granted, she had agreed to it back when Pip thought he was guilty of masterminding the exam scam – a relatively minor transgression compared with murder – and she'd agreed on the understanding that she would be present for the conversation. Pip sighed. There was no getting around it. Ms Peters had specifically said it would have to wait. She certainly wouldn't agree to Pip confronting a would-be murderer.

What if there was a way Pip could find out about Alan Geoffrey's movements that day without contravening Ms Peters's explicit instructions? She racked her brains. She wished she'd kept a lookout for him in Ruby's photographs. If she had the skills, she could hack his Google calendar. Or track him via his smart watch. Or... She drew a blank.

It was very pleasant under the tree on the log in the Marsh Field, with the dappled sunlight coming through the branches above and the sound of frogs and birds, even a bumble bee. Pip wished she could lie down on a blanket for a nap, but she had to get a move on. She was teaching PE in half an hour and she needed to get things set up. She stood, brushed leaves and lichen from the bum of her tracksuit, and walked over to the school, still thinking about Alan Geoffrey.

'Speak of the devil and he shall appear' was a saying Pip's grandmother was fond of. She also said the devil made work for idle hands, but presumably not at the same time. Anyhow, who should be lurking around the sports block when Pip arrived, but Alan Geoffrey himself!

'Hi, Alan,' she said casually. 'Waiting for someone?'

His deathly white skin blushed a blotchy red, but he said with studied cool, 'No. Not at all. Just getting some air.'

Chanel came round the corner, and greeted him with a sweet smile. 'There you are, I was just…' Then she noticed Pip. 'Oh, miss, Pip, gosh, I didn't see you. Hi. Gosh.'

That girl had zero poker face.

'So, Alan. How did you like the Fun Day?' asked Pip.

'It was all right,' he said. 'Didn't see much of it. I was in charge of online ticket sales, so I was busy all day in the office and at the ticket booth where they came to collect. Hardly got a chance to look around.'

If that was true, he would have had a hard time getting to the building site and back to steamroll Chanel's stepfather.

'I did see the llama escapade though, that was fun,' he added. Smirky little bugger. But if he had witnessed the llama drama, it was even less likely that he'd been down at the building site committing murder.

'I'll be off then. Bye, all,' he said.

Chanel watched him go. Pip tried to read her expression – longing? Love?

The rest of the class started to trickle over to the sports block, ready for the lesson.

'Just going to the bathroom,' Chanel announced. 'Back in a sec.' And she dashed off.

Pip called the girls to order and quickly instructed them to warm up with ten laps round the sports field – in the same direction, she emphasised, having learned from her previous mistake.

Then she went after Chanel, creeping along walls and peering round corners. She kept the girl in sight as best she could, hanging back and ducking into doorways to avoid detection. It didn't take long. Within minutes, as expected, she came upon the girl and Alan Geoffrey. They were caught in the very act of passing a piece of paper between them.

'What's going on here?' Pip asked in her best teacher voice. Chanel put the paper behind her back, but not nearly quick enough to fool an experienced investigator – or a long-time school note-passer – like Pip.

They both blushed furiously. Caught in the act! Maybe Flis's instinct and David Cole's accusation were right, and the two of them were having a 'thing', an improper relationship of some kind. In which case, Alan would move right to the top of Pip's suspect list – llama drama or not.

Pip held out her hand, palm up, expectantly.

'Might I remind you that I am a member of staff at this institution and that this letter is my private property,' said Alan, with such stern officiousness that Pip withdrew her hand. He put the folded-up piece of paper into his tote bag.

Pip knew she needed to play this one carefully. It was true, Alan was a teacher at the school and she had no rights to his personal correspondence. She had also been specifically told not to make accusations regarding the girls, or even to question them. But on the other hand, Chanel was a vulnerable young woman who had been through a terrible shock and bereavement. She might be under the thrall of this older man. Who might even have killed her stepfather. She felt she had a duty to interfere.

She took Chanel's hand in hers and said, 'I know that feelings can be powerful and confusing, especially when you're young. Sometimes, it even feels like love, but this is—'

'This is nothing like that,' Alan broke in angrily.

'Really, Pip, it isn't. Like I said to David when he found those messages, it's not what you think. I promise you. There's nothing… nothing funny going on between me and Mr Geoffrey.'

To be fair, both parties looked horrified at the suggestion.

'Then what are you doing?'

Chanel looked at Alan as if for permission. His face was fixed in a fury. She said nothing.

Pip tried again. 'Tell me then, what did you tell David?'

'I told him the truth. He believed me. He even laughed when he heard.'

'Heard what?' asked Pip.

The two of them looked into each other's eyes with a swell of emotions – sadness, resignation, embarrassment.

'Just give it to her, Alan,' said Chanel, with a sigh.

He put his hand into his tote, pulled out the folded piece of paper and handed it to Pip.

Pip opened the folded note with what she hoped was an authoritative flourish.

'"Recipe for my mum's chocolate cake,"' she read out. '"This one is sure to make you win."' Pip looked up. 'What is this?' she asked.

Alan's face was suffused in blotchy blushes by this point.

'I'm entering *Strictly Come Baking*,' he muttered, 'and Chanel has been helping me.'

Pip looked from one to the other. She was still confused. Chanel didn't seem like the best person to look to for baking guidance.

'My mum owns the bakery in the village,' said Chanel. 'She wins prizes and stuff. I help her out in the holidays. With the baking. Alan can't get help from a professional, so I've been giving him tips and getting some recipes for him, like. On the sly.' Now they were both blushing.

Pip knew the bakery in question. She drove past it on her way to the school, and always thought about stopping. It certainly didn't seem like these two were having a steamy affair, and David had known that. So maybe Alan was no longer a prime suspect for the murder, but he wasn't off the hook for the exam scam. If anything, this all showed that Chanel and Alan weren't above bending the rules when they wanted something.

Pip looked at Alan. 'While we're spilling the cocoa beans, why don't you tell me about the exam paper leaks then. Is that how you pay Chanel back for the recipes?'

Alan looked at her, his pale face a perfect blank. Pip was no mind-reader, but either he knew nothing about it, or he was Laurence Olivier's grand-nephew and the natural heir to his talent.

'What exam paper leaks?'

'Oh, come on, it seems to be an open secret amongst some of your young friends,' she said, gesturing to Chanel.

'Nope. No idea what you're talking about. Whatever it is, it's nothing to do with me.'

'I told you it wasn't him,' Chanel said.

'What wasn't me?'

With an angry glance at Pip, Chanel exhaled huffily and explained.

Pip mumbled awkwardly, 'Someone with tech skills is involved in it, so…'

'Well, it's not me,' he said. 'You'd better go look for your scam artist computer boffin elsewhere. Now if you've finished with your wild assumptions and accusations, I've got a class to prepare. See you around, Chanel. Thanks for the recipe.'

Chanel watched him go, and turned on Pip. She was furious, unsurprisingly. 'That was so embarrassing! How could you? You're as bad as David with your snooping and accusations. Except that David at least saw sense when I explained that there was nothing weird going on between me and Alan.'

'He believed you?'

'Of course he did.'

'What about the threats to report Alan to the school?'

'He was just worked up, is all. He was always like that, getting into a tizz. But he calmed down.'

'I'm sorry, Chanel. I didn't mean to embarrass you. I thought I was protecting you.'

'Well, you weren't. You're not my friend and you're not my mother. You're a PE teacher. Just teach PE and stop interfering in my life.'

CHAPTER 27

Pip drove home dull with exhaustion and with a deep sense of hopelessness. She'd failed in all her missions – to clear Claire's name, to uncover the mastermind behind the exam scam, and to find out who killed David Cole. And on top of that, she'd upset poor Chanel by crashing around in her life, just when the girl needed a friend.

She had that old familiar feeling of failure, of messing up, of being in the wrong job, or the wrong place at the wrong time, of not being good enough. Since she had found herself accidentally in the role of sleuth, and had one or two lucky breaks, life had looked up. She had her rent covered, and a sense of purpose.

But this was way over her pay grade. She'd give it to the end of the week, and if she didn't have any brainwaves – or a giant sack of clues, preferably marked with the word CLUES – she would say her farewells to Ms Peters and be on her way.

She turned on the radio, hoping for some cheerful music. Her little Mini's sound system – if you could call it that – was too old for Bluetooth, so she took her chances with whatever the airwaves had on offer. In one of the few instances of good fortune she'd had today, it was that old Katy Perry song about waking up in Vegas. Pip sang along. She remembered it well, because she herself had actually *been* waking up in Vegas when it was top of the hit parade a decade before. Being a croupier was a lot less fun than she'd expected. Terribly hard on the feet. And good heavens, the casino management was awfully unforgiving – it was just one little slip, a mere decimal place. All that shouting had been completely unnecessary. Well, the less said about that the better. It could have happened to anyone.

The six o'clock news headlines came on. An improbably jolly young woman ran through a litany of awfulness. A hurricane here, a kidnapping there. A cheerful description of an election somewhere faraway, the country now in the midst of a violent disagreement over the vote.

Vote.

Into her head popped Charles Eastleigh, on the day David Cole died, spitting out the words, 'I know what this is about. It's the vote, isn't it?'

She slammed her palm onto the radio's off button, cutting off the newsreader who was merrily regaling her listeners with the tale of an escaped elephant trampling a tourist in Thailand.

How could Pip have missed it? She was so taken with her theories about the exam scam and the girls that she hadn't properly heard the rest.

She tried to think back to what came next. It had all been so quick and muffled. David had said nothing that Pip could hear or recall, but she did remember Charles referring to the vote and then, furiously, something like: 'How dare you! I'm chairman of the board of this school.'

She pulled up at home with renewed focus. She had a new lead. Well, a lead to a lead, perhaps. Smokey Robinson came skittering towards her on his little grey paws as she opened the door. Most had changed her approach to Pip's long daily absences. She didn't get up from the sofa to greet her, but pretended she hadn't noticed her return, gazing fixedly to a point above the television through slitted eyes. Scooping up Smokey, Pip went over to the sofa, sitting down to stroke the mother cat. Most gave up ignoring her and purred deeply, vibrating under her hand.

'I'm dog-tired, cats,' she said, for her own amusement. Cats, for all their charm, had zero sense of humour. 'Long hard day. Not like you, kitties. Lazing about, waiting for scoff. Have you had supper?'

'Talking to the cats, are you?' asked Tim from the doorway. He must have been in his room when she arrived.

'After a day with scores of chatty teenage girls, I appreciate their complete lack of response.'

'I've spent all day in front of a screen.' He ran his fingers through his hair, giving it a cute rumpled look. 'These might actually be the first words I've spoken since I bought my lunchtime sandwich. I fed the cats, but I did it in complete silence. Like a monk.'

'You can do the talking, then. I'm wiped out. On the subject of food, I've had nothing but biscuits for days. Shall we toss that frozen lasagne into the oven?'

'Excellent idea. There's a bit of greenery. We can make a salad.'

They put the lasagne in to cook and retreated to the sofa where they slumped like two melting snowpersons. After a bit of urging, Pip updated Tim on the day's discoveries.

'*Strictly Come Baking*?' he asked, delightedly. 'That's classic. Your life is so much more fun than mine.'

'I'm not sure that death by steamroller classifies as fun. Anyway, this whole investigation has just been one dead end after another – if you'll excuse the pun – until now. Now I'm thinking that the vote could be a lead. It could have led to David's death. That property business sounds like a hornet's nest. There are all kinds of issues – objections from neighbours, bunny huggers, you name it. One of the teachers was saying…'

She stopped short in her tracks. 'The Marsh Field.'

'What?'

'David Cole's company wanted to buy the big wild field that belongs to the school. One of the teachers told me. Maybe that was the vote Charles was talking about. Maybe they were voting on that?'

'Sounds plausible. The board would probably have to vote on whether to sell or not.'

'A lead, Tim,' she said, grinning at him. 'I think I have a lead.'

'That's great, Pip,' said Tim. 'So you're investigating the murder too?'

'Oh no, not investigating. Just, you know…'

Admit it, Pip thought to herself, *you are investigating.* Despite Ms Peters's instructions to stay away.

'Well, maybe when you've found the murderer, you can get back to clearing Claire's name.' He said it with a smile, but Pip wasn't sure it was genuine. He sounded a tiny bit snippy, to be honest. She sighed. It seemed so long since that night Tim had almost kissed her, and here he was getting snippy.

'I'm working on that too, don't worry. Making good progress,' she said, with rather more confidence than she felt.

The following day, Pip arrived a little later than usual. There had been quite a wait as the morning traffic was stopped by a stationary hedgehog in the road. Pip would have picked it up, but the loud woman in head-to-toe Burberry whose Land Rover was at the head of the queue of cars was telling people not to interfere with nature. A few people got out to argue the toss on that – most felt that the hedgehog could be safely moved, although a minority, mostly old fellows passing by on their morning walks, were happy to watch it sit there, considering its options.

Finally, a man in a business suit got out of his Mercedes, stomped to the head of the line, said, 'For goodness' sake,' and moved the hedgehog to the kerb.

Pip's first goal, when she finally arrived at the staffroom, was to pounce on Amy, the Biology teacher, the font of all property-related knowledge, thanks to her brother-in-law. She didn't have to wait long. The young woman came in for pre-class coffee, loading her cup with two full spoons of sugar. 'Gets me through the morning classes,' she said to Pip with a laugh. 'Caffeine and sugar. The foods of the gods. How's it going on the sports side? All good?'

'Yes, great. They're nice kids.' Pip had poor small talk and a marked inability to bring a conversation smoothly towards the subject she wanted to talk about. Instead, she blurted out, 'So, Amy, I was thinking about what you said about the Marsh Field. Do you know any more about it? Has the school decided to sell?'

'I don't know. Last time I asked my brother-in-law, the school board hadn't made a decision. It was a bit of a battle, strong feelings both ways. Not an easy decision, I imagine.'

'I suppose so. In that case, I guess the board would have to vote on it.'

'I don't know much about the management side of the school, but almost certainly. I do know that a board meeting was scheduled for yesterday, but because of… you know… the incident… it didn't happen.'

Pip considered what this might mean in terms of her developing theory that this matter might have had something to do with David Cole's death. Her train of thought was interrupted by Candice, the Maths teacher, who came into the staffroom and made a beeline for Amy.

Candice mumbled a hello to Pip and turned to Amy with an apologetic smile. 'I'm sorry to be such a twit, but could you show me again about the Excel?' She drew her laptop out of her shoulder bag and put it on the table. 'You see, I'm trying to make a new row? I've clicked insert again and again but nothing happens. Anyway, look, it's just not working…' She opened the laptop and pointed as she talked. 'Here. I pushed this, but then the little gizmo thing doesn't come up so I can't make a new row.' She looked completely flustered, pecking and squinting anxiously at the laptop – she was certainly not displaying the nerves of steel you'd expect from a gambling ace. Or the computer skills you'd expect from the criminal mastermind behind the exam scam.

'I have the same problem,' said Pip in her friendliest tone. 'Not the best with technology.'

Candice nodded gratefully. 'It just mystifies me.'

'I'd have thought you maths boffs would all be good at tech.'

'Not me, I'm terrible. Amy is always saving me from disaster.'

Amy smiled. 'Candice, you can do it if you just keep calm. What did I say? One step at a time. The problem is you panic!'

The two women bent over the machine, Amy talking Candice through the process in a soothing voice. She must be a good teacher, thought Pip.

The bell rang, indicating ten minutes until classes and precipitating a clattering of teacups into saucers and saucers onto trays. Pip took her own cup over to the tray, her head full of questions. She'd made one useful discovery: Candice was useless at tech, which meant that she could be crossed off the list of suspects for the technology genius behind the exam scam.

She hadn't learned much from Amy that would help her in the murder investigation, though. She would have to ask Ms Peters about the Marsh Field and the board meeting and who wanted what and what was at stake. And whether it would be enough to get David Cole killed.

A horrible thought occurred to Pip. Whoever had killed David Cole was still out there. The Marsh Field was still in play. Would he kill again?

CHAPTER 28

Pip was about to leave the staffroom, and waved a general good bye to the few teachers who were still collecting their books and bags.

Janice, the English teacher, was one of the last to move, still sitting in an armchair, glued to her iPad. She looked up at Pip, then back to her device. 'I shouldn't think the head will be pleased,' she said sternly.

Pip turned to see if Janice was perhaps addressing someone behind her, but no. There was by now no one left in the staffroom but the two of them.

'I'm sorry, I don't know what you mean.'

'Speaking to the press.'

Janice swiped her device to find the top of the page and began to read out loud: 'The school has not issued a statement at this time, but the sports teacher who found Mr Cole's body, and who asked to remain anonymous, described the scene as gruesome. "I can't imagine why anyone would do such a terrible thing. And almost on school property. I have been having nightmares about it all week. It's just very lucky that none of the young girls were around to see the horror."'

'That was not me.'

'"The sports teacher who found Mr Cole's body"? Wasn't that you?'

'Yes, I found the body, but I didn't speak to any journalist. I wouldn't do that. I never said those words, not to a journalist or to anyone else. What are you reading?'

'The local community online newspaper. The *Kent Connection*. The copy editing is not to the standard one might like to see, but it does do a reasonable job of following the big local stories,' she said, putting her iPad into her copious bag, and hoisting it onto her shoulder as she stood. 'Mr Cole's death is right there on the front page, as you can imagine. Your comment, too. The head is going to be livid with you.' She paused for a moment, as if contemplating how livid Ms Peters would indeed be. 'Anyway, I'd best be off. Time and tide waits for no man. Shakespeare. *Julius Caesar.*'

With that, Janice made her stately way out of the staffroom, leaving Pip alone in utter confusion. Not a minute later, her mobile phone rang. Alexandra Peters. Pip's heart sank and she felt that too-familiar butterflies-in-the-stomach feeling that she got when she knew she was in trouble. She answered the phone.

'Would you come straight to my office, please. I need to speak with you.'

It was off to the headmistress's office for a dressing down, just like Pip's school days. Admittedly, the dressing down was often well deserved back then, but in this case, it was completely uncalled for. She knew for certain she had never spoken to a journalist.

This time, there was no waiting under the benign eye of Mrs Jenkins and the stern eyes of headmistresses past.

'You can go straight in,' said Mrs Jenkins, gesturing towards the open door.

Ms Peters was behind her desk, her mouth a thin line, a slight tremor in her hands betraying her anger.

'Was I not very clear,' she said tightly, without raising her voice, '*very* clear, that no member of staff was to speak to the press? That all enquiries should go via my office?'

'Yes, you were, very clear, but—'

Ms Peters held up her hand and continued. 'I don't want to hear any buts, Pip. This whole situation is extremely delicate from the school's point of view, and your comments have made that situation significantly worse. It creates the impression that this terrible incident was almost on our property, and our girls could have been in danger, either of physical harm or of witnessing a distressing murder.'

'I didn't say that, I promise,' said Pip.

'Well, whatever you said, this is what is in the newspaper. The phone has been ringing off the hook. I've had parents phoning, the national press. It's an utter disaster.'

'I'm sorry, but I—'

'It's no good you being sorry. Just stay away from the David Cole matter, and don't speak to anyone.'

'Actually, I have some new leads on that. I was thinking—'

'If you have anything of real value, I suggest you do the responsible thing as a citizen and hand it over to the police.'

'If I could just ask you one or two questions, about the Marsh Field.'

Ms Peters stood up and cut Pip off mid-sentence. 'No, Pip. Your involvement in this matter is over. You have until the end of the week to figure out what happened with the exams, or you can leave. This whole situation of having you in the school is becoming a liability. Now, if you'll excuse me, thanks to you, I have many, *many* phone calls to return.'

Pip left Ms Peters's office, shutting the door behind her, and, distracted and upset by what Ms Peters had said, almost ran into Mrs Jenkins who was straightening the old yearbooks on the side table right next to the door. Pip jumped when she saw her. 'Oh, sorry. Didn't see you there,' she said.

'Are you all right, dear?' was the secretary's concerned response.

'I suppose. Just a misunderstanding. Anyway, nothing to be done about it. That's the end of that,' was Pip's dejected response.

'Well, I'm sorry to hear that. If there's anything I can do to help, you let me know,' said Mrs Jenkins, returning to her desk.

'Thanks,' said Pip, her eyes unexpectedly pricking with tears at this kind offer. 'I appreciate it, but I've learned something about letting go in my time. I know when to cut my losses and move on.'

'I'm sure you're right, dear. Sometimes it's best to just let things go.'

Pip took a deep breath. She had until the end of the week to solve this mystery and clear Claire's name – and she was determined to do it. And if, along the way, she happened to figure out who killed David Cole… well, who could blame her?

First things first – to figure out how it was she was quoted in a newspaper when she knew that she hadn't spoken to anyone.

Pip opened up her laptop to google the online community newspaper and the article. There was no new information – neither the police nor the school were putting anything out. The quote from Imposter Pip was the only comment. Pip read it. It was exactly as Janice, the English teacher, had said. It didn't even sound like Pip! Anybody who knew her knew that very little made her lose any sleep. Not that the journalist – a Helen Garner, according to the byline – would know that.

Pip put her long legs up on the desk and leaned back in the chair. She closed her eyes, the better to think. Who would have spoken to the journalist and pretended to be Pip? And why? Pip couldn't think of a motive.

There was one way to find out. She scrolled to the Contact Us tab on the online newspaper, and there it was. 'For editorial enquiries and news tip-offs, contact investigative journalist Helen Garner.' Beside her name, an email address and a mobile number.

'*Kent Connection*, this is Helen.' The investigative journalist sounded not much older than Pip's students.

'It's Epiphany Bloom here, the sports teacher from Hurlingham House. I found the body?'

'Oh, hi Epiphany. Have you seen the story? It went live this morning.'

'I saw it. The thing is, Helen, that I have been maligned here. I did not give you that quote.'

'But you did.'

'I did not. And I think it's shocking that you would make up something like that.' Pip knew she wasn't exactly on the moral high ground when it came to making things up, but it was different when it was about a murder and in the newspaper.

'But you phoned me and told me those things. I wrote it down word for word.'

'Whoever you spoke to wasn't me. Do I sound like the person who phoned you?' demanded Pip.

Helen appeared to think about it. 'Actually no, I don't think so,' she said. 'Either that wasn't you, or you're not you now.'

'Well, I'm me,' said Pip. 'Someone else phoned you, but that person wasn't me.'

There was a stunned silence at the other end of the line. 'Well, that's impossible. You're lying. Who was it if it wasn't you?'

'You tell me. What did the person sound like?'

'Well, it was a woman.'

'Did her voice sound like mine?'

There was a further silence.

'I'll take that as a no,' said Pip. 'Did she sound young? Could it have been one of the students having a lark, do you think?'

'No, I don't think so. No. She sounded a bit older than that. I can't believe I've been tricked by some... Wait until I find out who—'

'Do you remember anything else about the voice? The accent, or the tone?'

'She sounded... I don't know, friendly? Helpful. Neutral, no accent that I noticed.'

'What did she say?'

'Wait, let me get my notes.'

There was a pause and the sound of scrabbling through items on a desk, then the flicking of pages.

'She gave her name – your name – Epiphany Bloom. I wrote it down here. But she asked me not to use it.'

'Did she say why you shouldn't use her name?'

'Just for privacy, it being a murder investigation and all.'

'But you felt free to say it was the sports teacher who found the body. I mean, who else could that refer to?'

'No, I asked her if I could say that and she said that was fine. "Perfect" was the word she used.'

'Surely you found that a bit strange,' said Pip. 'Not wanting you to use my name, but happy for you to identify me by my job anyway.'

'Well, now that you say so, I guess,' said Helen. 'But it's easy to be wise in retrospect, you know.'

Pip sighed. 'Was there anything else?'

'Really, nothing more than what's in the paper. It was a very brief conversation.'

Pip ended the call, frustrated at how little she had found out about the caller. It was a woman, so that narrowed it down to just a few million people. All the students were female, and ninety per cent of the school staff, so frankly, that was a supremely unhelpful bit of information.

She put her mind to the mystery of what the motive could possibly be for impersonating Pip and saying really very little. There seemed no sense to it. Could it be just a prank? One of the girls messing about? It seemed unlikely, and Helen did say the voice didn't sound like a schoolgirl.

Pip looked at the article again, reading the quote slowly. The words made it look as if the schoolgirls were somehow in jeopardy – just as Ms Peters had noted. Was whoever phoned trying to make the school look negligent? It was possible that someone was trying to make trouble for the school. And if so, why? Or was it someone trying to make trouble for Pip?

CHAPTER 29

The more she thought about it, the more likely it seemed that whoever had phoned the paper was hoping to get Pip into trouble with the school, and possibly out of the picture. Could it be tied to the exam scam? If Helen Garner was wrong about the age of the caller, it might have been Grace Faith or whoever her accomplices were. Maybe they were trying to get the interfering sports teacher fired so that they could go about their lucrative business undeterred.

But what if it wasn't about the exams? What if Impersonator Pip was keen to get Real Pip off the David Cole murder case? If so, the whole thing had worked out as intended. Pip was indeed off the case, and if she didn't solve the exam mystery, she'd be out of the school by the end of the week.

She had the feeling that the David Cole murder case was linked to the housing development, the Marsh Field, the vote and the board. She couldn't ask Ms Peters about it but Pip knew someone else who might know.

If Mrs Jenkins was surprised to see Pip back so soon after the meeting with Alexandra Peters, she didn't show it. Mrs Jenkins must be the perfect school secretary, thought Pip: competent, unflappable, efficient, discreet and able to wrangle all manner of office equipment – something that often eluded Pip herself.

'Hello, Epiphany. You've just missed Ms Peters, I'm afraid,' she said. 'She's gone for the day.'

Pip knew that, having lurked outside the office for some time waiting for Ms Peters to leave, but she feigned disappointment.

'Oh, that's a pity. I wanted to ask her a quick question.'

'Is it something I could help you with?'

'Thank you. Maybe you can,' said Pip. 'You do seem to know all about everything at the school.'

'Well, I do keep up. What do you want to know, dear?'

'I was wondering about the Marsh Field. It's such a lovely big space. What does the school use it for, apart from Fun Day? I was wondering if I could use it for sports things, you know, like running and exercise and so on. Do you think that would be OK?'

'Oh yes, that would be fine. It's just a nice big open space for the school to enjoy. The Art department uses it sometimes. The girls paint outside. And the Biology teachers like to go and catch tadpoles and so on. The place is full of them. In fact, there's a fellow there now, looking for rare frogs.'

Pip nodded – she knew Fwog Dude was poking around on some environmental impact study.

'Lovely, I'll take the girls over there some time for a run around. Isn't the school lucky to have it? I heard it might be sold for development, that there was talk of David Cole's company buying it for the residential estate. I do hope that's just a rumour,' said Pip, and then added with a grin, 'Staffroom gossip, you know how it is.'

Mrs Jenkins smiled. 'Yes, there has been talk of that.'

'It would be a pity,' said Pip, sitting down in the chair opposite Mrs Jenkins, arms folded, as if settling in for a good chat. 'Such a lovely unspoilt bit of wilderness.'

'Ms Peters thinks so, but it's really up to the board.'

'There must be all sorts of animals living there, poor things.' Pip racked her brain for names of wild animals, but they had all fled, perhaps in the ark. 'Ferrets,' she finally said. 'And those poor tadpoles. I don't know where they'd go. Or how. They don't even have legs.'

'I wouldn't worry just yet, dear. Some of our board members are very keen on nature and so on. One in particular – she is dead set against selling the field to the developer.'

'So this, Mrs…'

'Finnegan, Ethel Finnegan.'

'Mrs Finnegan. Is she the only woman on the board?'

'Yes, the other four are men. Why?'

'Oh, just interested. Glass ceiling. You know. Feminism. That sort of thing.'

'Well, it's all moot now. With poor Mr Cole, everything has been put on hold.'

Pip decided to push just a little further. She cocked her head to one side and said, as if the thought had just occurred to her: 'Mrs Jenkins. You don't think that David Cole's death has anything to do with the Marsh Field and the development, do you?'

'Well, goodness, dear,' said Mrs Jenkins in surprise. 'What an idea. I'd never thought… No… But now you mention it, it has been a *very* contentious issue. High emotion.' She thought for a minute. 'I suppose they might be connected.'

Pip reckoned she'd got about as much information as she could out of the secretary, and made her excuses. 'Well, I'm sure the police will be onto that connection. Gosh, I'd better get going, I see it's after three already,' said Pip, looking up at the wall clock behind the secretary's desk. 'I need to finish up a few things at my desk and I've just remembered I'm having dinner with my mum. I still have to get home and get spruced up.' She indicated her tracksuit, which was, in fact, looking like it had had as hard a day as Pip herself.

'Well, I'll be going too,' said Mrs Jenkins, turning off the photocopier and the computer. 'Have a good evening with your mum, Epiphany.'

*

Pip thanked her and hurried to her office. She had to drive home, change, and get to Henry's where he and Mummy were expecting her at seven thirty. On Henry's request, Pip had invited Jimmy to come with her. Jimmy and Henry got on like a house on fire. While Pip had been tied up with the police after the not-so-fun Fun Day, they'd bonded over doughnuts and llamas. It seemed weird – a seventy-something heir to a plumbing fortune and a mid-thirties ex-bouncer gym owner – but they shared a sort of open-heartedness that reached across the usual social boundaries. So she invited Jimmy, joking that she needed a bouncer to deflect Mummy, but the truth was that it would be nice to have him as her date-ish, friend, partner person.

Pip opened her computer to find a message from getyourbestmarks.co.uk. *Sally Llama. We are unable to process your application at this time.* What was that supposed to mean? Was there a technical problem? Were they onto her?

She couldn't think it through just then. She was under serious time pressure and she still had to answer a few emails, update her lesson plan for the week and put away all her personal items, as was school policy for teachers. It was close to four by the time she packed up and walked to her car. She followed a path that ran past the hockey field and under a little walkway outside the groundskeeper's offices, to the staff parking.

As she walked, Pip allowed herself to consider her romantic life, which somehow managed to be both complicated and entirely fruitless. The trouble was that Tim and Jimmy were two of her best friends and that she fancied both of them. They couldn't be more different. Jimmy had been round the block a few times, as he liked to say. He teased her and sparred with her and, she suspected, was as soft on the inside as he was tough on the outside. Tim spent most of his day in front of a computer screen, using that big old brain of his. You'd never meet a sweeter, more thoughtful guy.

And he was really very nice-looking. They were both so attractive, but so different. How was a girl to choose? And besides, she could never quite tell whether either of them *like* liked her, or just liked her as a friend.

An almighty crash shocked her out of her pondering. Just inches to her left was a great splatter of broken pottery and soil and a mangled geranium plant. Brushing dirt from her tracksuit trousers, she looked up and saw two pots filled with geraniums on a small ledge outside a window above the groundskeeper's offices. The one that would have sat between them minutes ago must have fallen just as Pip was walking underneath it.

Pip felt quite shaken by the noise and the surprise of it. She pressed her hand to her chest and felt her heart galloping like a herd of… something. Wildebeest maybe. She looked down again at the debris, noting a big pointed shard of pottery, and the hard heavy base of the pot. If either of those had hit her she would have been very badly injured. A blow to the head could have killed her. She felt quite faint at the near miss. Oh well, here she was, alive and healthy.

She let her heart rate settle and even gave a weak laugh. Imagine being killed in a freak accident with a falling flowerpot, like some cartoon character. What an embarrassing way to go.

CHAPTER 30

Jimmy had gone full dinner-with-the-parents, looking most respectable in a smart charcoal-grey jacket and an open-necked shirt of a paler grey, and carrying a box of After Eights. He was waiting for her outside The Glove Box. Pip's heart gave a little leap. The same leap it gave whenever Tim arrived home from work. Maybe it was nothing to do with the men – maybe she had some sort of heart condition.

Pip rolled down her window and said, 'Good evening, I'm looking for Jimmy, the owner. About your height, same shaved head, but kind of scruffy-looking?'

'Yeah yeah, very funny,' he said, pulling the door open and sliding into the tiny car. 'Thought I'd put my good duds on to meet the folks.'

'Folk, strictly speaking. And you've met her already. But you do look really good, and very dinner-with-parent appropriate.'

'Surprised to see I scrub up so well, are you?'

'Nah. And besides, I like Gym Jimmy just fine,' Pip said quickly, worried that she might have offended him. Tough guys could be surprisingly easily wounded, as she'd discovered in that brief long-distance relationship with the Navy SEAL while she was working as a radio operator in the navy. She'd really liked that job, but the Morse Code was so confusing and they freaked out when she got the dots and dashes confused. Could have happened to anyone, really.

'You look nice too,' he said, nodding approvingly at her black trousers and black leather ankle boots, and her silky animal-print blouse.

'I had about three minutes to change and toss some lippie on. I got away a bit later than I hoped from the school and you know what the traffic is like. Between the teaching, the exam scam and my side interest in the dead guy, I'm run off my feet.'

'This could only happen to you, Pip – one minute you're looking into little girls cheating; the next thing you know, you're trying to solve a murder case.'

'I'm most definitely not trying to solve the case. I just happened to be looking into a few aspects that overlapped with the other case. Anyway, not any more. Ms Peters has told me to step back.'

She explained about the mysterious impersonator.

'That is very strange. Who would do that? And why?'

'I think I can answer the why question, Jimmy. I must be onto something, getting close, and the person who phoned the paper was trying to get me into trouble with Ms Peters, have her take me off the case. The who is a lot more difficult. All I know is that it was a woman. My gut tells me it's someone who wants to stop me poking around in the exam scam or the David Cole murder. I'm thinking it has something to do with the development. In which case, whoever phoned is most likely someone who is on the anti-developer, anti-sale side of that issue. But who? That's the big question. There is a woman on the board who was vehemently opposed to the sale. I'm going to have to track her down.'

'So that whole stepping-back thing...' He grinned knowingly at her from the passenger seat, the beam of the oncoming cars' headlights bouncing off his shaved head.

'I am, yes. Absolutely stepping back. Just as soon as I've cleared this up. Jimmy, someone impersonated me! I need to clear my name. Then I'm done. I mean, I still need to clear Claire's name too, so I'll get back to that. Anyway, let's not talk about my business the whole way. Tell me about what's going on in your life.'

Jimmy updated her about his two daughters, Lily and Rose, now living with his ex in New Zealand. Lily had made the soccer team. Rose had a voice like an angel. The pride in his voice was tinged with sadness. He missed them.

'I'm hoping to get them here for Christmas,' he said. 'If everything goes to plan.'

'That would be really great, Jimmy. I hope it works out this time.'

She pulled up at Henry's house, an elegant four-storey divided up between himself, his daughter and a housekeeper. In an act of almost unprecedented astonishingness, she found a parking space right outside the door.

'Your lucky day,' said Jimmy, as they walked up to the door.

'Luckier than you know,' she said, pushing the buzzer. 'There was a freak accident today. I narrowly missed being killed by a—'

'Hello!' said Henry, flinging the door open and beaming in the doorway. 'Welcome, welcome. How marvellous to have you both here.'

He kissed Pip on the cheek and ushered her in, then grabbed Jimmy's hand and patted him affectionately on the shoulder.

'Come in, come in,' he said.

Mummy, Flis and Peter were in the sitting room, each already clutching a glass.

'What'll you have?' asked Henry, gesturing towards a groaning drinks table. 'I didn't know what everyone drank so I stocked up.'

'He bought four different whiskys,' Mummy said, in an indulgent fake-exasperated voice that Pip had never heard her use before. 'Two Irish, a Scotch, and something called a Kentucky bourbon, if you can believe that.'

Henry laughed uproariously. 'Oh, it's been ages since I had people over. I don't know what people drink these days. Is the gin craze still going? I got some anyway – one says botanical, whatever that means – and there's wine and beer of course, and mixers. And something called kombucha, which I heard Flis here has a taste for.'

'It's delicious, Henry, that's very kind of you to think of me, thank you,' Flis said, raising a glass of murky brown liquid in appreciation. 'Very good for the gut biome, too.'

'Well I never. What's that, then?' Henry asked, intrigued.

'Stomach,' Peter cut in quickly, patting his own. 'Can I pour you a glass of wine, Pip?'

He gave her a sly smile, pleased to have successfully headed off an exploration of digestive flora which he, like Pip, had heard a million times and could well do without. Pip accepted a half-glass of wine, and gazed around Henry's living room. She had been there once before, for a cup of tea in the kitchen, and she'd been so preoccupied with her search for the missing red dress from the *Pretty Woman* movie that she had barely glanced at the decor.

The place was lovely, with high ceilings and big windows. One wall was entirely covered in shelves, books interspersed with artefacts that appeared to be from all over the world. She wandered over to look at an intricately carved musical instrument placed near the shelf.

'It's called a marimba,' he said, coming over to join her. 'It's sort of like a xylophone. I picked it up in Zimbabwe. All these items were collected on my travels, back in my working days. Went everywhere, I did, representing the company. Loved the travelling.'

'I know you miss it.'

'Retirement life never suited me,' he said. 'I have to say, things have perked up a lot since I met you, Pip. And the llamas of course.' There was a pause, and he added, blushing, 'And your mother.'

They returned to sit on the sofas and chatted a bit, nibbling on the little bowls of cashew nuts and olives that Henry had put out on the coffee table. Flis launched into a long story about how her blog posts had been overrun with comments from anti-vax trollops.

'But how do you know that they're trollops?' asked Jimmy.

'Because they make rude comments, that's what trollops do,' explained Flis, earnestly. 'Trollops are undissenting in their comments.'

'Trolls,' muttered Pip to Jimmy. She was slightly distracted by how close he was sitting to her on the sofa, and how alluring the smell of his aftershave was. 'And she probably means that they're unrelenting, although I guess they might also not have any dissent.'

'That's what I said, Pip,' snapped Flis. 'You know how I hate it when you translate me to people.'

'Well, someone has to,' said Pip.

Luckily, Mummy came out of the kitchen and interrupted the argument. She called over to Henry, 'I think it's all ready, darling. Shall we bring everyone to the table?'

Darling? She never called Andrew McFee, her Gentleman Caller, darling. And certainly not Daddy, as best Pip could recall from years gone by.

Jimmy jumped up to help carry the steaming plates of lamb chops and vegetables.

They gathered around a gleaming oak table, set formally with polished silverware and crystal glasses, and roses that looked fresh from the garden. It was beautiful, a far cry from lasagne in the kitchen with Tim and the cats. Henry came round with the wine.

'I'll have a fizzy water, thanks. We came in the car, so no more wine for me. Wouldn't want to get into an accident.'

'Hey, Pip, speaking of accidents, you were about to tell me about your near miss today,' Jimmy said. He touched her hand as he said this, sending an unexpected bolt of electricity up her arm.

'Oh yes, I was. It was the craziest thing. I was walking under a sort of ledge with flowerpots on it, and one fell off. Huge thing. Missed me by inches.'

'Like the cartoons!' said Flis. Same childhood, same TV shows.

'Exactly. I would have been squashed just like the Road Runner. Seriously, though, I got a heck of a fright.'

'Good Lord,' said Mummy. 'How terrifying, darling. Thank goodness it missed you.'

'Yes, what a lucky miss. Pleased you are in fine health and here with us, dear Pip!' said Henry, raising his glass to her. Having filled his guests' glasses, he took his place at the head of the table, with Mummy on his right.

'On the subject of freak accidents, goodness, when we were at that Fun Day of yours, Pip, we heard about a terrible mishap,' he said. 'Other than… you know… the steamroller, of course.'

'Gosh yes, awful story,' said Mummy, laying a hand on his arm. How much time were these two actually spending together? It was all a bit strange. Mummy had no sooner returned from South America without Andrew McFee than she'd become besties with Henry. Pip wondered if she should be concerned. And if so, why. And for whom. Maybe herself, because her mother, who was in her sixties (sixty-five, but best not to mention) had a better dating game than Pip did. She returned her attention to Henry's freak accident story.

'One of the teachers was talking about it when we were at the school. It was a skiing accident, a couple of weeks back. This woman, she has something to do with the school, was in the States somewhere, one of those big cold places, Idaho perhaps. Got her skis caught in a moose antler in the snow, went over the top of it. Snap. Broke both her ankles.'

Henry went on, 'Poor woman is stuck in America. Can't travel with two broken ankles in those great big moon boots.'

'Very inconvenient, a foot injury,' said Flis. 'I had that ingrown toenail, remember, Pip? Could hardly walk.'

'Yes, and this woman is on various boards and so on,' said Mummy.

'Boards? Do you remember her name?' asked Pip.

'Can't say I do. Was it Finland?' Henry asked Mummy.

'I want to say vinegar,' said Mummy. 'But vinegar's not a name, is it?'

'Was it Ethel Finnegan, by any chance?' Pip asked.

'I think it might have been,' said Henry, cheerily. 'Something like that.'

Ethel Finnegan, the only woman on the board, the main proponent of the anti-sale, anti-development agenda, hadn't phoned the papers and impersonated Pip. Neither was she within a thousand miles of the place when David Cole was killed. Well, there was another suspect to cross off the list.

It was back to square one for Pip.

CHAPTER 31

'Swingball?' said Rizwana, eyes wide. 'I love swingball!'

'Cool, and a trampoline!' said Claire.

Pip had been so busy with her investigations that she had had no time to focus on planning the sports lessons. Ten minutes before the lesson was due to start, she opened up the sports cupboard in desperation, rooted through the hoops and balls and bats and – well, she didn't know what half the stuff was, to be honest – and selected a few sporty sorts of items.

'We're doing an obstacle course,' she said. 'High intensity cross training.'

Whatever that was.

'Come on, see what else you can find and help me set it up. Everything in a sort of circuit. Someone help Claire with that trampoline. Chanel, put those hoops over there, you can jump from one to the next. And the swingball, just a forehand and a backhand… There are some skipping ropes, we can use those.'

The set-up itself was good fun, the girls digging for interesting bits and pieces, tossing things to each other, laughing and sharing ideas. They stood back and surveyed their work, joshing and pointing, pleased with their ingenuity.

'It's not really *sports* though, is it?' said Grace Faith with her usual sneer. 'More like, I dunno, some silly kids' game.'

Pip felt the wind change, the laughter die down, the stress levels take an uptick, as the girls considered whether the smart move was to join in to back the Queen Bee, or to pretend they hadn't heard.

'It's just a bit of fun,' said Chanel, curtly. There was a moment of surprised silence, from which Pip deduced that a challenge to Grace Faith's dominance was rare, and then the social barometer changed again and the girls loosened up, with the exception of Grace Faith who threw daggers at her 'best friend'.

Pip gave Chanel a small smile and rallied the troops. 'Come on. Let's get started.'

The session was a great success. Not only were there no injuries – which Pip was pleased about, given her previous experiences – but the girls had a great time. Even the less-than-athletic ones got a good workout and emerged smiling and sweating.

As the girls headed for the changing rooms, Pip manoeuvred herself close to Chanel. 'Hey, Chanel,' she said casually. 'Thanks for the backup.'

The girl shrugged awkwardly.

'How are you doing? How are things at home?'

'OK, I guess. Sad, obviously. The accident.'

Pip was interested to hear that the steamroller incident was still being referred to as an accident.

'If you want to talk, you know I'm here. And Chanel, listen, I'm sorry about the other day. I was trying to help but I was out of line. I shouldn't have confronted you in front of Alan.'

Chanel gave her an almost-smile and a palms up gesture that Pip took to mean forgiveness.

'Thanks, Chanel, I'm glad we chatted. I felt bad about how we left things.'

'Yeah. Oh, and the exam thing? Word is that the, um, source has dried up. No response. No papers. Nothing.' Chanel scratched her neck. 'People are upset, I heard them talking about it.'

'The website is down?'

'I don't know. I haven't been on it, not after… This is just what I heard from, you know… people. I thought you'd want to know.'

'I do, thank you.'

This was an intriguing new development. Whoever was behind the exam scam might have got wind of Pip's investigations and shut up shop, temporarily at least. This would also account for the message saying they couldn't process her application. Back at her office, Pip went to her desk and opened up her laptop. She wanted to check out that website for herself.

Low battery. She stood up from her chair and bent down, reaching under the desk to plug the cord into the wall socket. As she touched it, a loud crack rang out and she felt a tingling surge of electricity run up her arm. Jerking herself away from the source of the shock, she smacked her head hard against the desk and crashed to the floor.

She came round to the sound of voices.

'Ms Bloom, are you all right?'

'Don't touch her. Keep back.'

'Is she alive?'

Pip tried to answer this last question – for she was indeed alive – but her woozy brain struggled with the words. A garbled sound came out, but her head was clearing. Ruby and Amelia were standing over her where she lay half under the desk. They peered down at her, their hands on their knees, their concerned faces like two moons in Pip's sky.

'Yes, I'm alive,' she said, with more success this time. 'I don't know what happened. I think I got an electric shock.' She still felt confused, and wondered whether she'd lost consciousness momentarily, but she managed to sit up.

'Amelia, go call for help,' said Ruby to her friend.

'I think I'm OK.'

Ruby ignored her.

'Amelia, go tell Mrs Jenkins there's been an accident with Ms Bloom here in the sports block.' Amelia nodded and ran off.

Pip was feeling better. Her head had cleared, although her right arm still felt odd and heavy and a bit tingly. There was a small burn on the skin of her fingertips where she'd touched the wire, and a very faint smell of seared flesh.

She remembered her original mission, which was to look up the website and see if Cheaters-R-Us had indeed gone to ground. She hoped her laptop hadn't been fried in the electrocution incident – she suspected not, as she had been shocked before she plugged it in. There'd be no checking now, anyway, seeing as she couldn't charge it.

Mr Seymour, the groundsman/handyman/fixer of all things, soon came hurrying – or as close to hurrying as he could, given his barrel-shaped body and his short, stocky legs.

'If you could all step right away from the power source,' Mr Seymour instructed officiously, without so much as a greeting.

Mr Seymour got down to his knees – it wasn't far – and crawled under the desk, Pip and the two girls watching from a safe distance. 'Well, I don't know what's been going on here,' he said. 'But this plug socket's a complete mess. The plate is loose for a start, and the earth wire has come out.'

'What does that mean?' Amelia asked. 'The plug wasn't earthed?'

'No. Goodness knows who put this in, or what happened to it. I've certainly never worked on this plug socket myself.' Mr Seymour turned to Pip. 'You're lucky you didn't get a worse shock. I reckon it's those big rubber soles on your running shoes that saved you from a very nasty incident. Even, I might say, a fatal one.'

*

Pip was processing this existentially alarming piece of news when the school nurse arrived. They hadn't met before, but there was no mistaking her – Nurse Garland looked the part, right down to the little upside-down watch attached to a brooch on her chest. She gave Pip the once-over, taking her blood pressure with a blow-up cuff, knocking her knee with a small hammer, peering into her eyes looking for who-knows-what – brain damage, perhaps? Small fires?

By this point, Pip felt as right as rain, so it wasn't a surprise when she got the all clear from the nurse, who was just as officious as Mr Seymour in her manner. 'I'm going to let you go home, but if you experience any dizziness, pain, shortness of breath or other symptoms, I want you to go to A and E immediately. Is that clear?'

Mumbling her agreement and her thanks to both of them, Pip put on her denim jacket and gathered her bags. She couldn't wait to get away from the two bossy authority figures, into her little Mini and on the road, where she could listen to music and calm her nerves. Her history was replete with hairy incidents and accidents, but two such near misses in two days really took the cake. Even for someone with Pip's dramatic history it was quite, well, shocking.

CHAPTER 32

The DJ on the radio station was hosting an all-female Golden Hour. Pip sat for a while in the car to listen. She loved this programme, even though somewhat horrifyingly, many of these so-called golden oldies – Christina Aguilera, Rihanna, Shakira – were familiar to Pip from her misspent youth. She always sang along to those with gusto, remembering her teens: the house parties, the clubs they accessed with fake IDs, the holiday romances in Cornwall and Portugal, smooching on the beach. Oh, those were the days.

Pip left the car park and started towards the village. She had barely warmed up, bellowing that she would survive, having not even got to the best bit where she instructed her errant lover to walk out the door, when she noticed a motley gaggle of people gathered on the side of the road.

Spotting the sign for the Executive Lifestyle Estate, Pip realised that she was on the far side of David Cole's site, where it adjoined the watery, boggy end of the Marsh Field. She'd only ever crossed into the site from the school side and the top end of the Marsh Field, so the approach was not familiar, but in the distance she recognised the stand of trees where Mummy and Sally the llama had been stationed. She tried not to look at the spot where she'd found Cole's body.

Pip muted Gloria Gaynor and slowed down. There was a little group of people holding signs, and a grubby young man seemed to be preparing to speak, a mic in one hand, the other hand fiddling with a portable speaker at his feet.

Her right foot lifted from the brake and hovered over the accelerator, preparing to spirit her away from the protest and towards a nice quiet sofa full of cats, but something made her stop on the side of the road and open her window. The little crowd raised their signs.

Stop the development!
Save our countryside!
NO to corporate greed!

(The author of that one had run into trouble in the sizing of the letters and the last word was squashed and angled, the letters getting smaller and smaller towards the end, the exclamation mark hovering above the letter D like a jaunty top hat.)

Pip sighed. She really, really wanted that sofa and that soft pile of cats, and a cup of tea, come to think of it, and perhaps a biscuit. But she also wanted to find out what had happened to David Cole, and she thought that this ragtag bunch of anti-development protestors might hold a clue.

Having unfolded herself from the Mini, Pip approached the group of protestors. She positioned herself next to the small scowling blonde woman holding the banner proclaiming a definitive NO to corporate greed and asked in a friendly voice, 'What's all this about then?'

'Property developers tearing up the countryside. There's some lot putting up more yuppie housing here. They got permission for this abomination…' She gestured to the architects' simulation on the giant billboard that loomed over them, depicting imaginary people enjoying their imaginary homes, set in a lush English countryside setting that was not only fake, but would soon be dug over to make more houses if the developers had their way. The woman continued with a scowl, 'Now they want the field too.'

Pip nodded. 'Would be a pity.'

'They'll stop at nothing. Money's all they care about.'

'Right. Who are they? Do you know anything about them?'

'City people,' she said, exhaling loudly from her nose. From the look on her face, she might have said 'arms dealers' or 'organ harvesters'. 'This greedy bunch have destroyed many an English village before this one.'

She looked fiercely at Pip. 'But it stops here.'

The grubby young man started to sing. It was appalling. The lyrics, for a start:

> 'This is to the Man
> You just think you can
> Own our momma Earth
> The planet of our birth
> Well, NO NO NO
> We're here to tell you GO!'

And then the so-called music. And the wailing. And—

A high-pitched shriek emerged from the amplifier. She clamped her hands over her ears and shuddered. Was an electrocution not enough suffering for one day?

The scream died down; she dropped her hunched shoulders and exhaled. She'd give it five minutes. Just take a walk around, chat to a few people, and see what she could find out. Ten minutes, max. She said goodbye to the angry protestor lady and moved on, taking a direction that would keep her as far as possible from the so-called music which had started up again; more ear-splitting warbling, more rhyming couplets.

She took shelter behind a van – it was a few decibels quieter – and who should she find lurking there, hands wrapped around a mug of tea, but Fwog Dude, aka Hamilton Cunningham-Smythe, of Cunningham's Cunning Critters. What good luck. He was the one

doing an environmental assessment of the tadpoles in the Marsh
Field. That recollection put a spring in her step and she hurried
over to him.

'Oh, Pip. Are you here for the pwotest wally?'

She turned to Fwog Dude and answered loudly over the din.
'Yes, sort of. I wanted to ask…'

The singer had kicked it up a notch for the chorus and they
could no longer converse, even by shouting.

'What?'

'What you say?'

'I can't…'

The 'song' finished finally, and Pip had barely had a moment
to appreciate the blessed silence when the cross-looking woman
she had been talking to started a call-and-response chant with the
audience.

'*What do we want?*' she cried.

On her instruction, the ragtag mob shouted back, '*Justice for
the Earth.*'

The shouting was quiet, relatively speaking, at least once you'd
had the grubby bloke caterwauling in your ear for five minutes.

'I think it's safe,' she said. 'Shall we walk around?'

'Yes, I do believe our eardrums are no longer in immediate pewil,'
Hamilton said, putting his tea mug down. Pip noted that it had
the Hurlingham House logo on it. Odd coincidence.

'So, what are you doing here?' she asked in a conversational tone.
'I remember you saying you were working on an environmental
impact study in the area. Is this it?'

'Not this specific one. I've been wetained as an independent
consultant by the council to look at the impact development in
the area more broadly.'

'*What do we want?*' came the call from the mic. The response
followed – '*An equitable future for all Earth's creatures*' – which Pip

felt could have done with some work, just in terms of catchiness. But what did she know?

'Are you here as part of the protest?' Pip asked.

Hamilton looked a bit shifty. 'It's all bit twicky, fwankly. I'm not pwotesing per se – that wouldn't be pwofessional, it would be a conflict of intewest – but overall, yes, I support their aims. This whole wegion is wich with flowa and fauna that is wapidly being destwoyed. In my own personal awea of intewest – fwogs, as you know – populations have been devastated. So if you were to ask me my opinion, I'd say it had all gone too far. It's time to put a hold on development.'

'*What do we want?*' the cross lady enquired.

'*An end to corporate greed and capitalism that harms!*'

Good luck with that, thought Pip, cynically.

The crowd had swelled now, presumably with people joining in on their way home from work or the school run. There must have been forty people or more. Some in wellies, some in gym clothes, a few in corporate attire, kids tagging along.

'Who are the rest of these people?' Pip asked.

'Mostly locals who just want to pwotect their area. The lady with the mic is Alison Walters. She's one of the organisers.'

The grubby singer was suddenly standing in front of them, flushed with success.

'Hey…?' he said to Pip, expectantly.

'Hi. Um, I'm Pip. I just came to…'

'Hey. I'm Bernard. Welcome, man, we need all hands on…'

While Bernard seemed to be trying to dredge the second part of the metaphor from deep in his brain, Hamilton continued. 'I was just saying that Alison is the leader, in so far as there is one.'

'Fierce,' said Bernard admiringly, having presumably forgotten about the hands and the deck.

'A little too fierce sometimes, if you want my opinion. Most of the people here are concerned citizens but she's a weal wabble wouser.'

Pip and Bernard both took a moment to process that last phrase. 'Rabble rouser, is she?'

'We need more people like that woman, man,' Bernard said, patting Hamilton on the shoulder. 'We're facing down the man, man.'

Hamilton stiffened and said imperiously, 'Perhaps so, *man*, but I dwaw the line at public violence.'

Pip's interest was piqued. 'Alison is violent?'

'She is, I'm afraid. And she encourages the others with her wiotous behaviour. Vewy dangerous.'

Could this dangerous Alison woman have had something to do with Cole's death?

Hamilton continued, disapprovingly, 'I don't appwove of her methods, but I must say, she'd got chawisma, that one. You'd never imagine that she's an owal hygienist.'

'An oral hygienist? Yes, that is a bit incongruous. But tell me more about her violent nature. What did she do? Who did she harm?'

Hamilton blinked and stammered a little. 'Oh no, not a person. I mean. Gosh. Not yet, anyway. She's nothing like that other mob.' Hamilton was, presumably, referring to the people who he'd been involved with the last time Pip met him, who had kidnapped Matty Price and murdered a girl called Livi.

'What did she do, then?'

'Um, well, once she, um she tore up a stack of fliers that the pwoperty company had printed. Weally woughly.'

Pip nodded encouragingly, although that didn't seem quite on the same page as flattening someone with a steamroller.

'And then she set fire to public pwoperty.' Arson! That sounded a bit more like it.

Bernard chuckled. 'It was a dustbin, dude. She set fire to a dustbin. With the fliers. It's recycling, like. Ashes to ashes. Karma. Show the man the can.' His eyes glazed over for a moment, and then he reached into his pocket for a scrap of paper and a pencil stub. 'Show the man the can,' he said, as he slowly wrote it down. 'You have to catch the genius as it flows from the source, man.'

'Yes indeed, it was just a dustbin,' said Hamilton, irritably bringing the discussion back on course. 'But she burnt it to a cwisp and that's against the law. And then did you see her kicking all the burning papers awound in that dangerous manner? The whole place could have gone up. People could have been hurt. And I've seen her shouting vewy angwily at the developers. I even saw her throw a pinecone, once. Hit a fellow on the back. She's got a temper, that one. She's a dangewous woman. You mark my words.'

A temper. Arson. Lobbing things at other people. Did her devotion to the environment stretch to murder?

'Gotta fight the fight, man. Can't do that with tea and biscuits.'

Hamilton blushed at the dig.

Pip got that niggling feeling that sometimes indicated a clue, or an insight, or something not quite right. 'Speaking of tea, I noticed you had a Hurlingham House mug. Funny thing. I've been working there these last few weeks. And they own the field the developers want to buy. How did you get the mug?'

'Oh yes,' said Hamilton, pleased to have a change of subject from Alison Walters. 'I've been conversing with the pwincipal. Lovely woman, just lovely. And clever. And lovely.'

He looked down at his shoes, blushing. *Oh my word, Fwog Dude has a thing for Ms Peters!*

'Yes, she's very nice. A good headmistress.'

'She's taken a weal interest in the environmental impact study. Smart woman, she is, and very… Yes, anyway, she pops down to see how we're doing with the sampling and to chat about things. Sends down tea and, um, yes' – he looked at Bernard – 'biscuits. Vewy kind.'

Bernard had lost interest and turned away. 'I'm gonna love you and leave you, yeah? Got another few tunes to do. Think I'm gonna debut my new one – "Money money, mess you up". Bye then, Kip.' He was wandering off before he'd finished his sentence, waving vaguely.

'Deck,' he shouted triumphantly over his shoulder. 'All hands on deck.'

'Alexandra's not keen on selling the land for development,' Pip said casually, making it sound as if she and Alex were old mates, and this was something they'd chatted about. 'So I suppose you have that in common.'

'Yes indeed. She's not keen at all. In fact, she's said they'd sell the field over her dead body. We have a lot in common, actually. She's very passionate about the enviwonment, a nature lover. Weally, we are vewy alike.'

Pip didn't know quite what to say to this – the frog-loving environmental scientist and the beautiful young headmistress seemed, well, worlds apart.

'We've had lots of conversation about the habitat. She's actually surprisingly interested in fwogs, for a lay person,' said Hamilton, admiringly. 'I tell you, Pip, that woman is a cut above. Not just in her, you know, she's, I mean…'

Hamilton definitely had a crush on Alexandra Peters. He struggled on. 'What I mean to say is…'

The rest of his sentence drowned, struggling under the waves of screaming awfulness that was the debut performance of Bernard's new work.

'That's it. I'm out of here,' Pip said, pushing her hands determinedly into her pockets.

CHAPTER 33

Her fingers touched paper. She ran her thumb absent-mindedly along the sharp crease and felt a prickle of recognition. It was the note she'd found in the steamroller and shoved into her jacket pocket before anyone saw it. A clue right from the scene of the crime! How could she have forgotten to look at it? She'd run off to that stupid staff meeting and then forgotten. If she hadn't decided to wear this jacket again today, it might have been lost forever. *Idiot, idiot, idiot.* Her arms resting on the roof of the Mini, she unfolded it, holding her breath. A grid. Numbers. It was a bingo card from the Fun Day.

Pip got into the car, the paper next to her on the seat. Did it mean anything? And if so, what? Her brain churned as she drove, grappling with the how and why and who and when questions. What did she know? For a start, the paper must have been dropped on the day of the murder, probably at around the exact time of the murder. Perhaps even *by* the murderer.

This thought gave her such a start that she almost scraped a Range Rover coming in the other direction on the narrow road. A furious-looking man shook his fist at her and shouted something she couldn't hear. Pip thought that was a bit of a cheek, seeing as his car was twice the size of hers.

She let her mind wander back to the bingo paper. Who would have had access to the cards? And who could have dropped this one at the scene of the crime? A cyclist ahead of her turned sharply right. She had to brake hard not to hit him. After the two near misses, she decided to slow down and concentrate a bit harder.

*

No sign of Tim – he'd told her he had a crazy day and not to worry about him for dinner, so after feeding the cats, Pip made herself a piece of toast and honey with a cup of tea. She sat at the kitchen table with her plate and mug in easy reach and started making lists in her holographic all-seeing third-eye notebook. She found making lists so comforting, even if the actual doing of the lists was often a bit of a disappointment and she didn't manage to do or solve or fix or find half the things she'd intended.

Naturally, the cats hated this list-making activity. It was so brutally un-cat-centred. Their human barely acknowledged them, the surfaces around her were hard and unforgiving, and her hands were so busy with that annoying pointy thing. Smokey jumped onto the table and batted Pip's pen gently as she wrote 'ACCESS TO BINGO CARD' at the top of a page, and underneath:

- Chanel (who was helping)
- Anyone who played bingo (!!!)
- Me!
- Anyone who passed through the office that day

She stared hard at the paper. It never helped, but she did it anyway. Really, this list was no use. It could be almost anyone. Smokey stared at the list too, and then gently bit the top of Pip's pen. Apparently he had no better idea than Pip did.

The bingo players were the first problem. There were at least twenty people there and it could have been any of them. She drummed her fingers on the table. *Hang on.* This sheet was blank. Anyone who had played bingo would have markings on their sheet. Whoever had dropped this hadn't played. She felt rather pleased with herself for knocking twenty suspects off her list in one fell swoop.

Strike. She crossed herself off too. Twenty-one. Smokey gave the pen a lick. He seemed pleased with the progress Pip was making.

Chanel. Chanel had been with Pip the whole time, helping with the bingo, the set-up and then the wrap-up. But even if she thought the girl was involved in the murder, which she didn't, the timing didn't work. She couldn't have got to the site in time. As for the office – well, again, lots of people could have come in and out.

Her process of elimination was interrupted by another bolt from the blue. What if it wasn't dropped by the murderer? What if Cole had dropped it himself? Could the paper have fallen from his pocket? She thought back to her brief encounter with the man who was to become the focus of so much of her attention. While she was printing the second lot of cards, David and Charles were arguing outside. And then they'd stomped off. There was no way that David could have had one of the final set of bingo cards. He could possibly have picked up one of the first set of cards, the one Pip had photocopied the day before without realising that they all had to be different. Gazing at the random arrangement of numbers, she couldn't tell whether it was one of the original set she'd printed, or the later set. If she could figure that out, she could narrow down the time period in which this paper was dropped. Which would help her narrow down who it could be.

Pip had a brainwave. Mrs Jenkins had printed them off her computer. She'd be able to tell which of the bingo cards this was. She'd ask her second thing in the morning. First, she was going to track down the oral hygienist behind the environmental protest. Pip knew from experience that environmental protesters are not always what they seem.

CHAPTER 34

Luckily for Pip, when she phoned first thing the next morning, Alison Walters had just had a cancellation and could see her at lunchtime. Pip felt she needed to check the woman out – she was the only person who had so far been tagged as violent – and the only way she could think to do so at short notice was to go and get her teeth cleaned. She was overdue for a cleaning anyway.

As she put down the phone, Pip did observe to herself that violence wasn't really a quality she wanted in an oral hygienist. She hoped that Alison restricted her anger to dustbins and developers, and didn't unleash it on her patients. Pip herself had had a run-in with a dustbin, those golden few weeks when she'd driven the rubbish truck. Those bins are a lot more troublesome than they look, once you get to know them.

Pip grabbed her laptop bag, kissed the cats, and yelled her goodbyes to Tim who'd been at his desk since the early hours, or maybe the late hours of yesterday, she wasn't sure. All she knew was that he was on a hectic deadline for a project – the nature of which was secret, as usual. She had her own busy day ahead, what with the bingo paper and the oral hygienist.

'Running late, gotta go. See you for supper?'

There was a muffled grunt that she took for a yes.

'I'll cook,' she said.

Another indecipherable shout from behind the door. She took that for a thanks. The traffic was the usual mess, but fortunately, she didn't have anything pressing to do for now.

*

Most of the sports lessons took place later in the day. She had planned on spending the morning devising lesson plans – the obstacle course was a hard act to follow, but she was thinking of a fitness session based on the Macarena. She'd had that bad experience with the Macarena in the bar in Ibiza, though, and wasn't sure she wanted to relive it in front of a class full of teenage girls. Then again, she didn't have to actually participate.

Before she left for her appointment, Pip went into Mrs Jenkins's office, hoping not to run into Ms Peters, given the uncertain status of their relationship, but rather to run into Mrs Jenkins and ask her about the bingo papers. Mrs Jenkins was in her usual place behind her desk, staring at her computer with a frown.

'Mrs Jenkins?'

The older lady started at the sound of Pip's voice. 'Oh, it's you, dear,' she said, closing down the spreadsheet she'd had open. 'Just inputting marks. Always such a botheration.'

'Just wanted to let you know I'll be out for a bit. I have a dentist appointment.' Pip felt that sounded more urgent than the oral hygienist. She pulled her face slightly, in an odd pantomime intended to indicate toothache.

'Oh dear, poor you. Toothache is horrible. I can see you are a bit swollen,' said Mrs Jenkins. *Bloody cheek.* There was nothing wrong with her face!

'Oh, Mrs Jenkins, there's something you might be able to help me with,' said Pip, as if the thought had just struck her. 'Remember when we printed off those bingo papers? Remember the first set, the one I copied all the same? I saved it on your desktop to print. Could you look on your computer and see if it's this one?'

Leaning in to Mrs Jenkins, Pip pulled the heavily creased paper from her pocket and unfolded it.

'Where did that come from?' the older woman asked, uncharacteristically inquisitive, gesturing to the scrap.

'Found it lying around.'

'Oh, well, I think I deleted the file,' said Mrs Jenkins. 'I don't like to have documents cluttering my desktop.'

'There it is,' said Pip, who had eagle-eyed it on the top right of the screen. 'It says "Pip bingo".' Actually it said 'Pip bigno'. Pip was a horrible typist.

'Oh yes, there it is. How lucky,' said Mrs Jenkins. 'I thought I'd cleared everything off.'

She opened it, and Pip held her paper up against it. 'Not the same. Thank you.'

It was one of the second set of bingo cards. David Cole hadn't dropped the paper, then.

'Why did you want to know?' asked Mrs Jenkins,

'Oh, just a hunch I had. Nothing very interesting.'

Pip knew she sounded evasive, but Mrs Jenkins didn't pry further.

'Well, good luck with the dentist!'

'Thanks, Mrs Jenkins. I'll be back by the end of lunch break.'

Alison Walters's practice was in the village closest to the school, a mere five-minute drive. Pip enjoyed the windy little roads and the hedges, and the village with its main street of shops – boutiques and expensive restaurants mingling with the grocer's and the hardware shop and an old-fashioned toy shop. She was tempted to stop at Chanel's mother's bakery, which had a board clamouring 'Try our Chocolate Muffins!', but it felt rather at odds with the teeth-cleaning mission.

She found a parking place right outside the oral hygienist's office and went in with butterflies in her tummy – because of the teeth scraping, or the case, or the dangerous angry woman, she wasn't sure. Alison was standing at the reception desk, chatting to the receptionist in a perfectly pleasant manner. She looked very professional in her white coat, which was absolutely spotless; no sign of blood, gore or fire damage.

She introduced herself, smiling, and said, 'If you could just fill in the form with your details, I'll be ready for you.'

Pip scrawled her particulars, and went into the room with the dentist's chair and array of shining metal things.

'I feel like I've seen you somewhere,' Alison said.

Pip frowned as she positioned herself on the chair and leaned back. 'Funny, I thought I recognised you too. Maybe at the shops. Or the school? Do you have children at Hurlingham House? I work there.'

'I do, my daughter started there this year. I might have seen you at drop-off. Or the Fun Day.'

Pip felt a prickle of nervous excitement. That put her squarely at the scene of the crime. She could have been at the school and dropped the bingo card. And Pip knew that she had a history of violence.

Alison continued, 'Hang on, that's where I know you from. Weren't you at the protest over at the Marsh Field?'

'There you go,' said Pip, as if it had just come to her. 'That's probably it. In fact, I remember now! You had a megaphone. You were one of the organisers, weren't you?'

'Just one of many. We're not an official organisation, just concerned citizens.' Alison was very warm now that she'd established they were kindred spirits. She pushed the button that reclined the chair. Gosh, it was pleasant lying back like that. Pity she was going to have her teeth scraped.

Alison pulled on a mask and reached for one of the shiny instruments. 'I'm going to start with the scaling.'

'I'd love to hear more about what's happening with the development on that field. I'm totally with you on this one – it would be such a pity to lose it to housing. We need to take a strong stand,' Pip said. 'I'll shut up now, but you go on.'

Alison explained about Betterworld Developers and the Marsh Field, which Pip of course knew.

'It's a very important area, with the frogs and so on.'

'Gursh uh her whoo.'

'They really don't need to build right there – there are other places, less sensitive.'

'Oh hhhgnin.'

'It makes me furious that they can get away with this destructive, greedy behaviour,' Alison said, digging under Pip's gums.

Pip nodded encouragingly, making what she thought was an agreeable gurgling noise in the throat. This was what she was hoping for. Fury.

Alison scraped away. Pip wished she hadn't drunk quite so much coffee.

'Hhhhmph. Red wine, coffee, tea,' Alison said, disapprovingly. 'You should try to cut down, or at least brush after drinking. Or even rinse.' Pip couldn't imagine any of that happening.

There was a break in the conversation while Alison went at Pip's teeth with a high-speed electric toothbrush, whilst suctioning water from the back of her mouth. She was gentle and thorough. Pip shuddered recalling some of her previous dental experiences, most notably the blacksmith/dentist who had proffered his services when she'd broken a tooth in Nepal. Finally, Alison finished and sent Pip to the basin to rinse with the lurid pink water.

'Great job, thanks,' said Pip, wiping. 'Hardly any blood and gore. Didn't hurt a bit.'

'It shouldn't. I generally believe that you can get further with gentleness than force.'

'Well, maybe not where greedy property developers are concerned.' Pip hoped this sounded like a casual observation rather than a call to war.

Alison laughed. 'Even there! Look, I can get a bit worked up about that, no question – although I'm really trying to keep my cool these days. But the only thing that's going to put a stop to this over-development is changing public sentiment. We need to inform and mobilise the community. That's what the rallies are about.'

'Is it enough though?' Pip asked. 'I mean, talking and singing is all well and good, but we're dealing with a very powerful enemy. They only understand force. I can see why protesters are tempted to break things and burn stuff.'

'Oh dear, don't mention burning,' Alison said, reddening with embarrassment. 'There was an accident with a dustbin once. I tossed a bunch of the developer's brochures into the bin and someone threw a cigarette in afterwards. The ink must have been highly flammable because the whole thing went up. I tried to stomp it out but it was too hot. The burning papers went everywhere. The grass was burned. What a mess. I still feel awful about that, destroying public property and putting people in danger. Not at all the sort of example I want to set. I insisted on reimbursing the council, of course. You'd be welcome to join us, but absolutely no violence or destruction of property will be tolerated, we're quite clear on that.'

Another thing that was quite clear was that she'd hit another dead end, thought Pip on the winding drive back to the school. Alison was not some violent madwoman who would stop at nothing to get her way. If she was still feeling bad about the accidental burning of a dustbin, it was very unlikely she had it in her to murder a man in cold blood. Even to save a pristine piece of marshland from destruction.

Back at her desk, Pip opened her laptop to find an email from Mrs Jenkins.

I hope the dentist wasn't too awful! Please pop by my office before you leave. I have a little something for you. Jacqueline.

Jacqueline, well who'd have thought? In fact, Pip had never given a moment's consideration to Mrs Jenkins's first name. She was one of those women who just seemed to have been born a Mrs.

After a thoroughly exhausting afternoon of the Macarena – not that Pip danced herself, of course, not after Ibiza, but it was exhausting just watching – Pip went to collect the promised 'little something'.

'Home-made Thai curried pumpkin and coconut soup,' said Mrs Jenkins, smiling and handing over a tub. 'Ms Peters made a big batch and brought it in for our lunch. There was more than enough for two and when I mentioned that you were going to the dentist, Ms Peters insisted I give you some.'

'That's very kind of her, and of you, thank you,' said Pip, genuinely touched by the gesture, especially when Ms Peters had been so cross with her before.

'Well, I know you're on your own and I know how it feels to come home after a long and difficult day and have to rustle up a meal for one.'

Pip felt sorry for herself in Mrs Jenkins's picture, forgetting for a moment that she came home to dishy Tim. 'Well, I do have—'

'Cats, I know! Wonderful company but not much help when it comes to cooking,' Mrs Jenkins said, with a giggle.

It had never occurred to Pip that Mrs Jenkins had a sense of humour. In fact, she'd given very little thought to Mrs Jenkins at all, something she felt momentarily bad about now that she'd shown her such kindness.

'You are so right. They are hopeless in the kitchen.'

'Well, don't give them any of that soup – it's quite spicy, not good for cats at all.'

'I won't. Thank you, Mrs Jenkins… Jacqueline… And please thank Ms Peters for me. I'm looking forward to supper.'

She remembered that when she'd left that morning she'd promised to cook supper for herself and Tim. She looked at the soup and wondered if it would stretch to two. It would do if she made a couple of cheese toasties, she thought, and they both loved those. Dinner sorted. Easy.

CHAPTER 35

They were like two zombies, she and Tim. He had been working full tilt for days, up half the night and early in the morning, catching a few hours of sleep in between long hours at his computer. As usual, he couldn't tell her the details of his work in securing companies' websites against hackers and thieves.

She was more forthcoming about her investigations into the death of David Cole, less so about her progress on the exam scam. She'd rather let it slide, what with the murder investigation, and Ms Peters's unavailability. And now the website seemed to have gone completely quiet.

'It's not quite wrapped up, but close, and I'm confident Claire's name will be cleared,' she said brightly, putting the soup into a pot to warm. 'Any day now, really.' She took out the cheese. 'Can you be trusted with a grater?' she asked Tim, who was sitting at the table, staring dully at nothing. 'Or are you too tired for sharp objects?'

'I wouldn't trust myself with a chainsaw but I think I can handle the grater.'

She cut four slices of bread while he grated a pile of lurid yellow cheese.

'Mayo,' she said, slathering it onto the outside of the bread. 'The secret of my sandwich success.'

She dropped the bread into a sizzling pan and sprinkled salt and pepper onto the mayonnaise.

'How are you not obese?' he asked in wonder.

'No one knows. It's a mystery.'

'Well, you're very lucky to look so great on fried mayonnaise,' he said.

She blushed as she stirred the steaming soup. She never quite knew if he was flirting or flattering or just being nice.

Tim poured the soup into two cups while she lifted the sandwiches onto plates and cut them in half. They both perked up at the steaming soup, fragrant with coconut, and the oily, cheesy toasties.

'Why don't we watch a movie tonight?' she said, in between spoonfuls. 'Give ourselves the night off, pick some silly romantic comedy, veg out.'

'I don't know, I should be working... But what the heck, let's do it. I'll see what's on,' he said, picking up his phone.

'It's got to be real trash though. Not some romantic French thing full of lingering glances and lingering lingerie. I want laughs. Mistaken identities. Missed trains.'

'Mmhh-mmhh, got you,' he said, chewing and scrolling and nodding. He swallowed. 'Ah, "When a lovelorn ghost from the 1920s moves into yoga teacher Savannah's studio..."'

'That'll do...'

'Or else we've got, "When Walter took his four huskies to Central Park, little did he know that..."'

'Huskies? Fine with me...'

'Oh, hang on. "Recovering from a break-up, Rosa wins a trip to a tropical island. On her first windsurfing lesson, a freak storm deposits her and the very annoying hot surf teacher on a tiny..."'

'Ooooh. Sounds good. They hate each other, right?'

'Oh yes, I'm sure. He's super annoying.'

'And he's super hot?'

'Yes, also super hot,' he said, holding his phone up to show her the poster, which featured an actual living Ken doll with a six pack so defined it might have been made of plastic.

'That's the one. Although I'm so tired I don't know how I'll keep my eyes open.'

'Did you *see* those abs?' Tim smiled, teasing Pip. She considered making a few suggestions about his own abs, but didn't have the energy.

'OK, maybe I can stay awake,' she said with a smile.

'I'm exhausted too.' Tim yawned. 'My head's swimming. Let's get this thing started.'

They made a mug of tea each and moved to the sofa. He pointed the remote control at the TV and up came the titles.

Pip felt herself drifting off, the words of the title scrolling blurrily in front of her drooping eyes, her head pulled down with an invisible weight to Tim's shoulder. She tried to force her eyelids open and lift her head, but she was too exhausted. She felt herself slipping down, down, down into a deep and dreamless sleep.

She was woken by movement. The pillow was moving. She reached out her hand to steady it and felt something firm, and not at all pillow-like. Her eyes fluttered, but closed again in the bright sunlight pouring through the window. She'd glimpsed denim. Another attempt at opening her eyes showed a button and a buckle. She forced her eyes to stay open long enough to help her confused brain process where she was. Her head was on a leg, a thigh. The leg was moving. She reached up, her hand feeling something silky… fabric… bare skin.

Someone groaned, a yawn.

'Pip.' Tim's voice came swimming towards her.

She lifted her head and looked up. He was sprawled on the sofa and she was lying on his lap. His arm was heavy on her shoulder, her hand up his shirt against his waist.

The feel of skin on skin jolted them both fully awake. Pip pulled her hand back, inadvertently running it over Tim's thigh. In embarrassment, she jerked her body away from him, just as he retreated to his corner of the sofa. Pip slipped inelegantly off the sofa onto the carpet with a soft thud. She was at eye level with his knees, and noticed a wet mark where she must have drooled on him in her sleep. Pip flushed in confusion and mortification. She had occasionally fantasised about waking up in Tim's arms, but in her dreams she hadn't left a patch of drool on his jeans. Actually, in her fantasies he mostly wasn't wearing jeans.

They looked at each other in shock and began speaking, their words tumbling over each other. 'I'm sorry… What happened… I must have fallen asleep… Did I… Were we…?'

Pip got up off the floor and staggered to the armchair across from Tim. The TV screen was frozen on the credits, Tim's laptop still attached with its cable. Two mugs of tea sat untouched and stone cold on the coffee table.

What had happened last night? Her head was thick and heavy as she grappled for a memory. They'd had supper. She struggled to remember what had happened after that, but her brain wouldn't cooperate. The movie, they'd watched a movie. She couldn't remember a thing about it.

'Did we even start the movie?' she asked. 'I remember sitting down…'

'I think so.' Tim rubbed his face and scratched his head, mussing his mussy hair. 'I must have been exhausted, I just passed out.'

'Me too. Crazy. One minute we're having supper and the next… Well, here we are. I feel like I've been run over by a stea—' She stopped herself just in time, remembering that in fact someone she knew had recently – and not metaphorically – been run over by a steamroller. 'A bus.'

He shook his head, as if trying to clear a fog. 'Me too. Actually, I feel like I've been on a bender. Are we sure we didn't accidentally have a bottle of tequila?' he joked weakly. 'And maybe a handful of Xanax? Because that's what it feels like to me.'

'Soup and toasties. We didn't even have any wine,' she said, rubbing her throbbing temples. 'This reminds me of the time when I was working at the cattle ranch, and I accidentally took a horse pill instead of my multivitamin. Completely passed out for most of a day. I felt like death when I woke up. Couldn't remember a thing. It was like my head was full of cotton wool and sharp objects.'

'I'll make some coffee,' he said, without moving from his position, slumped on the sofa.

'Good idea,' she said, not moving either.

She closed her eyes, just for a moment. Five minutes, she told herself, then she would hit the shower. And with that, she fell back into a deep sleep.

Pip woke to the sound of cups clattering, the tap running, the fridge opening – the familiar sound of Tim making coffee in the kitchen. Next came the smells – coffee, of course, and the delicious aroma of lightly burnt toast.

She stretched and yawned, to the annoyance of Most who had taken advantage of the presence of a dead-to-the-world human, and was stretched out across her lap with her head dangling off Pip's knee. Checking her watch, Pip saw she'd been asleep for nearly an hour.

Tim came through from the kitchen. 'I was just coming to wake you,' he said. 'Breakfast's ready.'

Pip followed him into the kitchen and eagerly sipped her coffee, feeling bad about staining her newly cleaned gnashers, but savouring the taste and the delightful anticipation of the hot caffeine and sugar hitting her bloodstream.

'Great coffee – thanks, Tim.'

'How are you feeling?'

'Bit dopey, bit queasy, but much better. You?'

'Yeah, same. Feeling mostly OK now. I fell asleep again too. I wonder if we're coming down with something. A flu, maybe.'

Slathering strawberry jam onto her toast, Pip considered his suggestion. 'Doesn't feel like a flu. Feels more like a gas leak. Or something we ate or drank. I felt almost drugged.'

When she said it, she was simply describing the feeling. But as soon as the words came out of her mouth, she recognised them as true. 'Tim,' she said, sitting bolt upright. 'Do you think we could have been drugged?'

'Pip, come on…'

'Seriously, think about it. We both passed out just about comatose. When we woke up hours later we had no memory of the evening before, and we felt like death warmed up. We felt drugged.'

'But with what? And by whom?'

It didn't take more than a few steps back into her blurry memory to work out what had happened. They'd had nothing but tea to drink. They'd eaten the same cheese and the bread the day before with no ill effect.

'It must have been the soup.'

Tim stared at her in disbelief. 'Really? You think so?'

'It's the only thing I can think of, and… Oh my God.' Pip turned ice cold. 'Tim! The accidents. The falling flowerpot. The electric shock. Tim, I think someone is trying to kill me.'

CHAPTER 36

'Think about it,' she said to Tim. 'The soup would have been a generous serving for one, and I shared it between the two of us. We each only ingested half the intended amount of whatever drug it was.'

'Oh God, imagine if you'd eaten it all.'

'I know.' Pip shuddered to think that the full dose might have been enough to kill her.

'Who gave you the soup, and why, and how?' said Tim, shaking his head in disbelief.

Pip explained about her visit to the angry environmentalist tooth cleaner, which raised a smile from Tim, even in the dire current circumstances. 'Honestly, Pip, the things you get up to.'

She explained that Mrs Jenkins had given her the soup from Ms Peters.

'So are you saying that Ms Peters tried to poison you?' he asked.

'I'm not saying... I don't know... It seems impossible.' She shook her head. 'And why? Something to do with Cole? Or... No, just no.'

'I hear you – she doesn't seem like a candidate for murder. I don't know her well, but after our meeting, I can't believe... And Mrs Jenkins?'

Pip shook her head. 'You've seen Mrs Jenkins. She's the archetypal school secretary. Efficient, competent, keeps everything running smoothly behind the scenes. She's been at the school forever and is going to retire at the end of the year. There's no way she would... I mean, why would anyone?'

She heard the panicky shrillness in her voice, her throat tight. She took a breath and said, more calmly, 'I'm wondering if someone else might have tampered with the soup? It was kept in the staffroom fridge. Someone might have overheard them talking, known it was for me.'

'Someone like who?' Tim asked.

'Another teacher? I don't know. I'm not thinking straight…' She shook her head to clear the fog.

They sat quietly, each in their own thoughts. Pip let her breathing calm, and her brain followed. Instead of scrabbling through the slim information she had on the events of the last twenty-four hours, she needed a new approach.

'Let's go back a bit,' she said. 'It started with the flowerpot… In fact, no, it started before that with the leak to the newspaper. That was the first attempt to get me out of the picture. Then the flowerpot, then the exposed wires in the plug socket, and now this.'

'Someone's getting increasingly desperate to get you off the scene.'

'Exactly. That must mean I'm getting close.'

'Close to what?'

'To finding out who killed David Cole?'

'Are you sure that this is about Cole? That it has nothing to do with the exam scam? Because, Pip, I don't want you to get hurt over that. I brought you into it but I never thought it would get dangerous.'

She waved his objections away. 'It's nothing to do with that. No one would try and kill me over some schoolgirls cheating on their exam. Besides, I'm pretty sure one of the girls is involved in it, and a sixteen-year-old girl is probably the least likely profile for a murderer.'

There was a pause at the word 'murderer'.

'What else do you know about who might have done this to you? Anything at all.'

'The soup came from Ms Peters. Mrs Jenkins said she'd actually handed it over herself.' Pip tried to picture what could have happened. Anything that wouldn't point the way it all seemed to be pointing.

She didn't want to admit it, she could hardly bear the thought, but she was rapidly running out of options, clues and leads. All signs were pointing in the same direction. She racked her brain, searching for other possibilities, other suspects. Reasons why it couldn't be.

Tim watched her, waiting, biding his time. She sighed, slowly acknowledging to herself the only possible answer. 'I guess… I mean… I can't imagine, but it must be…'

He nodded.

'Oh, bloody hell.'

'I know. I'm sorry.'

'Alexandra Peters tried to kill me.'

'It's unbelievable,' he said. 'As in, I can't believe it. Except…'

'Except that it's the only thing that makes sense, I know,' said Pip. She felt wide awake now; the adrenaline coursing through her veins was enough to take the edge off the hangover of Ms Peters's poisonous soup.

'The flowerpot.' Pip smacked her hand down on the kitchen table, startling Most who had been snoozing in the empty fruit bowl. 'There's only one route down to the car park, so that was an obvious move, probably spontaneous. The first attempt was probably spur of the moment. Maybe she just thought she'd injure me, put me out of action. Next…' She smacked her hand down on the table again, pleased with the effect. Most eased herself out of the fruit bowl and, with a look of disdain, leapt off the table. 'Then the electrocution. Obviously, she knows my office, knows where I work, the layout, the electrics. And that was a more serious attempt. I could have died. Seriously.' Smack. 'Then she sent me the soup. Who knows what was in it. A handful of tranqs. A mixed bag raided from the medicine closet in the secretary's office. Maybe Ms Peters has a drug habit of her own.'

She pushed herself back in the kitchen chair, leaning against the ladder back, until it was balanced on its back legs. She stayed there, suspended in space and thought.

Then she rocked forward, the chair legs smacking to the ground.

'Come on,' she said.

'Come where?'

She stood up. 'We are going to go finish this thing.'

CHAPTER 37

'And by finish this thing you mean…'

'I know what's going on, but I don't have actual evidence. I need to confront Ms Peters with what I know, get her to spill the beans on the murder.'

'How?'

'I'm working on it. I'll tell you in the car. Let's go.'

'But I need a shower. And you do too – have you seen yourself?'

Pip sighed. James Bond never got held up with the need to shower or use the toilet, but it always seemed to happen to her.

'OK,' she said. 'You go first.'

While Tim went to steam up the bathroom with his steamy presence and his steamy shower, Pip put the sofa cushions back in place and straightened up the coffee table. She picked up the mugs of cold tea and took them to the kitchen.

The television screen was filled with a fuzzy static that was disturbing to her addled brain. She rooted around for the remote and turned it off, then unplugged Tim's laptop.

As she lifted the laptop, she must have hit a key because the screen came to life. She wasn't snooping, really she wasn't, but a familiar name jumped out at her – Chanel Winters. She looked again. More names.

Rizwana.

Ruby.

Amelia.

It was a list of the girls in Claire's class. She glanced at the open tabs along the top of the screen: 'class list' and 'mark order'.

'Your turn,' called Tim, emerging from the bathroom with wafts of sandalwood steam. She didn't even try to cop a peek at his damp torso, just slammed the laptop closed and dropped it onto the coffee table.

'Thanks, coming.'

In the shower, she thought about what she'd seen. It seemed that Tim had been in the Hurlingham House computer system. But how? He was a hacker, after all, so the how was probably not that difficult. He'd said himself that schools often had lousy security. The bigger question was why? What would he be doing there?

Pip shampooed her hair, gradually replacing Tim's sandalwood scent with her own favourite, lemon blossom and almond.

She fleetingly entertained the thought that Tim was somehow involved in the exam scam, but that was ridiculous, she told herself, squeezing a blob of conditioner into her hand. Tim was one of the good guys. He was the one who protected a company's computer system, who kept the bad guys out. Besides, he'd brought her in to help clear Claire's name, she thought, massaging her scalp vigorously with her fingertips. There must be an explanation. She just needed to think of it.

The unwelcome thought kept coming back. As she soaped her shoulders. As she rinsed the conditioner from her hair. What was Tim doing in the school's computer system? He had been very busy of late, and quite secretive about his mystery client – maybe it wasn't a client at all, maybe he was busy with something else. Like managing his side hustle – selling exam papers. *Don't be ridiculous*, she told herself. The site was down, in any event. But the dark suspicions kept surfacing. She thought about Claire. If Tim was involved, what was Claire's role? Accomplice? Innocent bystander?

It didn't make sense. Tim had asked Pip to get involved. With the hot water pounding down on her shoulders, she tried to work through the logic. Assuming he was behind it all, Tim knew that Claire hadn't cheated, that her improved mark was the result of hard work. He must have felt guilty to have got her caught up in his scam. So he'd brought Pip in. He knew he could keep an eye on her, hear about what she'd uncovered. Perhaps he felt Pip wasn't smart enough to bust his clever scam, she thought, with a mixture of shame and sadness.

Her brain was still foggy from the soup. Her thoughts were as slippery as the soap and swirled like the sudsy water at her feet. She needed to think this through before she spoke to Tim.

Clean, dressed and somewhat more human – if still riddled with confusion – she joined him in the sitting room. Most was wedged between his thigh and the arm of the sofa and was purring blissfully, his ribcage rising and falling in time to Tim's long, firm strokes. He was so loving with the cats, surely he couldn't be a criminal? Also, he was so cute. He was quite smartly dressed in a pale blue button-down shirt that set off his dark hair to great effect. He looked neat and eager and dear and helpful, and Pip felt bad even thinking that he might be involved in something illegal. Still, better to be safe than sorry.

'I was thinking, it's probably better if I talk to Alexandra Peters alone. It's kind of you to offer to come with me, but really, there's no need.'

In surprise, Tim stopped stroking Most. The cat opened her eyes and gave Pip a furious glare – she knew who was to blame for this outrage.

'Pip, if you suspect Ms Peters is dangerous, you can't see her alone,' Tim said, with a frown of concern.

'I'll go to her office and talk to her there. Mrs Jenkins will be right outside. The admin block is busy. There's no danger. I'll tell her what I know, and record her response on my phone. Then we can go to the police with it.'

'I should come with you.'

'No – if you're there, she's less likely to say anything incriminating.'

'Pip, I'm coming.'

'No. I want to do it alone. It's important to me.'

'OK, fine. You go,' he said curtly. 'I'll see you later.'

She felt awful for hurting his feelings, but she didn't want him around until she'd figured out what was going on and what his role was. In the car on the way to school, she ran through a scenario in which Tim was behind the exam scam. 'Just hypothetically,' she told herself. 'A thought experiment.'

So, if Tim had hacked into the school computer system, he would be able to access all the teachers' work, in particular the tests and exams they set. He could easily take his pick of which ones to offer. He would also know all the girls' marks, and their email addresses. So he could monitor who was using his papers, and whether they were using them according to the rules. The website, the Bitcoin payment system and setting up a hard-to-trace IP address would be well within his capabilities.

Just because he could, doesn't mean he did, said the disbelieving part of her brain.

But I saw those open tabs, her more suspicious self retorted. If he wasn't running the scam, what was he doing with those documents? She couldn't think of any reason. Not a single one.

CHAPTER 38

Pulling into the car park, Pip tried to put the exam scam out of her mind and focus on the job at hand: confronting Ms Peters about the attempts on her life. She felt a prickle of apprehension, even fear, at the thought. She parked the car and pulled her bag into her lap, searching for her phone. She went into the voice note function and did a test recording: '*I met a traveller from a something land who said... blah blah blah.*' It played back fine. She tested it again, this time with the phone in her jacket pocket, continuing the verse: '*Two vast and something something of stone...*' She played it back. Still audible.

Walking to the office, Pip kept a sharp eye out for falling objects, trip wires, snakes, open pits covered with sticks and grass. She felt positively paranoid after her near misses, her heart pounding at the possible dangers, and at the thought of having to confront Ms Peters. Having made it to the office without mishap, she found Mrs Jenkins's desk empty and the head's door open, her office empty too.

She sat and waited, her heart rate slowing. She couldn't wait all day, she thought after a few minutes. She'd leave a note. Mrs Jenkins's desk was so neat and tidy, Pip couldn't even find a stray pencil or piece of paper. The pen cup held no pens – presumably because they were constantly being nicked by passing visitors – just a ruler, a nail file and a lethal-looking letter opener. Not much help opening emails, she thought, smiling inwardly at her own joke. She reached for the letter opener, felt the comforting weight of it in her hand, and on impulse put it into her pocket. There had been three attempts on her life already. Who knew how the meeting with Ms Peters would go?

She went round to the other side of the desk, where Mrs Jenkins would sit, and took a piece of paper from the printer. The desk's big central drawer was locked, so Pip felt around the smaller drawers looking for something to write with. Pip was amused to find an adult colouring-in book and a packet of luridly coloured gel pens tucked at the back. She smiled to herself at the thought of Mrs Jenkins waiting out the last months until her retirement, sneaking quiet moments to colour in scenes of flowers and birds and butterflies, fish and coral, a unicorn grazing in a meadow, in neon pink and luminous yellow. On the cover of the colouring book you could see little squiggles, each the shape of a curly 'J', where Mrs Jenkins must have tested out the colour of the pens. Really, it was so sweet.

Pip took one of the more legible, less ridiculously hued gel pens – a bright green – to write a note.

I need to see you. It's important. I've figured everything out. Call me when you're back in the office. Pip

The ink had tiny bits of glitter in it – hardly the professional look Pip would like to create – but she folded the note, wrote Alexandra Peters's name on the front, and left it in the centre of the headmistress's desk, where it wouldn't be missed.

While she folded the paper, she picked up her phone to call Tim. She knew she needed to confront him too, but she was avoiding it. She opened her contacts and hesitated. She'd talk to Claire instead, sound the girl out. She must know what Tim was up to. She would probably spill all the details if confronted. Realising that Claire wouldn't pick up – she'd be in class – Pip left her a voice note: 'Claire, it's Pip. I know what's going on with the exam papers. I think you know, too. We need to talk urgently. Call me.'

Pip sent the note and turned to leave Ms Peters's office, finding herself face to face with Mrs Jenkins who must have come in without her noticing. Pip gave a little shriek – her nerves were shot after the events of the week – and Mrs Jenkins looked just as startled, her mouth open in an O on a fast intake of breath.

Pip recovered first. 'Oh! Mrs Jenkins, there you are. Sorry if I gave you a fright. I was looking for Ms Peters. I need to see her. I left a note,' she said, gesturing to it on the desk.

Poor Mrs Jenkins was still flustered. 'See Ms Peters? I'll let her know,' she said faintly, her face pale.

'Are you all right?'

'Just need a minute,' the older woman said, breathing heavily. 'I didn't expect to see you. I… I didn't know anyone was here.'

'Sorry,' said Pip again, and waited awkwardly while Mrs Jenkins got her breath back.

'I'm fine now. Thank you,' said Mrs Jenkins, patting her chest. 'Ms Peters is at the Marsh Field with the environmental assessment people. I'll let her know you're looking for her.'

'OK, I'll be in my office,' said Pip. 'Please phone me if she can see me. I'll come back.'

Pip took another tentative walk, her senses still on high alert. As she entered her office, she looked up to make sure there was nothing perched on the top of the door, poised to brain her. She carefully avoided touching any electrical cables. She reached for the half KitKat she'd left on her desk drawer the day before, but thought better of it and chucked it in the bin. She hated the prickling feeling of dread that was now her constant companion. If Ms Peters was trying to kill her, she needed to hear it herself, and understand why. And if it was, as she suspected, to do with David Cole's murder, she'd hand over everything she knew to the police and get on with her life.

Her phone rang. It was the school switchboard number. Mrs Jenkins greeted her, sounding like her usual efficient self. 'Hello,

Pip. Ms Peters can see you this morning. She's still busy with the environmental impact people at the Marsh Field. She asks if you can meet her there at twelve.'

Pip agreed, relieved to be meeting her out in the open. Just in case.

'It looks like rain, apparently. She suggests you meet at the site office in case it's wet.'

As she got up to leave for her meeting, Pip wished she had a better weapon than the letter opener. Not a gun, of course; someone as clumsy as Pip should never touch a gun, as Mummy pointed out after that incident when her uncle Edmond had taken the girls clay pigeon shooting. Fortunately, his foot had healed quite well after the surgery.

Mace, that would be good. Except she didn't have any. Pip went through her gym bag and her cupboard, looking for likely items for self-defence. She found a small spray-on deodorant, Fresh Summer Breeze. Better than nothing. She put the deodorant in her other pocket, feeling rather silly but slightly better prepared. At least she was sensibly dressed in her tracksuit trousers and gym shoes and denim jacket. She could run if she had to. Although she hoped not to. She thought longingly of the half KitKat – the sugar would be welcome – but again decided against it. Time to go and confront Ms Peters and find out the truth.

CHAPTER 39

The door of the site office was ajar. Pip approached from the side, hoping to peek into the little wooden office before Ms Peters saw her. She didn't know what she would find, but felt that the element of surprise was always preferable to the element of surprised.

As she neared the door, she heard footsteps, as if someone was pacing the wooden floorboards. Interesting. Was Ms Peters nervous of Pip's arrival? The figure moved away from the door and back, away and back. Pip inched closer, and as Ms Peters moved towards the door this time, she glimpsed her. Except that it wasn't Ms Peters. The school uniform. Those dark plaits.

'Claire!' she said, blowing her cover and causing the girl to jump about a foot in the air and squeak like a parrot.

'Pip!'

'What are you doing here?'

'I don't know. Ms Peters asked me to meet her here at noon. I don't know why. Why does she want to see me?'

This was a good question. Why was Claire here?

Pip had asked to meet Ms Peters, but Ms Peters didn't know why. She might have thought it was about the exam scam. Had she somehow found out that Tim was involved in it too? Maybe she wanted to confront Claire about that, with Pip.

'Did you get my voice note?' Pip asked.

The girl shook her head. 'Haven't listened yet. I had to rush to get here in time.'

'Claire, I know Tim's involved in the exam scam. I know he hacked into the school's computer system. I think Ms Peters must have found out too and that's why she wants to see you.'

'Tim? Involved with a scam?' Claire snorted in disbelief. 'Never. He's, like, the best.'

'I'm sorry, I know it's hard to think about your brother being caught up in something like that, but I saw his computer, Claire. He had tabs open with all the class marks and things. It's no use denying it, I know he's involved.'

Claire sighed. 'There's an explanation,' she said.

'Yes, your brother has turned out to be another disappointment in the long list of disappointments that I call my life. But there's no time for that now.'

'That's not true,' Claire said, leaping to her brother's defence. 'Tim must have had a good reason for looking at those marks. The only possible explanation is that he wanted to help me. And to help you. That must be why he was on the website.'

Pip sighed. It made sense. More sense than Tim being a criminal. Pip herself had rather dropped the ball on the exam scam investigation once she'd started looking into the murder – and then she'd had her own brushes with death. Maybe he had just been doing a bit of investigating on his own. He had, after all, actually told her that he would look into the website. And Pip had assumed the worst! This was even worse than the time she'd been working at Harrods in the fish department and accused Beyoncé of being a secret shopper. It was the huge sunglasses that confused her.

She felt terrible about having doubted Tim. Good, wonderful, sexy, helpful Tim. It must have been those drugs in her system, making her paranoid. That and the repeated attempts on her life. Of course the father of her kittens would never run an exam scam. Just as soon as she'd confronted her would-be murderer, she'd clear the air with him, explain why she ran out this morning. Which reminded her. A would-be murderer, and also possibly the actual murderer of David Cole, was on her way to meet Pip as they spoke, and now Claire was here. Pip couldn't have the girl here when she confronted Ms Peters. It wasn't safe.

'You should go, Claire,' Pip said. 'It's all a misunderstanding. I'll explain the whole thing to Ms Peters.'

Claire argued feebly while Pip reached into her pocket for her phone. She pulled it out, along with the crumpled bingo sheet. She thought, fleetingly, that she was right back in almost the exact place where she'd found it. What an odd coincidence. Ms Peters had been one of the few people with access to the bingo sheets. It had served its purpose as a clue. She tossed the paper to the floor and looked at her phone. It was 11.55. Ms Peters would be here in five minutes. Claire needed to go.

Claire was wringing her hands. 'But Ms Peters... She's the headmistress and she said I must meet her... I don't know...I need to stay and see her. You can explain things and then we can go.'

Pip was feeling panicky. The exam scam was irrelevant: Ms Peters was a very dangerous woman. She needed to get Claire out of there.

'Claire, go. Go on, quickly, before she gets here.'

What had Pip been thinking, coming here to this remote spot to meet a murderer? That they'd have a little chat and Pip would leave with a confession recorded on her phone? This was typical of the ridiculous thinking that had got her stranded on top of the Eiffel Tower that New Year's Eve. She really needed to stop being so impulsive. Things could go badly meeting a possible murderer. And now Claire was tangled up in it.

'I dunno...' Claire said, not moving. 'I mean, why don't I just wait?'

Teenagers were so tiring, Pip thought, dropping her head in her hands and taking a deep breath that was meant to be calming but was on the way to hyperventilation.

Looking down at the floor, she caught a glimpse of something sparkly. It was on the bingo paper that she'd just dropped. A little squiggle on the back of the sheet, as if someone was trying out a pen, or scribbling to get the ink flowing. It was a pink squiggle, gel, shot through with glitter. It looked strangely familiar.

The colouring-in book. Mrs Jenkins's gel pens. But why would Ms Peters have a bingo card with a mark from one of Mrs Jenkins's pens? They weren't lying around. Pip had only found them because she'd been desperate for a pen, and looked in the drawers.

Unless it wasn't Ms Peters at all.

She looked more closely. The squiggle was in the shape of a curly 'J', the same shape that Mrs Jenkins had doodled on the cover of her colouring-in book. What if the bingo sheet Pip had found at the scene of the murder wasn't dropped by Ms Peters? What if it was dropped by Mrs Jenkins?

'Claire, who asked you to come to this meeting?'

'Ms Peters.'

'Ms Peters herself?'

'Yes. Well, not her exactly – Mrs Jenkins, the secretary.'

'She phoned me too,' said Pip, thinking aloud.

Pip's blood ran cold as she realised the full extent of what she had discovered. Ms Peters hadn't lured them here – Mrs Jenkins had.

Mrs Jenkins was behind the exam paper scam. Mrs Jenkins had read Pip's note to Ms Peters, and assumed that Pip had worked it out. She had lured Pip to this meeting at the site office. But why was Claire there?

Pip thought back. Mrs Jenkins had overheard her on the phone to Claire. What was it Pip had said? *I know what's going on with the exam papers. I think you know, too. We need to talk urgently.* Mrs Jenkins would assume that Claire knew about it too.

Mrs Jenkins had dropped the bingo card in the steamroller. She had killed David Cole. She had already tried to kill Pip three times. Pip and Claire were in terrible danger. 'Claire, get out. Get out now and phone Tim. Quick. You've got to go now.'

'It's too late for that, I'm afraid, dear,' came a voice from behind them.

It was Mrs Jenkins. She filled the doorway, dressed, as always, in the neat skirt and blouse, the sensible pumps with a low wedge heel, the low-maintenance haircut, the string of small pearls around her neck – but there was something different about her. She was standing up straighter and there was a look of determination on her face. Usually Mrs Jenkins faded into the background, but this Mrs Jenkins could never fade into anything. This Mrs Jenkins was a whole new ball game.

'Good morning, Mrs Jenkins.' Pip smiled. Maybe she hadn't overheard anything. Maybe Pip had this all wrong. Either way, how hard could it be for her and Claire to just walk away? This wasn't the Eiffel Tower after all.

'I was just saying to Claire that there was a misunderstanding about her exam results. Nothing that can't be sorted out, though,' Pip said, as calmly as she could manage. She took a step to the side, pulling Claire's arm, in the hope that they could slip past Mrs Jenkins. If she could pretend that this was all about the exams, and not let on that she had Mrs Jenkins pegged as the murderer, perhaps this could all be resolved without drama. 'But obviously nothing to do with you,' she added, with her most ingratiating smile.

Mrs Jenkins's face was a sneering mask. 'Oh, don't try and feed me a line, you silly woman. We both know you're investigating the exam scam.'

This took Pip by surprise. She was pretty sure that Mrs Jenkins had known nothing about the real reason Pip was at the school. But Mrs Jenkins was not what she seemed and she clearly knew a lot more than she let on – listening at doors, snooping at emails. Pip turned towards the door, gesturing to Claire to follow. 'Well, I'm sure you'll sort that out with Ms Peters. None of our business. We must be going.'

'Stop right there.'

Her voice was so authoritative that they did. They stopped in their tracks. Although Mrs Jenkins was about sixty, not exactly an imposing woman, and Pip and Claire could doubtless take her in a fight if they had to, there was something about her, some steely resolve, some underlying menace, that made Pip pause.

'Yes, I was running the exam scam,' Mrs Jenkins said casually. 'I must say, I thought you'd worked it out long ago. When you used the ridiculous name "Sally Llama", I admit I was stumped. I knew there was no girl in the school called Sally, let alone Llama. I thought maybe a girl was having a laugh at first. Girls are so tiresome. God, I hate them.' Mrs Jenkins shot a look of loathing at Claire, while Pip thought about what she'd just revealed.

'But then I told you about my mother's llamas, and Sally Llama actually came to the fete,' said Pip, remembering.

'Exactly. And then I knew what you and Alexandra had been gossiping about in her office all that time, without me. Thinking that I was just some stupid secretary. Bitches.'

'You realised I was investigating the exam scam.'

'Actually, I thought you'd have it all figured out pretty quickly after that. I gave you too much credit, it seems. Or, you gave me too little.'

That second part was true. Pip hadn't for one moment thought that sweet, efficient Mrs Jenkins might be behind the scam. She'd underestimated her abilities, too. 'You're great with computers. You have access to all the marks, and you observe the girls every day. You were the perfect person to run such a scheme. You knew how to get the information into the right hands, and how to manage it so that nobody cheated so much that they got caught. You knew which girls had the money, and which girls needed the marks.'

Mrs Jenkins looked almost proud. 'Yes, indeed. I had it all wrapped up. Alexandra thought I was just there to do her bidding, to keep the school running smoothly while she swanned around being the big-shot headmistress. Meanwhile, who was the clever one, huh? Who was the mastermind? Me!'

Pip's eye caught the bingo card at her feet again, the telltale squiggle of gel pen. She felt suddenly queasy. The exam scam was the least of Mrs Jenkins's crimes. If Pip's thinking was right, Mrs Jenkins was a murderer. She had killed David Cole. The only thing Pip had in her favour was that Mrs Jenkins didn't know Pip had figured that out. Pip's priority now was to get herself and Claire safely out of this building and away from Mrs Jenkins.

'You're frightfully clever to have run such a clever scam. You're quite right that we had no idea. And Ms Peters still doesn't, and I'm not going to tell her, because I will look such a fool for having taken so long to work it out. You have nothing to worry about as far as I'm concerned,' said Pip, smiling brightly. 'You keep your, um, earnings, and take down the site. I'll tell her it was unsolvable, the site has been disabled, and we'll never know who was behind it.'

Claire nodded eagerly, and said, 'I literally don't know what you are talking about.'

'There you go,' said Pip, taking Claire's arm again and pulling her towards the door. 'Sorted. We'll be off.'

'Not so fast,' said Mrs Jenkins, giving Pip a surprisingly hard shove away from the door. Pip stumbled backwards, pulling Claire with her. 'You're still taking me for a fool.'

'No, no, not at all,' said Pip, her eyes unwillingly drawn back to the bingo card on the floor.

Mrs Jenkins's eyes followed hers. 'Ah, the bingo cards,' she said. 'I have you and your complete and utter inefficiency to thank for alerting me to the fact that David Cole was also wise to the scam.'

'The conversation we overheard from the printing room?' said Pip.

'Yes. I suppose I should thank you for that. If you hadn't messed up the printing of the bingo sheets, I'd never have known he was onto me.'

'He thought he was onto Grace Faith. He wasn't onto you.'

'Really? Well, if he wasn't, he soon would be,' said Mrs Jenkins, dismissively. She seemed unconcerned by the fact that she'd steam-rolled a man for nothing. 'Once he tried to use the information to bully Charles into voting to sell the Marsh Field, I knew that things would, shall we say, gather steam?' She gave a weird evil laugh. 'My little money-making scheme would become public, someone would soon be digging deeper. I needed to stop him.'

'So you followed him to the field and…'

'And squashed him with a steamroller,' blurted out Claire, with horror.

'Oh, you make it sound so deliberate,' said Mrs Jenkins. 'He was there, I was there, the steamroller was there. The man was on his phone, like everyone these days. He should have had his wits about him. It's his own fault. Him and those idiots who made a keypad code of 1-2-3-4. They are the real culprits. I cannot abide stupidity.'

'We saw you after you'd done it,' said Pip, who had been playing back the day in her head. 'You were there when Sally the llama ran past. You'd already been on the building site.'

Mrs Jenkins clapped slowly. 'I thought you'd figure it out eventually. You're not stupid, even if you are a little slow. That's why I have to kill you. You were the only one who had enough pieces to put it together. I knew you'd do it eventually. With you gone, I'll be able to relax.'

'Now, really,' said Pip. 'You've been trying to murder me all week, and you haven't succeeded. So I think we can safely say that you won't murder me now.'

'Oh, but I think I will,' said Mrs Jenkins, with a small smile.

She took a lighter from her pocket. Full of surprises, she was. Pip had no idea she smoked. 'In case you get any ideas, you should know that while you two were chatting away, I primed this place for a big old fire,' she said, her eyes sparkling at the prospect. 'Sacking and turpentine all around this little office. This little *wooden* office. It could go up like a bonfire, really.' She flicked the lighter casually. 'We don't want any accidents.'

'I'm with you there. No accidents. Claire and I are happy to let this whole thing go.' Pip tried desperately to think of a way they could get round the old woman, and out of the door.

Mrs Jenkins ignored her and continued speaking, while flicking the lighter casually. 'It was going so well, until those silly girls broke the rules and you got involved. I was just a few months away from retirement. With my pension and my extra earnings, I was all set up.'

'I'm sure you can still have a very nice retirement. I hear Brighton is—'

'Don't patronise me. I don't want a very nice retirement in Brighton. I am leaving this dull, grey place and moving to the Seychelles. It's all arranged; we've got our visas, the money. Me and John Seymour. I'm going to write my novel and swim in the sea every day. He's going to buy a boat, run fishing charters.'

'Mr Seymour from maintenance?' asked Claire with surprise.

Pip imagined Mrs Jenkins with the stocky Mr Seymour, the odd couple living the good life on a tropical island, on the spoils of the exam scam. It would have been rather a charming romantic story, had it not been for the murder and fraud.

'Ah, how lovely,' said Pip, giving Claire a glance which she hoped signalled *RUN!*

Mrs Jenkins's face had taken on a dreamy look. 'Coconuts,' she said. 'I love coconuts, don't you?'

'Oh yes, lovely,' said Pip, feeling like she was in some mad cocktail party making small talk. Making small talk with the woman who had tried to kill her three times, and was working up to a fourth attempt.

'Coconut cocktails on the beach…'

'That sounds lovely.' Why could Pip not stop saying 'lovely'? 'I'm sure you'll be very happy there.'

'We will, and I'm certainly not going to let you two stop me.'

'Righto. Fair enough. Bon voyage, I say. Now, we really must be going, Claire, come on. Tim knew we were coming here and he will be here any minute looking for us.' She said the last words in a very loud voice, in the hope that they might make some impact on Mrs Jenkins, who still seemed to be away with the coconuts.

The dreamy look left Mrs Jenkins's face. 'He's not going to be pleased when he finds you,' she said, and flicked the lighter again. This time, she held the button down, the flame burning strongly between them. 'Or should I say, whatever's left of you.'

CHAPTER 40

The fire made the exact whooshing sound you hear in the movies. The sound of hot, billowing energy releasing as a devastating blaze.

Mrs Jenkins had stepped out of the door, bent to touch the flame to where she had poured petrol over a sack next to the door, then slammed it shut and locked it. The site office was tiny, a shed. There was nowhere to hide, no alternative exit. The wooden structure would go up in minutes, Pip knew. Although the smoke might get them first. It was pouring in through the floorboards at the front of the building, filling the space. Claire was shouldering the door with force, but it was not budging a crack.

Pip looked for tools. There was a spade, some planks. A bucket. A filing cabinet and a desk. A chair. A tool for stamping down the dirt. A length of webbing. Pip ran around the perimeter of the room feeling blindly for weak spots in the planks, but the little wooden office was alarmingly sturdy. The single window across from the door was fitted with a criss-cross of metal burglar bars. She pushed it open for the little ventilation it offered. Putting her face to the window, she took a deep breath of blessed fresh air before pushing Claire in front of her. 'Breathe,' she shouted. The girl gasped and gulped gratefully.

'Get back,' shouted Pip, and she slammed the spade against the window frame. Three blows, with the full force Jimmy had taught her in the gym, but it hardly shifted.

The flames were coming through now in spots to the front of the office, where the whole wall must be on fire. The room was filled with hot smoke. Pip feared they would die there, but put it out of her head. She couldn't let Claire die. She wouldn't.

Pip put down the shovel and pulled herself up onto the filing cabinet pushed against the wall furthest from the fire. 'Pass me the shovel,' she yelled at Claire. Claire looked bewildered, but after a heart-stopping moment, she grabbed the shovel and handed it to Pip, who was now standing, balanced precariously, on the filing cabinet. Using all her recently gained upper body strength, she hit the shovel hard against the galvanised metal roof. She felt a bit of give, a metal sheet pulling against the nails that held it to the wooden roof truss.

'Claire, get a plank, anything – come up here and help me. We can loosen the roof,' Pip shouted, coughing out the smoke and dust between words.

The girl took a huge gulp of the fresh air by the window, grabbed a plank and clambered up onto the filing cabinet next to Pip. The cabinet shuddered slightly but held, and Claire started banging at the roof with the plank, while Pip continued to hit it with the shovel.

When she could bear the smoke in her lungs no longer, Pip jumped down for a few deep breaths by the window, then climbed back up, wielding the spade in desperation. She felt a tear in her shoulder at the same time she felt the metal pull from the truss. The sheet clattered to the ground.

Sky. The two of them looked at it in wonder for a moment. Sky and fresh air. Then they looked at each other. Claire's face was streaked with soot and the traces of tears – from crying or coughing Pip didn't know. Pip imagined she looked much the same.

'Go, Claire. Go. I'll help you up.'

'But, Pip—'

'Come on! Now!'

Pip got ready to hoist Claire up, as she might have hoisted her onto a horse, the girl's foot in her hand. With a great shove from

Pip and a valiant pull, Claire launched herself up onto the wall, hanging over it, her legs dangling inside, but her head and shoulders at least out of the office.

'Jump. The fire's on the other side still – you'll be fine.'

'I can't,' said Claire, sobbing. 'It's too high.'

'You can. Take your leg over. Claire, now! Get away from the fire.'

With a mighty effort, Claire pulled herself so that she was perched on the edge of the wall.

'Go. Over you go!'

'Pip, what about you?'

'I'll be fine. I can get over. Drop. Claire, *drop*.'

And with that the girl disappeared, a faint shriek against the almighty noise of the crackling timbers. Pip couldn't worry about how she'd fallen or landed. She was undoubtedly safer there than Pip was, alone now in the burning building. She was a good bit taller than Claire but even so, the edge of the wall was out of reach.

Claire's face appeared at the window. Pip could see her shouting but couldn't hear her. She gave the girl a thumbs up, displaying a confidence she didn't feel.

Pip stood on the filing cabinet for a moment, considering her options. She had none. It was as hot as all hell now, the flames having engulfed the whole side closest to the door. She needed to get out. But unlike Claire, she had no one to hoist her. She was going to have to jump.

She bent her knees, counted to three, and jumped. She crashed against the wooden wall, one arm over, her feet scrabbling for purchase. The thick rubber soles with their good grip got some traction on the wooden planks and she managed to push herself up a bit. Pip pulled with her arm and pushed with her toes and got her other hand onto the top of the wall. She heaved a bit more of her chest up next. Every part of her was aching, her fingers screaming in pain, but she pulled again, this time getting both arms over. The air was clearer here and she could see flashes of grass between the billows of smoke. With a last mighty effort she hauled a leg onto the top of the wall and let herself tumble through the grey, onto the ground below.

CHAPTER 41

Claire was shouting at her. Pip wished she would stop. Why couldn't the girl just leave her alone to lie here, trying not to move her aching body?

'Get up!' Claire was shouting.

Pip rolled onto her hands and knees, and stayed there for a moment, coughing.

Claire shook her shoulder. 'Can you walk? We need to get away from here. The smoke.'

Pip nodded – the girl was right – but standing up seemed like a bridge too far. Her chest hurt from the smoke or the coughing or both, her shoulder was injured in some way she couldn't determine, and she'd landed heavily on her right leg and hip. She got to her feet gingerly. 'Where is she?' asked Pip, gasping. A three-word sentence was all she could manage but Claire knew who she meant.

'I don't know. She was gone by the time I got out.'

The ground was drier than it had been on the Fun Day, but still she thought she could see a series of depressions which could be footprints.

'If these are her prints, she went towards the school. This way.' Pip gestured away from the burning site office in the direction of the Marsh Field, still coughing smoke from her lungs. She took a deep breath and set off after Mrs Jenkins, holding on to Claire's shoulder. She hobbled the first few steps but her bad leg loosened up as she went, and soon she was able to walk almost normally. Her chest started to clear as she gulped in fresher air.

'Are we going after her?' Claire asked, with some apprehension, understandably – the woman had, after all, tried to burn them alive.

'I need to find her. Who knows what she'll do? That woman is crazy dangerous,' Pip said, somewhat redundantly under the circumstances. 'We don't know who she might hurt next.'

They would need to hurry if they were to catch up with Mrs Jenkins. She'd had a good few minutes' head start. She was older, yes, but she had not been locked in a smoke-filled room, or fallen from the roof onto the hard ground, as Pip had. Pip tried to put on a little jog. Her hip and knee expressed their unhappiness, but held up. Her head was clearing and she realised she hadn't called for backup. Then she realised she had no phone.

'Claire! My phone! I left it in the office.' Pip took a moment to inwardly bemoan the loss of her very cool tabby-striped phone cover – luckily, her three million kitten pics were safe in the Cloud.

'I've got mine.' Claire pulled it out of her pocket.

'Phone the police. Tell them it's an emergency. Tell them to contact Inspectors Goodall and Truman. Oh, and the fire brigade!'

As she said it, sirens could be heard on the road and she caught a flash of bright red between the trees, on the road, coming towards the site. Someone must have called the fire brigade already. A small crowd of curious schoolgirls had gathered by the school fence to gawk at the flames and the billowing smoke emerging from what was left of the wooden site office.

Claire phoned as they trotted towards the trees on the border of the site and the Marsh Field, close to the marsh itself. The ground was getting increasingly muddy as they neared the water, and Pip could see the trail of footprints quite clearly. It headed into the little grove of trees.

'On their way,' Claire panted, shoving her phone into the pocket of her school trousers.

They stopped at the entrance to the woods and looked at each other.

'I'll go,' said Pip. 'You stay here.'

'Not likely,' said Claire. 'I won't let you go in there on your own.'

'OK, but stay behind me. And be quiet,' Pip said, finger to her lips. 'I'd prefer she didn't see us coming.'

She stopped again. 'Wait!' she said.

Digging into the pocket of her denim jacket, she pulled out the mini can of spray-on deodorant and handed it to Claire.

The girl blushed, shaking the can. 'Sorry, I'm sure I smell awful. The smoke.'

'Gosh, no!' Pip said, embarrassed. 'Not that. It's for protection. Like mace. Spray her in the face if you have to. I've got this.' Pip held up the letter opener. It had looked sharply dangerous on the desk, but now it appeared pathetically flimsy and quite unlikely to open anything tougher than an envelope.

Pip's eyes met Claire's, and she could see that the girl was scared. But there was no choice.

'Come on.'

It was pleasantly damp and cool amongst the trees, not that Pip could enjoy it with the adrenaline coursing through her veins, making her head feel light and heavy at the same time. The footsteps had petered out but there was a path, which she followed, with Claire sticking close behind.

They walked as quietly as they could, stepping lightly, their ears and eyes straining for any sign of Mrs Jenkins. Pip stopped suddenly, sending Claire barrelling into her. She emitted a 'hhmmmff' sound, then put her hand over her mouth.

'Do you hear something?' whispered Pip.

They stood still and listened. There was a very muffled sound of voices – at least one of them male, judging by the low tone.

They crept towards the noise, bent over, hearts beating. It was lighter up ahead, a clearing in the woods perhaps, and the voices were getting louder.

'Is it feeling better? That was a nasty fall and your ankle is swollen. I don't understand why you were running like that.'

It was Ms Peters! Who was she talking to?

Pip stopped holding her hand up to stop Claire behind her. She dared not go closer, she'd be spotted. She would stay and listen for a moment first.

'Oh yes, fine now. I must go. I'm in a hurry.'

Mrs Jenkins!

Pip felt a surge of fear or excitement or both.

'I do wecommend caution. I had a weally nasty wolled ankle once, wambling in the wiver enviwoment of the Wockies.'

It was Fwog Dude! What the heck was going on?

'I'd better be on my way.' Mrs Jenkins's voice had taken on a slightly desperate tone.

Well, that wasn't going to happen. Pip moved forward, stepping into a clearing where she saw Ms Peters and Hamilton sitting on a fallen log, a small picnic of a thermos of tea and a packet of chocolate digestives between them. Pip didn't have time to process what that meant, exactly. She was focused on Mrs Jenkins who had turned from where she must have been standing and was moving gingerly but surprisingly speedily through the trees.

'Stop her,' Pip shouted, startling the log-sitters so that they spilled their thermos of tea onto their laps.

'Pip. What are—?'

'I'll explain later,' Pip shouted to Ms Peters. 'Mrs Jenkins is not what you think. She's dangerous. We need to stop her.'

Mrs Jenkins had a badly twisted ankle. Even in Pip's condition, it wasn't much of a chase. Within minutes she had caught up to her. The older woman turned to Pip, strangely calm.

'I am going to the Seychelles,' said Mrs Jenkins. 'It's all been arranged.'

'It's over,' Pip said. 'No Seychelles.'

'It's all *arranged*,' she said serenely, her face a blank. She continued in the same reasonable tone, like a zombie. 'The tickets are booked. I have bought a sunhat.' She patted her head as if to illustrate, and then turned away from Pip, heading down to the marsh. 'Now, if you'll excuse me.'

Pip reached for her. 'Mrs Jenkins, please stop. You are not going to the Seychelles. The police are on their way.'

Mrs Jenkins put on a burst of speed, setting off at a hobbling run across the field towards the marsh, Pip coming after her. Claire, who had been watching in frozen silence, followed. It was a matter of a few bounds for Pip to catch up with her again. She launched herself at Mrs Jenkins's back, the two of them landing in the boggy ground.

'It's over,' Pip said once more, her arms slipping as the muddy woman tried to get away. 'Just stop.'

Mrs Jenkins had squirmed out of her grasp and was struggling to her feet, escaping her sensible pumps which were stuck in the mud. She gave Pip a hard kick with her stockinged foot, sending her off balance, splashing down into the mud and water, and got up.

Mrs Jenkins was on the move again, with Pip close behind. Pip lunged at her, bringing them both down into the mud.

'Get off me, you bitch,' screamed Mrs Jenkins, getting to her feet. 'You and your interfering, you're going to ruin everything. You should be dead! I should have put another pill in that soup.'

Mrs Jenkins aimed another kick at Pip, with her good foot. Pip turned on her side in the mud, to avoid the foot to her face. Mrs

Jenkins took advantage of Pip's position and sat down heavily on her, trying to force her face down into the mud and water. Pip used every ounce of strength she had to turn her shoulders and pull her face from the mud to take a breath. She looked up at Mrs Jenkins – her sensible hair a filthy wreath of spikes and bits of grass, her neat skirt soaked and riding up her thighs, her blouse covered in earth and her pearls, miraculously, gleaming on top of the whole mess.

Pip felt for the letter opener in her pocket. She felt a mixture of relief and apprehension when her fingers touched its smooth blade. She gasped for air and hauled herself out of the bog with a great sucking squelching sound, pain shooting through her injured shoulder. She pulled the letter opener from her pocket. She'd never stabbed anyone before, but she knew she was going to have to do this. She slashed wildly at Mrs Jenkins.

Pip's face was covered in mud, her eyes streaming – she couldn't see where the blows landed but she felt nothing solid. She coughed the dirt and water from her throat and stabbed again, slicing only fresh air each time. Mrs Jenkins sat heavily on Pip and pushed down on her neck with her forearm, her full body weight resting on her throat, surprisingly strong in her rage. Her pearls dangled in front of her face as Pip struggled for breath, pulling her arm back, lifting the letter opener for another plunge. Air again. Air.

Then she felt one of her stabs make contact, a soft resistance of flesh against the blade and a surprised grunt from her opponent. The pressure on her chest and neck lightened as Mrs Jenkins loosened her grip. Pip's lungs filled with air and oxygen and cool and relief and… what was that? The scent of Fresh Summer Breeze?

Mrs Jenkins rolled off Pip, coughing and wheezing, revealing the welcome sight of Claire with her deodorant spray, which she'd discharged fully into Mrs Jenkins's face. Pip turned her head to see Ms Peters running up behind Claire, her braids bouncing, shock on her face. And then Hamilton, still holding the silver cup from the top of the thermos flask, trying not to spill his tea.

Mrs Jenkins was lying exhausted in the mud, her right hand pressed against her left forearm, where Pip had nicked her. The flimsy letter opener lay broken beside her.

Pip was alive and she was safe.

CHAPTER 42

Ms Peters – Alexandra – tapped her spoon against her wine glass, pushed her chair from the table and stood up. The people around the table put down their artisanal bread and Himalayan salted butter, broke off their conversation and looked up expectantly.

There was Mummy, with Henry by her side, as he always seemed to be these days. Flis and Peter, smiling up at her. Tim, looking unbelievably gorgeous, his eyes glinting between the full dark lashes, flicking towards Pip every few seconds, communicating his admiration, his gratitude, his… attraction, maybe? Lust? Claire by his side, a few scrapes and bruises still showing, although nothing as dramatic as Pip's. Jimmy catching her eye, grinning, proud as punch that his boxing lessons had come in handy. Charles, the chairman, with his pretty blonde wife.

'Hello and thank you all for coming,' Ms Peters said, smiling broadly at the table. They all smiled back. The most enthusiastic smiler was Hamilton, Fwog Dude, who seemed – astonishingly – to be Ms Peters's new beau. He glowed and smiled in admiration at the brilliance of everything she said, starting with 'Hello'.

'It's become a tradition for me to take the chairman of the board and his partner for lunch at the end of the school year, but this year I decided to do things a little differently. As you know, this has been an exceptionally unusual final term. The school faced some devastating blows, most terribly, the loss of David Cole, a parent at our school and a member of our community. We also faced a serious assault on our school's integrity.'

There was a sombre moment while they acknowledged the dreadful events of the past few weeks, before Ms Peters continued in a more upbeat tone. 'The reason you are all here is that I want to thank and pay tribute to Epiphany Bloom. We are so grateful to have had her assistance in these very difficult times.'

Everyone turned to look at Pip. Jimmy gave a wink. Mummy smiled, bemusedly – she was always faintly surprised when Pip was praised, and even now looked as if she was half expecting the other shoe to drop. Henry – as dapper as always, in a three-piece suit with a cheerful pocket square – shouted an enthusiastic, 'Hear, hear!'

'She managed to solve both the mystery of who was running an exam scam in my school and who killed poor David Cole – as you know, the perpetrator was one and the same – and we have since handed the matter over to our local police. As some of you might already know, our erstwhile school secretary, Mrs Jenkins, is in custody. She is facing a number of charges, including murder. A full investigation into the exam leaks is underway. I am pleased to say that this is being handled very discreetly, so the school's reputation is not sullied. Pip, thank you for your service to our school.'

There was a smattering of applause, a few raised glasses and some murmured congratulations. It wasn't entirely clear what the protocol was for celebrating someone who had solved a horrible murder.

'Gosh, I almost forgot. Pip, we have a gift for you! Where is it now? Girls?'

Pip had already received a handsome payment from the school for her efforts, so she was surprised to see Ruby and Amelia appear from an adjoining room of the pub, Ruby with her camera slung around her neck, Amelia carrying a flat, wrapped rectangular present. Pip accepted it and tore at the paper. Sally the llama careened crazily across the field, Pip herself chasing after her in the background. It was the photo from the Fun Day.

Pip stood up, surveying the bright expectant faces of her friends and family. She took a moment to gather herself before she spoke. 'Thank you, Alexandra, and thank you, Ruby, for this wonderful photograph,' she said. 'It's astonishing to think that it was only two weeks ago that Sally slipped through my fingers – thanks to Henry's special coconut conditioner – and led me to the body of David Cole. It was, as Alexandra said, a terrible loss to his family and the community, but I'm pleased to have played a part in bringing his killer to justice, and to ensuring the integrity of this fine school.'

After a bit more clapping, they settled down to peruse their menus – the pub, for all its wooden beams and ancient bar counter and pots of geraniums, was well known amongst the foodie set for its hot young chef, who had moved from London to follow her dream of creating a gastro pub experience in the country.

Tim, sitting next to Pip, put his hand on her arm and said, awkwardly, 'I need to tell you something, something a bit... Awkward.'

Was he finally going to own up to their intense physical attraction? There had, after all, been an almost-kiss at his cousin's engagement party, foiled by Pip's mushroom allergy.

'The thing is, I... um. I mean, it's not a biggie, but I do need to mention it.'

'It's OK, Tim, just say it.'

'There's something I feel bad about. I didn't have faith in you, you see. The exam scam. You were so busy with all the different, um, threads. The murder and so on. It didn't seem you were making much progress. I went behind your back and hacked the school computer system. Just to take a look. The mark order list and so on. I should have told you. I mean, I was trying to help Claire. And you. But I should have been upfront about it. And of course you solved everything anyway. So I was wrong.'

Pip considered countering his confession with one of her own – that she'd looked at his computer and not been upfront about what she'd seen there – but decided against it.

'Oh, that's OK, Tim. We all make mistakes. Let's not worry about it. I know you meant well,' she said magnanimously.

Further discussion was, fortunately, halted by the appearance of Alexandra Peters, who sat down on the other side of Pip.

'Pip, I'm so pleased to see you in good health and strength. Are you sure you are quite well?'

Pip had spent a night in hospital recovering from smoke inhalation and her various injuries. A week later, she still had a full tropical sunset of bruises and grazes, mostly along the right side of her body where she'd fallen from the roof of the site office.

'Absolutely. On the mend,' she said. 'I'll be sleeping on my left side for a while, but there was no serious damage. It looks worse than it is.'

'I've always told Epiphany that she needs to be more careful, a big girl like her,' said Mummy with a nod, relieved that she was back on familiar ground where Pip was messing up.

'Magnolia,' called Henry, beckoning to Mummy from down the table. 'Do come and listen to this. Jimmy here has the most marvellous stories about his nightclub days. Bouncing, apparently. He knows all sorts of fascinating characters and he's had some ideas about the llamas, too.'

Mummy excused herself and went to speak to Jimmy and Henry, her hand resting on Henry's arm. Pip smiled, and so did Ms Peters.

'I don't know if this is quite the moment, but I did want to put an idea in your head. A proposition,' said Ms Peters, looking a little nervous. 'I know you're not actually a teacher, but you're so good with the girls and they do seem to respond well to you. I wondered if you might consider staying on at the school. We could think it through, but perhaps some sort of position encompassing extracurricular activities, a sort of big sister, guidance and such.' She smiled. 'Obstacle courses, musical chairs, that sort of thing.' She'd clearly done her own investigation. 'You might even decide to study, get a teaching diploma.'

'Gosh, Ms Peters...'

'Alexandra, please.'

'Alexandra. I don't know what to say. I do love the girls and working at the school, and it would be even more enjoyable without someone dropping flowerpots on my head and trying to electrocute me.'

'Well, we would love to have you, although I'm sure you have lots of other options and opportunities.'

Um, no. Zero options. No opportunities, currently.

'Please do think about it.'

'Really, Alexandra, that actually sounds wonderful. I think I would like that very much. Let's meet next week and talk about how it might work.'

Flis came barrelling up and interrupted their conversation.

'I am so proud of you!' she gushed, giving Pip a huge hug.

'Thanks, sis,' Pip said, blushing. 'Ms Peters was just saying I might want to stay at the school, work with the girls, perhaps study teaching.'

'She's quite wonderful with children,' Flis said, addressing the headmistress. 'My children adore her, they call her the gilly aunt. They think that when people say "Oh my gilly aunt" they actually mean Pip.'

'Giddy,' mumbled Pip, but she was smiling. She hadn't known that about the children.

'Yes,' Flis continued merrily. 'She does this hilarious voice. That thing you do with your nose, Pip. Has them in stitches. Go on, Pip, do it for Alexandra!' Pip demurred, blushing, and Ms Peters left the two sisters together, promising to pick up the conversation the next week.

'You! A teacher!' said Flis, excitedly. 'Well, you could knock me over with a fender.'

'It's feather. Knock me over with a feather.'

'Don't be silly, Pip. It has to be a fender. You couldn't knock someone over with a feather.'

'That's the point. The speaker is so surprised that even a feather could—'

'Oh, well anyhow,' Flis said, waving her hand dismissively. 'I think it's wonderful.'

They were interrupted by another tap-tap of knife against glass.

'One last thing,' said Ms Peters. 'I wanted to mention, just in conclusion, that Hamilton and his team have completed their environmental impact study and the area is considered too important for it to be lost. In fact, a very rare and endangered frog species has been found in the wetland. It seems it is the first time that such a specimen has been found so far south in the British Isles. There will be no development on the Marsh Field.'

Fwog Dude had found a rare frog, and won the love of a beautiful, kind woman! Now, there was a fairy-tale ending, if ever there was one.

Pip glowed with good feeling – the job offer, her friends and family, even the frog. It was all rather wonderful. A happy ending, at last.

She felt her phone vibrate in her pocket. She reached for it. An unknown number. Why did Pip feel that the best course of action right now would be to kill the call? That it could only bring trouble? She hesitated, then hit the green button.

'Ms Bloom, it's Chanel here. I'm on the set of *Strictly Come Baking* with Alan and we have the best news. The chocolate cake – Alan won!'

A LETTER FROM KATIE

Dear reader,

Katie Gayle is, in fact two of us – Kate and Gail – and we want to say a huge thank you for choosing to read *Death at the Gates*, the third Epiphany Bloom cosy mystery. If you enjoyed the book, and want to keep up to date with all Katie Gayle's latest releases, just sign up at the following link. Your email address will never be shared and you can unsubscribe at any time.

www.bookouture.com/katie-gayle

We hope you loved Pip's adventures, and if you did we would be very grateful if you could write a review and post it on Amazon and Goodreads. We would love to hear what you think, and it makes such a difference in helping other readers to discover Pip too.

You can find us in a few places and we'd love to hear from you – Katie Gayle is on Twitter as @KatieGayleBooks and on Facebook as Katie Gayle Writer. You can also follow Kate on Twitter at @katesidley and Gail at @gailschimmel.

Thanks,
Katie Gayle

 KatieGayleWriter

 @KatieGayleBooks

Printed in Great Britain
by Amazon